I0743563

Death of the
Chinese Field Hands

Anne Louise Bannon

Healcroft House, Publishers

Altadena, California

Healcroft House, Publishers, a subsidiary of Robin
Goodfellow Enterprises,
Altadena, California
United States of America

Copyright 2020 by Anne Louise Bannon

ISBN: 978-1-948616-13-3

Library of Congress Control Number: 2020909995

ACKNOWLEDGEMENTS

I am continually amazed at how blessed I am in my friendships and acquaintances, and at the same time, terrified that I will forget to thank someone utterly critical to this process.

I am particularly indebted to my acupuncturist Dr. Vie Lu, who has patiently answered so very many questions about Chinese medicine.

If Maddie seems like a better doctor in this volume, most of that is thanks to Dr. Paula Bernstein, PhD, MD, who volunteered to serve as my medical consultant. After her help getting me through a host of Nineteenth Century medical journals, I've come to the conclusion it's a miracle humans survived as long as they have.

Thanks go to my dear friend and editor, Carol Louise Wilde. I may groan at her corrections, issues, and suggestions, but she is almost always right, and my work is the better for it.

Once again, the librarians of the History Department of the Los Angeles Public Library were wonderfully helpful. Scott Zesch's book, The Chinatown Wars, was not only invaluable, but Zesch was incredibly responsive and kind when I had additional questions, including when I should have seen one of the answers in the book's notes.

Finally, I have to thank my primary historical consultant and husband, Michael Holland. He continues to answer my questions and offers excellent insight and plenty of good humor. I couldn't ask for a better partner in this endeavor and in life.

DEDICATION

To my mother, Connie Bannon, the first and best of my teachers.

DRAMATIS PERSONNAE

Some of the characters in this story have the real names of people who were living in Los Angeles in 1871. However, since this is a work of fiction, they are technically fictional characters who may, in varying degrees, bear some resemblance to the real people they are named after. Those with real names I have noted. As for anyone else, the reader may assume that he or she is fully the product of my fevered imagination.

RANCHO DE LAS FLORES

Maddie Wilcox, owner, winemaker, physician

Sebastiano Ortiz, winery manager, husband of Olivia, brother to Enrique

Olivia Ortiz, cook, and wife of Sebastiano

Enrique Ortiz, vineyard manager, husband of Magdalena, brother to Sebastiano

Magdalena Ortiz, housekeeper, and wife of Enrique

Armando Ortiz, son to Magdalena and Enrique

Hernan Mendoza, field hand, husband of Maria, cousin to Emilio and Pascual

Maria Mendoza, maid, wife of Hernan

Rodolfo Sanchez, field hand, husband of Anita

Anita Sanchez, nanny, wife of Rodolfo

Emilio Mendoza, field hand, brother to Pascual, cousin to Hernan

Pascual Mendoza, field hand, brother to Emilio, cousin to Hernan

Wang Fu, field hand, physician

Wei Li, field hand, brother to Wei Chin

Wei Chin, field hand, brother to Wei Li

Juanita Alvarez, personal maid to Maddie

MADDIE'S FRIENDS

Angelina Sutton, undertaker's wife who prepares the bodies for burial

Walter Lomax, a deputy on the city police force

Regina Medina, madam, sister to Thomas Mahoney

LADIES OF LOS ANGELES SOCIETY (and their husbands)

Mrs. Carson, she and her husband Mr. Carson are presumed to have existed. Mr. Carson owns a stationery store

Mrs. Glassell, she is presumed to have existed, as her husband, Andrew Glassell, was a prominent attorney in town at the time, he also founded the Glassell Park neighborhood and helped found the City of Orange, California

Mrs. Judson and her husband, the banker Mr. Judson

Mrs. Hewitt and her husband Mr. Hewitt may have existed. They own and run the buggy manufactory

OTHER ANGELENOS

Doctor Skillen, a local medical man

Lavina Gaines, daughter to Robert Gaines, sister to Timothy Gaines

Robert Gaines, land agent, father to Lavina and Timothy

Timothy Gaines, land agent, son to Robert, brother to Lavina

Mr. Sedonez, saloon keeper

Efrem Smith, ranch hand for Mrs. Costa

Mrs. Costa, wife of a ranch owner and employer of Efrem Smith

Mr. Dillman, a carpenter in Regina's employ

Mr. Valdez, an Indian laborer
Mr. Gluck, a laborer
Mr. Ah, head of one of the Chinese companies
Mr. Alverno, a court clerk
Mr. McKinley, a land agent
Mr. Sanford, a teamster
Old Man Pugh, a former miner
Robert Leighland, a former ship owner
Mr. Shapiro, owner of a mercantile
Doc MacKenzie, another local medical man
Mr. Handley, insurance agent to Maddie Wilcox

AUTHOR'S NOTE

One of the great difficulties in writing a work fiction set in the Nineteenth Century with any authenticity at all is the incredible bigotry of the period. Negative attitudes toward people of color were commonplace and accepted by almost everyone, attitudes that, today, are hopefully considered shocking and inappropriate. The term Negro, for example, was the polite way to refer to a person of African descent.

Because this novel is based on an act that was considered shocking even for that time – the lynching of eighteen Chinese men simply because of their race – there are attitudes expressed by characters in this book that today are considered offensive. I have softened them somewhat because they are so shocking to our modern sensibilities but have not eliminated them.

If we are to make racial prejudice truly a thing of the past, then I believe we must face that past head on, even when it's shocking and inappropriate.

CHAPTER ONE

When I first began the Herculean labor that writing my memoirs has turned out to be, I had fully intended to avoid relating the terrible events of the autumn of 1871. I had (and have) little taste for recounting the horrors we experienced the awful night of the riot and the weeks that followed.

However, my sweet grandniece often says that there may be lessons learned in the relating of the darkest times of our lives. Given that she spent the Great War in France, serving as a nurse on the front lines, I don't doubt her wisdom in that regard. Furthermore, not to relate these events would be a grave injustice to the memories of those who lost their lives during those weeks. And so, I begin.

It had been a long day that Tuesday, October 24, in the year of Our Lord 1871, and it was a blessing for my three Chinese field hands that it was. The day started with bringing in the last of the grapes for the angelica. My vineyards and winery were my principal support in those days. We had already harvested the cabernet and merlot two weeks before and the wine would soon be ready to move from the vats in which the grapes had fermented into the casks where it would age. The grapes for the angelica were always harvested last, as they did not ripen readily. Indeed, even when some of the grapes had already turned to raisins, there were still several green grapes among the clusters.

As the sun slowly sank toward the horizon, Wei Li and Wei Chin were still walking in the vats with several of the Ortiz children, crushing the grapes in preparation for fermentation. Both were unusually tall for members of their race, with long, thin mustaches. Both had shaved the front of their scalps and wore the rest of their hair in long, braided queues down their backs, as did the vast majority of the Chinese did even while here.

Wang Fu, who was more traditionally statured and always wore a bright blue cap, worked alongside my partners in the venture, Sebastiano and Enrique Ortiz. I was wearing my red poplin work dress and moving the cleaned baskets to the back part of the winery barn.

We heard the first of the gunfire around five-thirty.

"Sounds like the big fight has started," Hernan said, playfully nudging Wei Li.

Hernan Mendoza was one of the other field hands on Rancho de las Flores. He'd just brought in the last baskets of grapes. Wei Li grunted and kept walking the vat.

Wang Fu had told us earlier that there were rumors that there would be a fight that day between two rival companies on the Calle de los Negros, where the Chinese principally lived. The companies were home organizations that, by themselves, helped the Chinese who came to our fair shores navigate a society that was to them utterly strange and even barbaric. But as so often happens, there was a criminal element known as Tongs that became attached to some of the companies. It was rumored that one of the companies had hired Tong assassins from San Francisco to fight against the leader of a rival company.

Even so, we were not terribly concerned at first. After all, Los Angeles was a very rough place in those days and the sound of gunfire was almost pervasive. However, that evening, not only did the reports continue, they grew as if more and more guns were being fired.

"You would think there was a war on," Sebastiano said, shaking his head.

"It may be," said Wang Fu quietly. He looked up at the Wei brothers, who looked frightened but did not say anything.

I wiped my hands on my apron. "That most certainly means there are injuries. I'd best get my bag and head over there."

Enrique and Sebastiano groaned quietly but did not bother to deter me. It would have done no good and they knew it.

"I go with you," said Wang Fu. His accent was getting much better, but it was still very heavy.

He had been trained as a physician in his native China and was becoming quite a help to me.

Armando, Enrique's son who was seventeen at the time, burst into the yard. Dark had settled by that point, and Armando was returning from his job at the Pico House hotel, around the corner from the Calle de los Negros.

"Wang Fu! Wei Li! Wei Chin!" Armando looked around, frantically. "Are they here?"

"We are in the grapes," Wei Chin said, nervously laughing.

Armando gasped. "You can't go home. There's a mob. I saw them take Ah Wing, one of the kitchen boys. They're calling for a lynching!"

"But what did this Mr. Ah do?" I asked.

"He didn't do anything!" Armando gulped, his face ashen in the light of the lamps scattered about the yard. "Leastways, I don't think so. But he was trying to run away, and some men caught him and Marshal Baker found a gun on him. They were screaming to lynch him and all of the Chinese, too. I was hoping our fellows would still be here, so I ran as fast as I could."

"Maddie," said Sebastiano. "Maybe we'd better wait to take care of people until things settle down."

I frowned, then shook my head. "That might be too late for the worst injured. But let us not throw all caution to the wind. Wang Fu, why don't you stay here? We can have the casualties brought here and you can tend to them. Enrique, you can keep guard. Sebastiano, shall we?"

"Let me get my guns," Sebastiano said. "Armando, get yours and the rifle."

Both the Wei brothers and Mr. Wang looked at me and Mr. Wang spoke first.

"There is the Lee wash house and laundry," he said. "That is where we live. Please find Lee Won and Lee Ma. They are good people. If as bad as Mr. Armando say, they will be safe with you."

Both Sebastiano and I readily agreed. However, by the time we made it to the Calle de los Negros, it was worse than what Armando had said.

I have tried again and again to forget that most terrible of nights. Even now, two score and ten years later, I cannot escape the horror, the acrid stench of human blood and fear, the screams, the harsh laughter of the mob.

Sebastiano insisted that we skirt the group crowded around the Coronel adobe, which we later learned was at the center of the riot. Torch light flickered against the shadows of the men, as they cheered and yelled all manner of curses at the Chinese within the adobe. The other buildings on the Calle de los Negros were dark, although one would catch the occasional glimpse of a flickering torch inside a window. Raucous shouts confirmed that there was looting going on.

Near the end of the calle closest to the Plaza, we found the Lee wash house. It, too, was dark. Sebastiano called out and slowly slid into the door. He came out a few minutes later, shaking his head.

"They're gone?" I asked, my mouth going dry.

Sebastiano shrugged. "There is no one inside."

Even as I fervently hoped that meant the family had escaped, I knew that was by no means certain.

"Where could they be?" I asked.

I hurried into the house, pulling up wash tubs and checking behind corners, but Sebastiano was right. There was no one home.

Shaking, I went back to the street and toward the crowd near the Coronel Adobe, almost stumbling against an overturned wagon. There was another cheer and more gunfire. I ran behind the wash house, but there was no one there, either. The cheering grew louder again, and my heart sank.

I went back to the street, determined to search every building until I found the Lee family. Sebastiano emerged from an adobe across from the wash house. As I ran over to him, Armando trotted up from the plaza behind us and leaned against the wagon bed I had almost fallen over.

Suddenly, the boy put his forefinger to his lips and pointed down at the wagon. Muffled sounds of hushing came from within the wooden box that had formed the bed, then silence. We could hear more loud laughter and cheers from the other end of the street. I nodded at Sebastiano and Armando, and we circled the wagon slowly, certain that whoever was underneath the overturned box was terrified beyond all reckoning. I knelt next to the wagon box.

"We're here to help you escape," I said slowly and softly. "We will not harm you. We will bring you to safety."

There was dead silence within. I nodded at Armando and Sebastiano and they slowly raised the box. Huddled inside were two women and three men. They drew back in terror as they saw me.

"Lee Won? Lee Ma?" I asked. "Wang Fu, Wei Li and Wei Chin sent us to find you."

The oldest of the three men looked at me warily. "Wang Fu?"

There was more shouting and the bouncing light of torches slowly made their way toward us.

"Yes, Wang Fu," I said. "Hurry. We must get you to safety."

One of the women chattered at the old man, and he nodded.

"I Lee Won," he said. "We go."

We hurried along the adobe on the eastern side of the plaza, hoping to find Alameda Street and get back to the rancho. But a crowd suddenly burst into the plaza and came straight toward us, so we slunk up in front of the Pico House and went cautiously along the Calle Principal toward the jail. It was a very long way around to the ranch, but we hoped we'd be able to go around the worst of the riot.

Just beyond the new Merced Theater, we realized that there was a mob coming from behind us. We ducked into the nearest street to hide, little realizing what a terrible mistake we'd made. We pressed ourselves into the doorway of a darkened adobe, but we could still see the corral at Aliso and Los Angeles streets. Three bodies dangled from the gate's crosspiece, black against the flicking orange light of the torches. Men were binding a fourth struggling man, slipping the noose over his neck, while what looked like a boy danced on the top of the gate.

I couldn't help it. I burst from our hiding place, screaming at the men, but they did not hear me. Two other men tried to make themselves heard as they confronted the crowd, but they were pushed back or ignored.

I started to rush forward, but Sebastiano held me back.

"We cannot help them," he growled softly. "Not now. We must save Wang Fu's friends."

I looked back. The two men continued their fight to be heard over the mob and I had to give Sebastiano the truth of his reasoning. Loathe as I was to admit it, there was nothing I could do there, although it still grieves me to this day that I didn't try harder to stop the mob. We slipped our small group back up to the Calle Principal and were debating which way to go when a group of about eight men suddenly bore down on us, guns drawn.

"You'll give us those heathens," the leader called out in between all manner of foul words. I could barely make out his face in the dark and the flickering torchlight, but his exceptionally full beard was dark, with the ends waving in the evening's breeze.

"I most certainly will not!" I said, positioning myself in front of our little band of refugees.

"Either hand them over or we'll shoot you like dogs," the leader crowed.

The men behind him laughed. Terrified, not only for myself, but for the people I guarded and my dearest of friends, I pressed my lips together.

"Shoot her, McKinley," growled one of the men behind the leader, I couldn't see who. "It's that lady doctor. She'll finally get what she's got coming to her."

It was not a sentiment with which I was unfamiliar, but it had never been used as an excuse to kill me before. The leader raised his gun. Armando and Sebastiano both cocked theirs.

"Hey, look over there!" a third man cried. "Let's go get after some of that!"

I have no idea if the men had, in fact, seen something more enticing or whether they merely didn't want to shoot us. Nonetheless, the men dashed off, although one lingered a moment, his face lost in the shadow of his hat. The torchlight glinted off the gold anchor watch fob that dangled from his vest pocket. Then he was gone, running after his fellows.

I swallowed and looked at Sebastiano. He nodded.

From there, we kept to the dark corners and eventually made it back to the rancho, thoroughly shaken but unharmed in body. I couldn't help looking back at the Calle de los Negros, and the glow of torchlight that hovered over it. I do not think I have ever felt as helpless as I did that night.

There was a great deal of chatter among our Chinese field hands and our guests in that so very odd language of theirs. In addition to Mr. and Mrs. Lee, an older couple with graying hair, there was Lu Ang, a spindly fellow who could not stop shaking, and An Wu and An Mei, a young couple. An Mei was Mr. and Mrs.

Lee's daughter and had only recently married Mr. An.

Wang Fu was very relieved to see the Lee family, but the Wei brothers seemed more concerned about something else. I asked Mr. Wang what that might be, but he shrugged as if he didn't want to tell me.

Among my household, Enrique's wife, Magdalena, seemed very perturbed to find that the "Chinos" were going to be spending the night in the large barracks house where most of my hands and their families lived. Sebastiano and Enrique each had an adobe to house their respective families. The barracks housed both Rodolfo and Anita Sanchez, and Hernan and Maria Mendoza and their growing family, along with Hernan's cousins Emilio and Pascual Mendoza. I was not happy with Magdalena's attitude, but was saved from remonstrating with her by Armando. We had often teased Magdalena that her darling son could tease her into doing anything he wanted. But that night I was profoundly glad of it. It must have been the resilience of youth, for Armando was able to translate to his mother the horrors we had witnessed in such a way that her prejudices were abandoned in favor of the Christian charity that I normally associated with her.

It was a sleepless night, nonetheless. That much I had anticipated, and, as I expected, I tossed and turned as the clock on my wardrobe chimed out hour after hour. I did not expect the nightmare that came upon me in the last hour before dawn.

I must interject that the past two volumes of my memoirs contain a serious error. At the time I wrote them, I was dependent on my memory and the letters I had written to my sisters to reconstruct the events I related, as my journals from that period in time had been burned up in a fire. So, I hope I may be forgiven for not remembering that I had, in fact, heard about Mr. Pasteur's germ theory and Mr. Lister's work in antiseptic surgery by that time. That I had not yet done my first true antiseptic surgery may account for the lapse.

In addition, while both Mr. Pasteur's and Mr. Lister's theories seem obvious now, they were not at all obvious at the time of which I write. I do recall being very intrigued by the idea of disease and infection being caused by invisible organic particles called germs, rather than by miasmas or malaria, or bad air. Mr. Lister's article that had been published in the California Medical Gazette had so intrigued me that I rushed over to the home of my friend and colleague, Dr. Skillen, to discuss it with him.

However, now that I think about it, there had also been an article about the advantages of using alcohol on wounds, and another on using plaster of Paris to make splints for broken bones. As Dr. Skillen employed wine as part of his poultice for gunshot wounds, we became quite involved discussing whether it was the alcohol or the herbs or the gunpowder that were the most effective parts of the poultice. I also expressed an interest in using plaster of Paris for splints, but Dr. Skillen seemed unimpressed.

The dream I had began happily, with my rush to get to Dr. Skillen's home as quickly as I could to discuss the articles that I'd read. I couldn't wait to hear what Dr. Skillen would say about Mr. Lister. I pushed my roan mare, Daisy, into a canter, under the brilliant cerulean blue sky that Los Angeles is so famous for. As I approached Dr. Skillen's house, the sky darkened and I saw rows and rows of tombstones erupting out of the ground, with even more people rising up behind them. No matter which way I looked, there was someone looking at me in accusation, and I knew that I could have saved that person's life. The young mother I had performed a caesarian section on to release the infant that was too big to pass from her womb, only to helplessly watch the mother die the next day as the contagion raged. The man whose leg I amputated that had festered and festered and he died in agony. The boy who had been shot in the gut and whose last night on earth was spent in fevered pain.

I woke up gasping and perspiring in spite of the chilled pre-dawn air. I swallowed my fear back. It had, after all, been naught but a dream. I had no idea then that the dream would continue to haunt me, and even now still does. I wanted to go back to sleep, but it was so close to the hour when I normally rose that it seemed pointless.

The sun that morning rose over the pueblo upon quite the grisly spectacle. Eighteen men in all had been lynched in three different locations. Many of the men had been mutilated as well. The bodies were cut down and the inquests began.

I went with the Wei brothers and our guests to the jail, where they had laid out the bodies. There were only 200 Chinese in the pueblo, and, not surprisingly, they mostly knew each other. Mr. An was horrified to find that one of his cousins was among the dead. Against our advice, Wei Li and Lee Won insisted on going back to the Calle de Los Negros. When we met them back at the rancho, Wei Li said something to Wei Chin and both brothers seemed relieved. Mr. Lee, however, was deeply saddened, telling us through Wang Fu that the wash house had been completely destroyed and the small amount of money that he had saved had been stolen.

The funeral for the victims was held that same day. I attended with Mr. Wang and his fellows. It was a curious event, with much atonal wailing, yet it was deeply affecting, and somehow reminded me of the nightmare I'd had that morning.

Among the good citizens of Los Angeles, most denied any involvement, some legitimately, others less so. As the days went on, those of the more settled class blamed the ruffians and transients in the pueblo. The newspapers published hypocritical essays on the rule of law, particularly given the stories they'd published in the weeks prior to the riot denouncing the Chinese as rogues.

One of my rescued guests, the spindly Lu Ang,

was gone to Wilmington by the end of the day after the funeral, presumably to catch the next steamship to San Francisco. Whether he stayed in California or returned to China, we never found out. The Lee family, however, had little choice but to stay, as did their son-in-law and daughter. With a sudden dearth of laundries (which at the time were mostly run by the Chinese), they actually did rather well, although it was not easy for them.

Wang Fu chose to stay, for which I was heartily glad. The Wei brothers, however, informed me that while they would wait until spring, they would be leaving to go back to China. Wei Chin, whose English was significantly better than his brother's hastened to reassure me that this had been planned before the riot.

"We come here to make money to take back to China," he explained. "So our family live easy. We have money now. We go. We wait 'til spring because no storm on ocean." He smiled impishly. "And we like you, Miz Wilcox. We help you prune vines, then we go."

There was naught I could do but give him my blessing.

A week passed and there was significant talk of witnesses and indictments. Still numbed by the shock of it all, we clung to the rhythms and tasks of everyday life. The wine for the angelica fermented. We racked the cabernet and merlot wines together and made a lovely claret, as I recall. I went on another crusade to teach housewives the importance of sanitation in the home, which was ill-received. We tried to pretend that everything was normal. So, I didn't think anything of asking Wei Li to take our goats and pasture them in the far end of the vineyard that day, the first week of November. None of us did.

Until Wei Li didn't come back.

CHAPTER TWO

It was a chilly afternoon when I sent Wei Li to pasture the goats. I had a fire going in my parlor's fireplace. Wang Fu was showing me how he diagnosed illness by taking a patient's pulse. It was a practice that was becoming very popular among the Americans in the pueblo, and given that Dr. Wong, the other Chinese doctor, had been among the eighteen murdered Chinese, Wang Fu was attracting considerable interest and business as a result.

As I have already noted, Mr. Wang's stature was more closely aligned to that of his fellow Chinese. In addition to his blue cap, he wore his hair in the traditional style, with the long queue, although his face was clean-shaven. The calm mien of his nature set him apart in many ways, but he also carried with him a slight sense of mischief and a spark of lively intelligence.

I didn't particularly understand the basis of his practice of pulse-taking, but found it at least as effective as anything I'd been doing, which is to say, not very effective at all. But we doctors did our best.

We were practicing on Maria, who was married to Hernan. Most of my household at that time was related to one or another of the other members. Maria helped Magdalena Ortiz with the housekeeping. Magdalena was married to Enrique.

Wang Fu had his hands firmly on Maria's wrists and held his eyes closed so that he could concentrate. Maria looked befuddled, but amused, as she tried to hold still and relax. Slowly, Wang Fu opened his eyes and smiled very warmly at Maria.

"We have some good news," he said. "You are expecting another baby."

Maria looked shocked, then counted in her head. "Yes, I may be."

"How could you have known that?" I asked.

"But, Maddie, I am late," Maria said.

It was the unusual custom in our household to address each other by our first names. It had started when I hired Sebastiano and Enrique, who are brothers, and found that whenever I called for Senor Ortiz, the brother I was not seeking was the one who inevitably answered. As we grew to be greater friends, I began to insist that they address me by my Christian name, as I did the rest of the household.

My beloved and profoundly missed mother had always treated her servants with the same respect she gave everybody, and as her staff deeply loved her, I had long ago resolved to imitate her example. It comes to me now, after looking at the letters my sisters had saved, that Mother may have been a Quaker, possibly in secret, as our family was mostly staunch Congregationalist.

Which is neither here nor there. I was about to question Wang Fu further when Sebastiano came into the parlor from the outside. It is an oddity of adobes that the front parlor almost always opens to the outside of the house without any foyer.

"Maddie, didn't you ask Wei Li to take the goats to pasture on the south end of the vineyard?" A worried frown creased Sebastiano's face.

"I did," I said, glancing out the window. Darkness was beginning to fall and shadows had deepened in the parlor. "He should be back by now, though."

"The goats are in the yard by themselves," Sebastiano said. "Rodolfo is putting them in their pen. But we can't find Wei Li."

That the goats had found their way back to the main yard area near their pen was not so terribly odd.

Goats do have that ability. Nonetheless, Wei Li was not so careless as to let them roam on their own.

Wang Fu stood up, alarm radiating from him. "Where is Wei Chin?"

"In the winery, looking for Wei Li," said Sebastiano.

There was a knock on the door and Maria scurried to answer it. She admitted Pascual and Wei Chin.

"We can't find him," Pascual said. "The last time anybody saw him, he was taking the goats to pasture in the vineyard."

We usually let the goats pasture in the vineyards once the weather became cooler (it seldom gets truly cold in Los Angeles). By that point, the vines had lost most of their leaves, but there were plenty of weeds, which the goats dealt with very efficiently.

It was very worrying. Wei Li was completely trustworthy, but accidents were far too common and there was reason to be concerned that he had somehow come to grief.

"Get the lanterns," I said. "It will be full dark by the time we get out that way."

Between the last of the daylight and the lit lanterns, we could see which path Wei Li and the goats had taken by the tracks left by the goats' sharp little hooves. Wang Fu and Wei Chin called out in Chinese, but only got silence in return. As the darkness grew, the short round leafless vines looked like little bundles of sticks in the lantern light.

We stopped walking near the fence at the southern border of the rancho. From there, Sebastiano, Enrique, Hernan, Pascual, Emilio, and Rodolfo spread out between the rows of vines, waving their lanterns. But it was I who had the misfortune to trip over Wei Li's legs. Wang Fu and Wei Chin ran up as I righted myself. Pascual brought the lantern over and ran the light along Wei Li's body, only to drop it as soon as he saw Wei Li's head.

I picked up the lantern, looked, then quickly waved everybody back away from the body.

"But—" began Enrique, as Pascual ran up the row and emptied his stomach.

"Yes, it is misfortune of the worst sort," I said. "But come no closer or your tracks may obliterate the ones the killer left behind."

"Killer?" Wei Chin choked.

"Yes, I'm afraid." I bent and shone the lantern on Wei Li's face to see what I could discern.

He had been choked to death; his protruding tongue bore witness to that. But more horrifying was that Wei Li's queue had been cut off and wrapped tightly around his throat. The dry dirt still bore witness to the struggle, and I could see boot prints heading back toward the fence. The goats had very effectively mowed the weeds and the ground was quite bare.

Wei Chin and Wang Fu lifted their voices in a horrid atonal wail. Hernan looked as though he wanted to shush them, but I shook my head. However grating we found the noise, they needed to let out their grief, which had been made only that much worse coming so soon after the horrors two weeks before.

I went back to inspecting the ground around Wei Li, then, satisfied that I could see nothing more, I signaled the men forward.

"Kindly avoid stepping over here and over there," I said, pointing to where I had seen the tracks.

I placed my lantern next to one of the ones leading away to the fence and looked at it. The shadows created by the lamplight highlighted the impression left behind. It was from a boot, and it looked like there was a hole in the sole, under the toe. Also, the imprint of two or three nails was made clear by the way the heel had been worn down.

I decided not to hope for Nature to spare the tracks from disturbance. So, I got a piece of paper and a pencil from my leather bag, which I had made sure to bring with me, as I had many of my medical supplies in it. I would have rather made a plaster cast of the footprint, as I remembered reading somewhere that someone had done something similar in Pompeii. But I didn't have any plaster of Paris with me, as it was far too heavy to carry a sufficient amount to make a cast for a broken bone and most people tended to have it on hand, anyway. I drew carefully, estimating the size of the boot in comparison to the bottom of the lantern, much as I had been taught to do in my anatomy classes.

The other tracks bore witness that there had only been one trespasser, although it was possible that they had been made by one of my employees. I couldn't imagine them wearing boots in such poor condition as these, as I made a point of paying them fairly well, but it was possible that the hole had merely been overlooked. Both Enrique and Sebastiano were rather notorious for overlooking rips, tears, and holes in their clothing and shoes.

While I was making my drawing, Hernan and Emilio were tenderly gathering up Wei Li's corpse. Wei Chin was still lost in his sobs, but Wang Fu appeared to be coming to himself.

"I would like to take him to my friend, Mrs. Sutton," I told Wang Fu. "Would that be all right? We'll bury him tomorrow if that's what needs to be done."

"We can take him straight to graveyard," Wang Fu said.

"I know." I sighed. "But I would like Mrs. Sutton to look at him as well. Maybe she can find something that will help us to find out who did this."

Wang Fu nodded and spoke gently in Chinese to Wei Chin. Wei Chin seemed past responding, but eventually muttered something to Wang Fu.

"He says we can take him to Mrs. Sutton," Wang Fu said.

Hernan and Rodolfo had gone on ahead to get the carretta, which they hitched to one of our mules. We put Wei Li's body in the back, as we'd found him. I'd insisted on that and meant no disrespect. I merely hoped that my dear friend Angelina Sutton would find something that I had not. She was the undertaker's wife, and it was her business to prepare the bodies for their funerals. She also had a keen eye and a lively curiosity, and as such, could tell me a great deal about the circumstances of a death in the pueblo. Indeed, she had alerted me to a murder that everyone had thought was an accident.

One of the Ortiz boys had been sent into the pueblo ahead of us to alert Angelina, so she was ready when our little cortège arrived at the back of her house. We laid Wei Li out on the table and Angelina shook her head.

"So much violence," she sighed. "At least, he doesn't look as bad as the others."

"What others?" I asked.

"Those eighteen Chinamen." She shook her head again. "I went by the yard where they had laid them out for their kin to identify them." She looked up at me a little guiltily. "Since I knew the time of death, I wanted to check the state of rigor mortis."

Angelina was making a study of rigor mortis as a way of determining when someone died. It seemed as though it would be a useful thing to know. You must remember, there was no such thing as crime detection as we now know it. There are few enough police now who will search the body or the scene of the crime to look for evidence. We had no idea back then that was what we were doing. We were simply trying to find things out because we needed to.

Angelina shook her head in dismay again. "The bodies had been terribly abused, both before and after death. They may have been only Chinamen, but no decent human being would have treated a dog that way."

I had heard some of the details and was glad when Angelina chose to spare me them. Wang Fu shuddered, and I was grateful that Wei Chin didn't seem to understand what Angelina was saying. Neither of the Wei brothers spoke English well at all, although Wei Chin made more of an effort. I wasn't sure how much he understood of what Wang Fu told him.

I had Rodolfo and Hernan take Wang Fu and Wei Chin back to the rancho. While the Lees were already re-building their laundry, they hadn't rebuilt the rest of the house yet and Wang Fu and the Wei brothers had been staying in the barracks house.

It was one of several buildings on the property. We had a barn for the animals, plus the winery building. But there were also the three adobes, one in which I lived, and the two for the Ortiz brothers and families. The barracks house had quite a few rooms on two levels. Indeed, we often ate supper inside the main room when the weather was foul.

Sebastiano had come along with us and stayed behind with me.

"This is how you found him?" Angelina asked, looking more closely at the body, then pressing gently on his forehead.

"Yes," I said, trying not to start crying.

"Despicable," she whispered again. She began carefully removing Wei Li's clothing, then stopped. "He's been shot. Look at this, Maddie. Someone shot him in the lower back."

She turned the body on its side so that I could see the bloodied back of his shirt. Once the shirt had been removed, I could see that the bullet had pierced Wei Li's back next to his spine at his waistline.

"I was wondering how this villain could have caught Wei Li by surprise," I said. "We found him in the vineyard and the vines aren't more than three feet tall out there."

Angelina rolled Wei Li back, then looked at his face.

"Hm. It looks like someone smoothed his face out,"

"It would have been one of my people, and I'm not surprised," I said. "It was quite ghastly, with his tongue sticking out."

"But look here," Angelina said, lifting up one of the eyelids. "Hemorrhages. They happen a lot when someone is choked. But they wouldn't happen if someone had already died. So, the bullet didn't kill him."

"That seems very odd." I looked sadly down at Wei Li's body. "If this killer had a gun, why didn't he finish the deed by shooting again? Why go to the trouble of strangling him?"

"Maybe he wanted to lynch him?" Angelina gently pulled away the braided hair from Wei Li's throat, then pointed out the ligature mark underneath. "He was definitely strangled."

"You would think we'd seen enough of that already," I said with a sigh.

"Yes, one would." Angelina made a face. "But Mr. Sutton was saying just the other night that while one doesn't want to support vigilantes, the Chinese are such rogues that it would save the courts a lot of time if they simply strung them all up as a matter of course. And in front of Chin Tai, too."

Chin Tai was Angelina's messenger boy.

"What a horrid thing to say," I said. "Especially in front of one of such tender years."

"And yet, it is so commonly said all over the pueblo."

"However commonly believed it is that the Chinese are rogues, it is nothing more than poppycock. Chinamen are no better nor no worse than those of any other country. And many are a great deal better than some." I blinked back tears as I thought of Wei Li working in the fields and the winery.

Angelina shrugged. "Still, with so many in the pueblo who feel they have a grievance against the Chinese, how are you going to go about finding who killed your man?"

I sighed, feeling utterly deflated. "I haven't the least idea." I got out my drawing of the boot track. "This was one of the tracks leading away from the body. It would seem likely that it was made by the killer. But I can't look at the bottom of everyone's feet, can I?"

"You could ask Mr. Mendoza, the cobbler, who had boots like that," Angelina suggested.

"I suppose that's a start. But it will have to wait until after the funeral. We should have it tomorrow. Wang Fu will help."

"That's good because I don't think Mr. Sutton will." Angelina shrugged. "I think I have an extra sheet for a shroud. Will that be enough?"

"It's better than what the others got," I said, feeling no little rage at the thought. I shook it off.

The funeral the next morning was somber and, unlike the one the week before, attended solely by the Lee family and my household. We wore white cockades on our arms rather than black, as the Chinese considered white the color of mourning. There was the atonal wailing and the smoke from the Joss sticks that made several of us sneeze. I'd offered what few roses that were in bloom, and the Lees scattered the petals, with Wang Fu explaining that they represented money to help Wei Li manage in the spirit world. I knew that eventually, after the flesh had rotted, the Chinese would dig Wei Li's skeleton up and send it back to China so that his bones could rest with those of his ancestors. I didn't entirely understand this obsession with their ancestors, but it was their way.

We invited the Lees back to the rancho for a luncheon, but they declined. When we got back to the rancho, Wei Chin went back to the barracks and stayed there.

"Perhaps we should go back to work," Wang Fu said, staring disconsolately after his countryman from where we stood in the yard in front of my adobe.

I sighed. "It seems somewhat disrespectful, and yet I cannot think of else to do." I looked at him. "You don't seem to be grieving so greatly anymore."

Wang Fu winced. "I, like you, am angry. We are not enemy. Yet so many people hate us. Even Negroes hate us. And why? Because they cannot understand us, and yet, your ways are as strange to us as our ways are to you. But we do not hate you or wish to harm you. We only want to make money to bring home to China, so our families have good lives."

I frowned as a truly horrid thought swept through me. "Mr. Wang, this may be a terrible thing to consider, but could Wei Chin have done this to his own brother? Perhaps he wanted to keep more of whatever money they'd made."

Wang Fu looked sadly at the barracks house. "I have wondered, too. But Rodolfo and Wei Chin were working together all afternoon. How could Wei Chin have gotten to that part of the vineyard, killed his brother, then gotten back so that nobody noticed?"

"That's right." I nodded. "Were they very close as brothers? It seems so, yet I know so little about them."

Wang Fu pressed his lips together. He seemed to be struggling with something.

I looked at him severely. "Do you know who could have done this?"

"If it was an American, no, I do not," Wang Fu said quietly.

"Good Heavens," I gasped. "Could it have been a Chinaman? Did you not say that your queues are almost sacred? Why would one of your fellows cut his queue?"

"Queues are not sacred," Wang Fu said. "They are sign of unity. To keep all Chinese united, we wear our hair this way. But you are right. To cut off our queue would mean we cannot go home."

"That seems like a very nasty way to remind Wei Li that he would not see his homeland again."

"It could be." Wang Fu again pressed his lips together.

"No better nor no worse," I grumbled. "Are you thinking of someone among your fellows who might have killed Wei Li?"

"Perhaps." Wang Fu looked at me. "However, you cannot ask questions. I can."

"You will share what you find with me, then?" I asked.

Wang Fu sighed.

"Please, Wang Fu. It would not be good to seek out a vigilante's justice. It would only cause more fear and anger among the Americans."

"Yes, it would," Wang Fu said. "But I am afraid the courts will not help. We cannot even testify there. I know some do get justice. But not for murder and not without strong witness."

I heard the rumbling of a buggy and horses, and sure enough, I saw a familiar rig with two jet black horses with an elegant, high-stepping gait coming toward the rancho. Pascual had seen the approaching buggy, too, and hurried to open the gate. The buggy rolled in, its driver sitting tall and perfectly dignified.

Of course, seeing a woman drive a buggy was scandalous enough. But there was so much that was scandalous about Regina Medina, that driving herself was the least of it. She was easily the most notorious madam in the pueblo at the time. Her house was particularly popular among those men who were the most influential and affluent.

It still amazes me to this day that Regina and I had become fast friends in spite of my deep disapproval of how she made her living. However, she had little option to do something else. As she often reminded me, with a great deal of justice on her part, her girls also had no other option. It was the sorry state of affairs in our world at the time that there were few opportunities for women who found themselves cast out or otherwise bereft of spouse or other family.

Regina was uncommonly tall and did not scruple to hide it. If anything, she made herself look even taller by wearing her shiny black hair piled high upon her head, and then wearing a tall top hat upon her tresses. Her other signature was the lace jabot she wore around her neck at all times.

Her riding habit that day was a dark purple

bombazine and I remember it particularly well because the skirt was far narrower than most others in the pueblo, with rows of ribboned ruching leading to what would become a bustle in the next few years. Regina was well known for always wearing the very latest of dresses. How she got the modes ahead of anyone else was one of her many secrets and one I never learned. But many a respectable woman had been humiliated to discover that her new dress of the very latest style had already been modeled by Regina weeks, if not months, before.

Pascual stepped forward as Regina stopped the horses. He held the lead horse's head while Regina tied the reins to the buggy's brake. A moment later, Regina daintily stepped down from the buggy. Wang Fu nodded at me and went out to the garden where we grew a variety of medicinal herbs along with vegetables for the household. Regina came over and took me by both my hands.

"Oh, Maddie, what a horror!" she said in her breathy voice. "I came as soon as I heard. How can it be that those miserable brutes have yet to slake their blood lust?"

"I have no idea," I said, leading Regina inside my adobe to the parlor. "It is extremely disturbing, to say the least. But I'm surprised that Wei Li's death has gotten about."

"It's all anybody is talking about." Regina smirked, then settled herself on the sofa and removed her gloves. "Or rather they're avoiding talking about it. You know how it is. All the supposedly righteous of our citizenry carrying on about what a disgrace all these ruffians and low characters are to our fair community and the rule of law. Never mind that the vast majority of those esteemed fellows did absolutely nothing to stop the lynchings. Indeed, I suspect some of them even participated. But to have it happen again. How terrible."

I sighed. "We don't know that it was connected to

the riot. Admittedly, it seems highly likely. However, there may be something else involved besides anger at the Chinese."

Regina lifted a perfectly arched eyebrow. "Could it be some form of internecine skullduggery? As I understand it, the riot was started because of a fight amongst the Chinese themselves."

"That is what Wang Fu has told me," I said. "Did you hear this among the souls you sheltered?"

Regina, who knew all too well what it meant to be despised by society, had hidden possibly the larger part of the Chinese population in her house, roughly sixty people. It was a profound act of charity from one who had no reason to be charitable. It never ceased to bewilder me that those who most vehemently claimed to be Christians seemed the least likely to act in accord with our Blessed Savior's charity, whilst those, such as Regina, who did not practice Christianity were often the most likely to fulfill the dictates of our Gospel to love our fellow man.

"About the riot, yes." Regina sighed as she looked longingly at the decanter of angelica that sat on my sideboard. "It was definitely a fight between the two companies. However, the news about your field hand only caused more fear and consternation." She shook her head. "Sadly, I have such a terrible time with their language. Although, if I am brutally honest, and when am I not, I do not do much better with Spanish, which at least sounds more like our own."

"And how many Chinese are you still housing?"

"Five, I think. Most of my refugees seem to have either left for elsewhere or have moved back to Negro Alley."

Negro Alley was the more polite way to refer to the Calle de los Negros, which is the way I described the street as I had been in Los Angeles long enough to learn Spanish and to use the old street names. There was the coarser version of the street's name, but I preferred to avoid it, never mind that most of my fellow citizens did not.

Regina looked me over shrewdly. "I gather from your questions that you have no idea who killed your field hand."

"Sadly, no, I do not," I said. I flirted briefly with the idea of pouring some angelica, but it was still very early in the day and while Regina had quite the head for liquor, I still had work to do and would have been quite impeded in those efforts if I drank as much as the two of us could consume in a visit. "Wang Fu has just now said that he will ask questions among his fellows, as I clearly cannot." I sighed. "I am not sure how I will ask the members of the lower element in the pueblo for information. Even should I find occasion to speak with them, they are hardly likely to tell the truth."

"As for the occasion, I'm sure you'll be patching any number of them up tonight, when all the usual fighting starts," Regina pointed out with considerable justice on her part. "And as for the lower element, I wouldn't worry about discerning who is lying and who isn't. Those fellows can't keep their stories straight no matter how hard they try. But don't be too quick to dismiss some of our more respectable citizens."

"I have no intention of doing so," I said. "However, it is easier to ask them questions as I have more occasion to talk to them. The hard part will be separating the general antipathy toward the Chinese from actual intent to cause harm."

Regina pursed her lips. "That will not be easy, indeed. I have a carpenter fellow working for me who has not been at all kind about my refugees. And I have good reason to believe he was among the rioters that ill-fated night. Perhaps I shall see what I can discover about Mr. Dillman. When was your field hand found?"

"Just after dusk, but according to Angelina, he'd probably been killed an hour or two before that."

"That's very interesting," said Regina. "Mr. Dillman left my house just after one o'clock last Friday, and without making any excuse for his absence. Nor had he finished his work. I was quite perturbed."

"He must have come by here by chance, then, as he could not have known Wei Li would be pasturing the goats in that part of the vineyard." I got up and fetched my leather bag, which had been left as usual next to the door. "I found several footprints of a rather singular boot. Here's the drawing I made of it."

Regina took the drawing and lifted an eyebrow. "That is quite singular. I just wonder how I am going to manage looking at the bottom of Mr. Dillman's boots." She suddenly smiled. "Actually, I do believe I know of a way. I shall spare you the particulars."

I did not say so, but I was grateful. I did not like to remind Regina of how I disapproved of her profession. Nor did I need to, any more than she had needed to explain to me how she expected to get a look at the bottom of Mr. Dillman's boots.

"But I am puzzled," Regina continued. "Assuming that we can prove that this is Mr. Dillman's boot, does it automatically follow that he killed Mr. Wei?"

"I can't imagine what he'd be doing in my vineyard if he didn't. That is where I found the prints. They were leading toward Wei Li's body, then leading away."

"Yes, but will the court let you testify to that?"

I sighed. "They will let me testify. But I will probably need Sebastiano or Enrique to testify also."

It was vastly unjust, and I'd had the problem before. At least I didn't face the problem that the Chinese did at the time. They were prohibited from testifying against any American.

Regina and I both looked again at the decanter of angelica, then looked at each other. She sighed deeply.

"It is too early, isn't it?" she asked.

"I deeply regret it but, yes, it is," I replied. "Besides, it's Saturday, and as you noted, I should be quite busy this evening."

"Alas and alack," said Regina. She rose gracefully and donned her gloves. "You must, indeed, keep your head clear in order to deal effectively with all the chaos, which means that I have done all that I can here." She kissed my cheek. "I do hope it will be a quiet night for a change, or at least a reasonably easy one."

"I hope the same for you," I said.

We moved outside, and I headed to the gate as Regina mounted her buggy. Some minutes later, I closed the gate behind her and turned back to my adobe.

I was wearing a relatively new walking suit, made of a lovely soft worsted wool that had been dyed a deep indigo. The bodice was shaped by a variety of cunning plaits and trimmed in ruffles. The skirt was similarly trimmed and swept back, although still rather full. Given the day and time, I probably should have changed to my red poplin work dress. However, I decided that there was no time like the present, which meant that a visit to Mr. Emmanuel Mendoza was in order.

Mr. Mendoza was the uncle of three of my field hands: Hernan, who was married to Maria, and Hernan's cousins Emilio and Pascual. The senior Mr. Mendoza made and sold shoes near the schoolhouse on Calle Segundo. There were additional cobblers in the pueblo, but I had an entree with Mr. Mendoza, thanks to his nephews, that I did not have with the others.

I would have walked off on my own, but both Enrique and Sebastiano caught me trying to leave the rancho. I had run into some trouble the year before and it had been decided by my household that it was not safe to let me move around the pueblo alone, especially not at night. Granted, sunset was several hours off, the clock having just struck two of the clock.

"It is broad daylight and I am only going to Mr. Mendoza's shoe shop," I protested.

Sebastiano shook his head. "It is Saturday."

"I am well aware of that," I said. "But it is quite early yet."

Enrique laughed. "It never is that early. We all know that the second someone calls, you will go. And then someone after that, and the next thing we know, it will be midnight with you trying to get home by yourself."

Unfortunately, Enrique had the right of it, although I had many times walked the streets in the earliest hours of the morning and come to no harm. I had also narrowly escaped harm more than once and often enough that it was to my benefit to have someone accompany me, however irritating that was.

I waited just long enough for Sebastiano to get his six-shooter while Enrique and Emilio saddled Daisy, my roan mare, and the mule. I had planned to walk, but it was somewhat quicker to ride. Besides, there was no telling whether I would get back to the rancho before supper or not.

My pique notwithstanding, it was probably just as well that Sebastiano had decided to join me that day. As we left the rancho, I got the odd feeling that we were being watched. As I thought about it, I realized that it was not the first time I'd had that feeling. There were not a lot of vantage points in the immediate area of the rancho's gate that would allow for such unseen observation. However, there was one small hill and not far off a huge oak tree that could provide some cover for an observer.

Sebastiano and I pulled up shortly in front of the small shop. It was but one of three different shops in the brick building that had been covered in whitewash. The window was filled with all manner of boots and slippers. Most of the shoes that Mr. Mendoza sold had been purchased in pieces from some manufactory, I know not where it was. Then Mr. Mendoza would assemble the pieces, often adjusting the fit and decoration to the needs and taste of the person buying the shoes. I had only the winter before come to start buying my shoes from Mr. Mendoza, although my hands, not surprisingly, had been patronizing Mr. Mendoza as long as they could remember.

Mr. Mendoza was of medium size but stooped from years bending over a cobbler's bench. His body and face were fairly round, and white speckled his dark hair and beard. He smiled warmly at me as I entered.

"Good day, Senora Wilcox," he said in Spanish. "What brings you here today? Did that rascal of a dog dine on your boots again?"

The rascal of a dog was ChiChi, one of those small Mexican dogs. He was a light tan in color with the amazing ability to jump almost straight up, often as high as my waist. It looked as though he were floating. While I do not hold with dogs inside the home as they are not sanitary, however delightful they may be, I'd had to make an exception in the case of ChiChi who was so small he could easily escape the barn. Unfortunately, that meant the local coyotes were apt to try to eat him. We had almost lost the poor little thing that previous spring. So, while we allowed ChiChi and our two other dogs, Negrito and Beauty, the run of the yard during the day, as soon as the sun set, ChiChi was sequestered in my adobe, while the other two dogs stayed in the barn.

Alas, ChiChi had quite the appetite for my boots, whether I happened to be wearing them or not.

"He did nibble on my heel yesterday morning," I said. "However, that is not why I'm here today." I pulled the drawing of the boot from my bag. "Have you repaired a boot with a sole that looked like this?"

Mr. Mendoza looked at the drawing. "No. I would remember a hole that big." He looked up at me, blinking quickly several times. "Why are you looking for that particular boot?"

I pressed my lips together. "I cannot say."

Mr. Mendoza nodded. "You are looking for the man who killed your Chinaman."

"He did not belong to me," I replied. "But, yes, he did work for me."

"Well, I have not seen this particular hole, but I will tell you if I do." He looked at the drawing again. "The owner should be coming to me soon enough." He mused as he handed me back the piece of paper.

"Indeed, it should be fairly easy to find the person whose boot this is."

"How?" I asked. "I can't go about the pueblo demanding that people show me the bottoms of their shoes."

"No. Of course not. But anyone with a hole this size will probably be limping from all the things he's stepping on through that hole."

"That is true," I said. "However, plenty of people limp who have perfectly sound shoes. Still, it might provide a hint as to which men I should be looking at more closely." I slid the paper back into my bag. "Gracias, Senor Mendoza. Please let me know if you see anything like this."

I left the shop feeling most disgruntled. Men who limped were not in short supply in the pueblo. But then, Mr. Mendoza had made a good point. That hole was sure to make walking at least a little bit difficult.

CHAPTER THREE

That Saturday night, it was clear that the pueblo was still reeling from the events two weeks before. Most of the ranch hands, teamsters, and other itinerant laborers seemed intent on proving their good behavior. It was both a blessing and a problem. There were fewer fights as a result, but those fights that occurred were much more severe.

I only dug bullets from three men. But we lost a shepherd, a Mr. Beltran, in a knife fight at Mr. Uribe's saloon. I'd had the good sense to go home before the violence started and change into my red poplin work dress and had brought a couple extra aprons with me. Both Mr. Beltran and the man he'd been fighting had originally been removed to the back storeroom behind the saloon. The owner, Mr. Uribe, bought a great deal of my angelica and some of my other wines, as his saloon was quite popular, especially with a great many of the local laborers.

The storeroom was a large room, with stacks of crates of varying heights lining most of the walls, a small writing desk next to the door leading to the saloon, itself, and a long table that was generally pushed next to the crates on the far end of the room.

Mr. Sedonez, the man who tended the bar, was out front, as usual. The man who had engaged with Mr. Beltran (and presumably killed him) was a Mr. Gluck, and he, also, was wounded. His clothes were made of coarse homespun and while they were not quite in tatters yet, they soon would be. His hair was wheat colored, what there was of it, and his face round. I had reason to believe he was one of many laborers who often made their way through Los Angeles at the time.

He was unconscious as he lay on the long table that Mr. Sedonez had kindly set near a stack of crates that now held several lanterns, all lit. Mr. Beltran's body had by that time been removed to the Suttons' funeral parlor. Or perhaps not. As he was beyond the need for my help, I paid him little mind not out of a lack of caring, but out of the necessity of patching up Mr. Gluck.

He had several rather nasty cuts, including one down his cheek, that went all the way into his beard. It being the most serious, I tended to that cut first. I shaved the beard away, poured carbolic acid over the cut, and sutured it closed, holding my breath against the vapor of stale beer that he emitted. It was not pleasant to breathe, but it was better than having to dose him into silence.

I was not alone as I worked. Sebastiano stood guard. Policeman Walter Lomax watched with his usual laconic mien. Three of Mr. Gluck's friends stood guard against the two friends of Mr. Beltran, which I thought was a bit unnecessary, Mr. Gluck's friends being considerably larger than Mr. Beltran's.

The final observer was Old Man Pugh. He'd been a miner in the early days of the Gold Rush, had supposedly struck it rich, then lost everything as so many had. He was toothless, his beard and hair were thin and a yellowed white. It was hard to say how tall he was, as he was bent over as if carrying the weight of a heavy load.

The old timer often appeared when I was trying to stitch someone back together, usually offering an outsized account of whatever affray had caused my patient his injury. Mr. Lomax liked him even though Mr. Pugh's memory was so bad that he was useless as a witness in court. However, in the brief aftermath of a fight, Mr. Pugh could be counted on to point out who did what to whom and from there Mr. Lomax could find more reliable witnesses.

"That there Mr. Gluck," Mr. Pugh told me as I looked at Mr. Gluck's arm and determined that the scratch there merely needed to be bandaged. "He coulda' taken on two of them shepherd fellows. And a meaner fellow, you never did see."

"Who drew first?" Mr. Lomax asked. He was a broad-shouldered man, with a square jaw that was generally clean-shaven, and brown hair.

Mr. Beltran's friends promptly screamed that Mr. Gluck had drawn his knife first, while Mr. Gluck's friends screamed that Mr. Beltran had. Mr. Pugh simply cackled, his breath as laden with the yeasty fustiness of stale beer as Mr. Gluck's.

"They drew together," Mr. Pugh said. "They both drew together."

"Over what?" Mr. Lomax asked, ignoring the other men in the room.

"Them dagnabbed Chinamen," Mr. Pugh said. "Ole Gluck there said that Beltran had helped with the lynchings and should be indicted with them other fellows. Beltran swore he was trying to stop the lynchings and that Gluck was holding them Chinese fellows down, so the men could get the ropes over their heads."

I was trying not to pay attention to Mr. Pugh. In the flickering yellow light of the single lantern in the room, I could see Mr. Gluck gasping for air, and it looked as though his lips were growing darker.

I opened his shirt and looked for signs of a wound on his chest but found none.

"Sebastiano," I said quickly. "Help me roll this man over."

Sebastiano heard the urgency in my voice and leaped to my aid. Mr. Gluck gasped again as we rolled his bulk onto his stomach. I pulled the roughly woven and stained shirt up his torso and motioned for the lantern. Mr. Lomax, who had seen me work many a time before as well, knew immediately what I wanted and grabbed the wanted lantern, shining its weak light on Mr. Gluck's back. Sure enough, instead of the even rows of ribs, visible even through Mr. Gluck's bulk, there was the dark of a bruise over one rib midway down Mr. Gluck's back, and a depression where the next lower rib should have been.

I may be a doctor, but I am a lady as well, and it is particularly incumbent upon me to behave as such at all times, as there is enough prejudice against women doctors as it is. There are moments when even the most decent and placid of my male colleagues will swear like hardened sailors. This was one such moment. Alas, I could not swear, but I very much wanted to.

I grabbed some more carbolic acid and rubbed it across the bruise, then poured more of the disinfectant over my scalpel and immediately went to work, cutting him open and straightening out the two broken ribs. I eased the bone that had pierced Mr. Gluck's lung away from that organ and watched the lung re-inflate. Whether it would remain inflated had yet to be seen. I, quite reasonably, should have despaired of the man's life. However, I set the rib bones and stitched him closed. Then, as the patient's lips began to darken again, I pulled a trocar, a thin, pointed tube that was used to drain all manner of growths and wounds, out of my bag, and after dosing it, pushed it carefully into the patient's chest. I wiped the wound down with more carbolic acid, then had Sebastiano and Mr. Lomax hold Mr. Gluck up so that I could wind a bandage around him and the trocar.

The wounded man continued breathing. I looked up. One of Mr. Gluck's friends had disappeared, as had both of Mr. Beltran's friends. I shook my head. They could cause all manner of mayhem, cutting and shooting each other up, but a little surgery turned them into jellies. The men who had taken Mr. Beltran to the undertaker's came back about then, bearing the stretcher they'd used.

"We should take him to the Sisters of Charity," I

told Mr. Gluck's two remaining friends. The sisters ran the hospital in the city and were good and kind nurses. I pointed to the nearest man. "You and your friend, get Mr. Gluck onto the stretcher. Gently! Bring him to the house and tell the sisters that I shall be along shortly. Gently!"

I supervised just long enough to make sure that the men handled Mr. Gluck with care, then took off my bloodied apron. Mr. Pugh was wheezing and chuckling softly to himself.

"It was that Beltran who started it, you know," he told Mr. Lomax. "I heard him calling Gluck out. He said Gluck had held the men down during the lynchings. Gluck is big. He can do things like that."

"Did you see Mr. Gluck the night of the riot?" I asked the old man.

"I absolutely did!" Mr. Pugh insisted.

I glanced over at Mr. Lomax, who shrugged.

"I seen all of them fellows," Mr. Pugh went on. "Efrem Smith, Valdez, McKinley, Leo Dillman, Raymond Sanford, all them fellows. They were whooping and hollering and hung at least three of them Chinamen over by the buggy manufactory. Mr. Hewitt tried to tell them to stop on account of there being ladies in the house. But they didn't listen. They didn't. There were even some of them fancy folk. You know them. The kind that look down their noses at you and me because they're so much better than us because they have money. Well, I'll tell you, they're no better than we are. Not in the least. They did nothing to stop them lynchings. And a couple of them even helped. Then they go parading around telling us about the rule of law. How we're no better than beasts because we lynched a few Chinamen, and most of them won't even let a Chinaman wipe their shoes."

Mr. Pugh suddenly gagged, coughed, then expectorated onto the floor. He pulled a grimy handkerchief from his pocket and wiped his mouth with deep satisfaction.

I looked over at Mr. Lomax, who again shrugged. I finished wrapping my tools in my apron and stuffed everything into my leather bag.

We disentangled ourselves from Mr. Pugh, who was still fulminating on those of our wealthier citizens holding themselves up as better than everyone else.

"What do you think, Mr. Lomax?" I asked as we walked toward the hospital.

"About what, Mrs. Wilcox?"

"About Mr. Pugh's list of fellows who were part of the riot. I know several men were arrested, but were any of them the men Mr. Pugh named?"

"No."

I glanced at Sebastiano, then sighed. "Are any of those fellows limping?"

"Not that I've noticed," Mr. Lomax said.

I stopped walking and turned on him. "I'm looking for the man who killed Wei Li. I have reason to believe that one of them might have problems walking because of a hole in his boot."

"Not if you stuff enough newspaper in the bottom," Mr. Lomax said.

I felt my one ray of hope fade away. "Then how am I to find this fellow?"

"I looked at Gluck's boots. They're whole, but not new," said Sebastiano.

"You're looking for boots?" Mr. Lomax asked.

"I found several footprints," I said, beginning my walk again. "From a very singular boot with a hole in the bottom."

"Oh."

Fortunately, he did not ask how I was going to look at the soles of everyone of whom I was suspicious.

We arrived at the hospital and I checked on Mr. Gluck. Mother Superior, a very tired-looking woman with a pinched face, was not entirely happy to have yet another invalid to care for, let alone having been awakened at such a late hour. I could hardly blame her. Every indigent fool who came to harm ended up on her doorstep, and the good Christians of the pueblo often lagged in the support of her mission.

Mr. Gluck, for his part, continued to breathe. I explained to Mother Ynez what had happened and what I was concerned about. She agreed and had one of her nuns sit with Mr. Gluck.

The hospital clock was striking three of the morning at that point, so Sebastiano and I made our way home.

I managed to get to Sunday services on time, although I largely dozed through Reverend Elmwood's sermon. It could have been one of his better ones. He did occasionally find a theme that would stir one to betterment. But that was a rare occasion, indeed, which is why I often found myself getting quite sleepy during services. I would have quit attending completely, but I do believe that if one is to call herself Christian, the very least she can do is attend church once a week.

Dinner was waiting for me after services. Most of the people on the rancho were Mexican, and thus Catholics, so we ate an early dinner on Sundays because they fasted from the night before until after their services. Wang Fu and Wei Chin joined us, and if it wasn't an entirely merry feast, at least it was pleasant enough and I do hope that Wei Chin found some comfort in it.

Later that afternoon, I went to check on Mr. Gluck. He was sleeping when I got there, but still very much alive. I had to admit that I was impressed by his fortitude. The nurses had re-wound his various bandages and had, I must confess, done an even neater job than I had. The good women did not complain, nor would they. Still, I got the impression that Mr. Gluck was not the most temperate of patients.

The next morning, I discovered that there might be a small leak in the ceiling that required the immediate assistance of a skilled carpenter. Or, more accurately, I decided that I wanted to speak with Mr. Dillman. So, I sent a note to Regina, who promptly sent him along.

He was a tall, slender man with well-formed shoulders, fair hair, and green eyes. He seemed congenial enough, but as I spoke with him, I noticed a certain braggadocio in his bearing, as if no one could possibly know more about carpentry than he. I explained my concern and he smiled and hitched up his pants.

"I'll take care of it," he said. "Why don't you just hurry along? You don't need to worry your pretty little head about a thing."

I couldn't help it. I glared at him.

"Mr. Dillman, you should be aware that the very minute someone tells me I shouldn't worry my pretty little head about something, I find that I should worry about exactly that."

His eyes flashed angrily. I do believe he was not trying to pull the wool over my eyes, but I could also tell that he did not appreciate my remonstrance. Still, he found a small ladder and began to inspect the beams of my ceiling. Given that the adobe was fairly new (it had been constructed the spring before), Mr. Dillman did not find anything, nor did I expect him to. Unfortunately, I was not able to get a good look at the bottoms of his boots either.

"That's a good sound beam, Miz Wilcox," Mr. Dillman announced.

"Thank you, Mr. Dillman." I smiled again. "Mrs. Medina speaks quite highly of your work."

I, in fact, did not know what Regina thought of Mr. Dillman's work. But as she generally hired the best she could find, and as he had not been dismissed, I felt I could assume that she was at the very least satisfied. Nor would she mind me using her supposed thoughts as a way to begin a conversation with Mr. Dillman.

"I expect she does," Mr. Dillman replied.

"Do you like working there?"

"Oh, it's good enough, except for all the Chinamen she had over there. Couldn't find a pot to—" He stopped suddenly. "Begging your pardon, ma'am."

"I expect it was quite crowded over there for a time."

"And I do not like them Chinese. That weird noise they make when they talk. And they're taking our jobs, too."

"You seem to be well enough employed," I said.

"But I know plenty of fellows who aren't." He looked around. "You don't have any of them around here."

"I lost one of my field hands recently," I said.

"Probably run off to go back home. I wish they all would."

I paused and looked at him. "Did I not see you on the road that runs past the southern edge of my rancho on Friday afternoon?"

He looked at me a little warily. "I don't know what you mean."

I forced myself to smile. "I merely saw someone and wanted to know if it was you."

"I didn't come nowhere near this place," he said with some vehemence. "Why would I?"

"Perhaps you were passing by on the way to someplace else. People go along that road quite often."

"Well, it weren't me. I got no business out this way and don't want any." He sent a quick glance at my door.

"A carpenter who doesn't want business?"

"That's not what I mean," he snapped. He grabbed his hat from the hall tree next to the door. "Now, good day."

He scrambled out the door. I watched from the window as he paused, hitched up his pants, then hurried through the yard to the gate. The odd thing was, I realized that I had, indeed, seen someone on the road near my rancho that day, albeit in the morning. However, I dismissed the thought. After all, as I had pointed out, it was not unusual to see people on that road.

I went to find my gloves and found they were lost again. Juanita Alvarez, my personal maid, shook her head when I asked her for them.

"You could have looked in the drawer where they belong," she chided me.

I did have a tall bureau in my bedroom, which did have a drawer that held my gloves. However, I had a bad habit of leaving whatever gloves I'd been wearing near my leather bag, which often meant the gloves fell to the floor. Or sometimes ChiChi ran off with them. Or I failed to take off my gloves until I was in my study. In short, my gloves seldom landed in the drawer where they belonged, unless Juanita found them and put them away.

Juanita was a young, very pretty woman, and very dear to me, although I'm afraid I did take her very much for granted at times and would eventually come to rue it when she left me to get married. I couldn't have realistically expected her to forego marriage to stay with me and we did remain friends ever after. But even to this day, I do miss her chiding and often wise perspective.

I had on my newest riding habit, made of dark green linen and wool. The skirt was swept back and the bodice decorated with velvet ruching. I did have a dark green hat and veil to match but wore my black riding gloves with it. I got those from the bureau while Juanita had Emilio saddle Daisy and a mule for Damiano and Juan. Damiano was Sebastiano and Olivia's youngest son and the second youngest among the five children that survived. Juan was the fourth of Enrique and Magdalena's six surviving children. The two cousins were thirteen and looked much alike, having their fathers' broad shoulders and square faces.

The boys would be riding alongside me that day as I made my errand to the hospital to check on Mr. Gluck. They waited by the mule, bickering over who would ride in front. Emilio hushed them and said they would take turns and pointed out that the boy riding behind had the primary responsibility for shooting whoever attacked me. I felt very annoyed because I knew Emilio wasn't entirely teasing.

The boys and I rode off, arriving shortly at the hospital. Mr. Gluck was awake, if looking rather pale. I was surprised that he wasn't chained to his bed, as he had killed Mr. Beltran. However, the good sister told me that the witnesses to the fight had assured Mr. Lomax that Mr. Beltran had drawn his knife first. Hence, Mr. Gluck had killed Mr. Beltran in self-defense and there seemed little point in having a trial to determine what was manifestly obvious.

"Good day, Mr. Gluck," I said briskly. "How are you feeling?"

He looked away from me and grunted.

"I would imagine that your cuts and your ribs are causing you a fair amount of pain," I said.

I loosened the bandage on his cheek. There was some reddening, but not the putrid ooze of contagion. It is, sadly, not clear from my journals at which point I began to accept germ theory as fact. However, by that time, I had certainly embraced the efficacy of both carbolic acid and alcohol for the treatment of wounds.

I lifted his nightgown and listened to his chest with my stethoscope, then checked under the chest bandage. I had removed the trocar the night before and that wound was also healing quite cleanly.

As I wrapped a fresh bandage around Mr. Gluck, he regarded me with a sullen stare, as if he couldn't bear to have me touch him and yet was powerless to stop me. That, alas, was not an unusual reaction. But then he surprised me.

"Do you think I am guilty?" He asked.

I looked at him, curiously. "We are all guilty of something."

"But I helped," he said, sadly. "I helped lynch those Chinamen. What that dagnabbed shepherd said was true."

I pressed my lips together and took a deep breath. "What happened?"

"I was in the saloon. They came in and said Bob

Thompson was killed. That the Chinamen had killed him and that we were going to go after them." He sighed very deeply. "I don't know why, but I like a good fight. I have nothing against the Chinamen. But a good fight is worth something. Then they said they were going to lynch the Chinamen. I don't know why, but everyone was so wild, and I was, too. I held the Chinamen as they struggled so the others could get the nooses around their necks. I don't know why I did. I just did. It wasn't even a fight. But I did it. I don't know why, but I did it." He looked at me, his eyes brimming with sorrow. "I am not a saint. I like a good fight. But in a fight, there is someone fighting you. This. There was no fight. What have I done?"

That horrid dream from the night after the riot flashed through my head, and it seemed as though Wei Li had joined my accusers. I swallowed and stepped back. Gluck's contrition seemed very real, and as a Christian woman it was my duty to forgive him. But I could not. I simply could not.

I swallowed again. "Shall I have a priest or minister come to you?"

It was the best I could do.

He coughed. "A priest would be good. I need to confess my sins."

I checked the bandage on his arm, then stood over him.

"There was another Chinese man, killed only this past Friday."

"There was? Was there a fight?"

"No. He was shot in the back."

Mr. Gluck shook his head. "That was not me. I don't like to shoot people. That is not a fight. I like a good fight."

I left his bedside, shaking with fury. I did ask the nurse to call a priest for Mr. Gluck. But that was all I could do.

CHAPTER FOUR

My soul and mind were in such a state as I left the hospital, I insisted that Juan and Damiano take the mule and Daisy and ride on ahead without me. I needed to walk. It was the only thing I could think of to calm myself.

The boys looked at each other dubiously. They did not want to disobey me, but they also desperately did not want to disobey their fathers, and I suspect they had a difficult time discerning whose fury would be worse to face. However, mine was not only present but was a rare enough occurrence, I like to think, that it must have seemed the more frightening prospect. In any case, the boys chose to ride slowly just ahead of me.

I strode from the hospital to the Calle Primavera and then down Calle Segundo to the Calle Principal. Outside of the American Hotel, I stumbled into another woman. So blind was my anger, I failed to see who she was at first.

"Oh, pray excuse me, Mrs. Wilcox," said the soft voice.

I blinked. "Oh, Miss Gaines."

It was Miss Lavina Gaines, the only daughter of a local land agent. She was a lovely young thing, about seventeen at that point, with brown ringlets that bobbed becomingly around her round, pert face.

"I'm afraid it is I who must beg pardon from you," I said, recovering myself. "I was not watching where I was walking."

"You're very kind, Mrs. Wilcox."

"As are you, Miss Gaines. I trust all is well with

you?"

"Well enough," she said, trying so very hard not to betray that all was not well with her. Indeed, she seemed to be on the verge of tears.

Lest she lose her battle and present an unseemly display on the street, I gently tugged her into the hotel. We found a quiet corner where we could sit unobserved.

I might not have done so, but Miss Gaines' mother had died some years before. The girl did have friends among the young women of the pueblo, but this seemed to be the sort of thing that required a more mature listener. I would normally not have seen myself as fulfilling that requirement, but there seemed to be no one else. In addition, the burden of a young heart seemed to be an almost pleasant distraction from my current worries.

"You're too kind, Mrs. Wilcox," Miss Gaines said once we were seated. She pulled a handkerchief from the small beaded bag that matched her cunningly-made pink walking suit. "It's my father. He wants me to get married."

"And you do not wish to?"

Miss Gaines shook her head. "I'm perfectly happy to marry. I just do not wish to marry the men my father wants me to. They are all so old!" The tears finally burst forth. "I do not want to be ungrateful. But I do not wish to marry a gray-haired old man. And some of them are quite awful. They are like so many of Father's friends. They present themselves as fine, upstanding citizens and they are anything but. I know of one fellow, he is a drunkard. One fellow has a hole in his soul. At least three more are likewise not nearly as wealthy as they pretend to be. And the worst of it is that Father wants me to be well-cared for in case he dies. That's why he wants me to marry and why he picks the men he does."

"But why can't he see what you see?" I asked, feeling decidedly disgusted.

"I've asked him, and he keeps telling me that I'm a silly, senseless thing and that I should trust him."

Alas, I was in no mood to be charitable.

"What utter nonsense!" I snapped. "You are easily the most sensible young woman I have ever met."

I might have exaggerated in that moment, but Miss Gaines was exceedingly sensible for a young woman of her years, as well as kind and very selfless when it came to her miserly father and despicable brother.

"But what am I to do?" she asked.

"I would most strongly advise you not to marry someone you don't want to."

The poor girl quailed. I took a deep breath and steadied myself.

"Miss Gaines, am I to understand that you fear being put out on the streets without support if you go against your father's wishes?"

"Mother told me I must obey him, and that he would be well within his rights to put me out if I did not do his bidding."

"He might be within his rights, but only an ogre would do such a thing. Has he threatened to do so?"

"Not in so many words." Miss Gaines sniffed. "But he does frequently complain about what an ungrateful and unkind girl I am."

I sat up straight. "You must not believe that. Indeed, you are far kinder to both him and your brother than either of them deserve." Even though we were in a public place, I took her hands in mine. "Miss Gaines, I, too, was in your place. I had graduated from medical college and when my father found out, he was so ashamed of me, he wanted to throw me to the streets. I was terrified. The only relief my father offered was for me to marry Albert Wilcox, the son of my father's best friend. I did not like Mr. Wilcox. He was vaguely stupid, dishonest, and had no interest in me. He simply needed a wife and had always liked me from a distance. I did not think I could make my way as a physician, so I made the mistake of marrying Mr. Wilcox. And the first thing he did was to drag me out here. He had no regard for me. He only wanted me not to embarrass him by not telling anyone I was a doctor. He had also promised me all his belongings should he die first and had written me a letter saying so. I expect he realized that I needed some convincing to marry him. But I have no doubt that had he'd gotten around to making a will before he died, he would have reneged on that. I knew what sort of man he was and still agreed to marry him, to my everlasting regret. I have made a life for myself here, and Our Good Lord was kind enough to take him off my hands within months after he bought the rancho. So, I do understand your fear. However, I beg you to learn from my bitter experience and do not marry a man simply because you think you have no other alternative."

"But I don't have any other alternative."

I took a deep breath. "You do. If your father throws you out, you will come live with me." I swallowed. "It is the very least I can do. We will manage quite well, and I am sure I can find some gainful employment for you until such time as you find a man worthy of you."

Miss Gaines blinked her eyes and began crying again. "Mrs. Wilcox, what a kind and generous offer! How can I ever thank you?"

"No thanks are needed yet," I said, pulling myself up straight. "It remains to be seen what course your father will follow. He may yet see his way to being more understanding."

"Still, I am much relieved." Miss Gaines dabbed at her eyes. "Knowing that I shall not be left to ruin. I do so want to be the dutiful daughter my mother wanted me to be. But I cannot face the kind of husband my father wants for me." She looked at me and sighed. "Why is it that we are to obey and trust the men in our lives even when it is clear that they have no regard for our feelings? I know my father loves me and only wishes good for me. But I cannot honestly believe that he has the first understanding of what that good is, especially given how easily his own friends have pulled the wool over his eyes."

I shook my head. "I cannot say, my dear. We are supposed to trust that our menfolk really do know best. However, I have found few who seem to. Indeed, when some man tells me what my best interests are, it is almost inevitable that those same interests are to his benefit and not necessarily to mine." I smiled and got up. "Now, I am afraid that I must see to other duties."

"Of course." Miss Gaines rose as well. "Thank you ever so much, Mrs. Wilcox."

"Feel free to call on me whenever you wish." I said, gathering my bag about me.

We left the hotel together, and she hurried off to her father's home. I paused on the street. Juan and Damiano waited nearby, Daisy and the mule's reins in hand. I couldn't help but smile at their plan for staying close while allowing me my chance to walk and to see to another. It was exactly what I had needed. For all that Miss Gaines' troubles had annoyed me, hearing her plea and being able to allay her fears had done my mood a world of good.

However, as I stood on the street, wondering what to do next, I again got the feeling that my movements were under observation. Perhaps I had seen someone one too many times out of the corner of my eye. I could not say.

I dismissed the thought, but that left me at a bit of a loss as to what to do next. There were many people I could have called on, but few, if any, who would be apprised of the state of various boots in the pueblo. But then, as I considered, it occurred to me that there were two women in the pueblo who might know more about the state of someone's boots than one would suppose.

Mrs. Carson and Mrs. Glassell were the two most virulent gossips in the pueblo. They delighted in knowing everyone else's secrets, never mind that they seldom revealed their own. Nor, if I am completely honest, was their supposed knowledge all that accurate. Still, it was possible that one or the other had observed something untoward.

I made my way to Mrs. Carson's home first. It was a grand house, painted a pale yellow, with a sweeping porch. I knocked at the door, and was not surprised to learn that Mrs. Carson was not in. I had already seen the curtain of the parlor window twitch, which led me to believe that Mrs. Carson was, in fact, in but did not wish to see me. I was not surprised. She seldom spoke to me unless she encountered me on the street or when she required my services as a doctor for her husband or herself.

I smiled at the Negro maid and left for Mrs. Glassell's, where I was admitted to her front parlor. Mrs. Glassell was in her favorite chair, holding court, as it were. She was a very round woman, with graying hair, and wearing a lawn tea dress with a pink figured rose pattern that did not compliment her skin coloring at all.

"Oh, dear, dear, Mrs. Wilcox!" she gushed, holding her hands out to me.

I took them briefly, then seated myself on the sofa next to her.

"What horrors we've already been through," Mrs. Glassell went on. "And now, to have them revisited on your ranch. My heart goes out to you. It truly does."

"Thank you, Mrs. Glassell." I paused, catching the gleam of interest in her eyes. It suddenly occurred to me that I would need to be careful of what questions I asked of her, as she clearly was more interested in what conclusions she could draw from them than giving me any real answers. "Your concern is quite kind."

"I assume you're on the hunt for the low character that did this to your Chinaman?"

"Naturally. But there are a great many people who could have killed Mr. Wei," I replied.

I debated showing her the drawing of the boot print. If Mrs. Glassell saw it, everyone in the pueblo would know what I was looking for in a matter of hours. On the other hand, I had shown the drawing to several people already. Perhaps it would help if others were looking for the boot, as well.

"I do hope you can help me," I continued. "We found a rather singular boot print in the vineyard where Mr. Wei was killed. It seems highly likely that it belongs to the killer."

"A boot print?" Mrs. Glassell asked. "But in what way is it singular?"

"It had a rather large hole in the sole and was quite worn on the heel," I said.

"Good Heavens. There must be any number of boots in the pueblo in such disrepair."

"That is, unfortunately, true. It does not make my task any easier, I assure you."

Mrs. Glassell snorted. "Indeed, it doesn't. Unfortunately, I don't see how I can be of help to you."

"Just because the boot is badly worn on the bottom does not mean that it is as badly worn on the top," I replied.

Mrs. Glassell sat back in her chair in affront. "Surely this bit of deranged behavior happened among the ruffians of the pueblo rather than its civilized citizens."

"More than likely," I said with a conciliatory smile. "However, I cannot make that assumption out of hand. Which is why I was hoping that you would have some idea of who is, shall we say, putting on a better show of his wealth than perhaps he is entitled to."

"Another simple task," Mrs. Glassell said, rolling her eyes. "Even Mr. Carson is prone to exaggerating about his holdings." She paused. "You will not say so to Mrs. Carson, will you? I would not want her to be embarrassed."

"Of course not," I said. "I fully intend to keep this interview in the strictest confidence and hope you will do the same."

"Naturally," Mrs. Glassell said with a satisfied smirk. "You know me. The very soul of discretion."

I bit my tongue and smiled.

"But what an interesting observation," she continued. "I don't doubt Mr. Judson could be counted among those who appear better turned out than they are. Just between the two of us, Mrs. Judson complains bitterly to me that he will keep shirts until he can no longer keep them on his person because they are so riddled with holes. He says, according to her, that there is no point in throwing away a perfectly useful garment as long as the mends do not show."

Mr. Judson owned one of the largest banks in town and was a one-time member of the city council. I knew his wife rather better, though not to the point of such confidences. It would not have entirely surprised me if he proved to be so miserly, however I had no reason to believe that he was.

"And Mr. McKinley. The land agent." Mrs. Glassell nodded eagerly. "I've heard rumors about him not being as successful as he would have you believe. Perhaps he's hiding a few holes in his boots."

I'd heard the name recently but couldn't remember where or how.

Mrs. Glassell didn't seem to notice. "Oh, and that other land agent, Mr. Gaines. They say he's quite a miser. There might be a reason why. And then you could also consider Mr. Montero, the tanner. It stands to reason he wouldn't find the time to repair his boots, never mind how much leather he has. Or Mr. Handley, the insurance agent. You know how terrible a business that is. Let me think. Let me think. Ah. Mr. Fletcher, come to think of it, he's a land agent and a lawyer. Then Mr. Costa, he has that ranch to the east of here. He travels so much. You would think he wouldn't need to if the ranch is doing so well. And Mr. Shapiro, of the mercantile. Now, there's a business one would think is successful, but is probably not. I've found dust on several of the bolts of fabric in there." She paused, then smiled almost wickedly. "And let us not forget Mr. Hewitt."

I sat back, almost surprised. "Mr. Hewitt?"

Mrs. Glassell nodded. "You do know his little secret, don't you? He presents himself as staunch and sober a fellow as can be and we know he's not sober."

I sighed. "I'm afraid so. But he manages it well."

Actually, he didn't. His wife, Mrs. Hewitt did, even as she was terrified that someone would find out that it was she that ran their buggy manufactory rather than him. It was not surprising that Mrs. Glassell had noted his problem.

"In addition," I continued. "He protested against the lynchings, admittedly for not wanting them that close to his home. But he did protest. Why would he then go and kill a field hand?"

Mrs. Glassell put up her hands and shook them. "I wouldn't have the faintest idea. I dare say, you're the only one who would know the answer to that. Or be able to find it."

"I hope not," I said.

"Be that as it may," Mrs. Glassell said. "Everyone knows you are very clever about these sorts of things. I, for one, am completely confident that you'll find your Chinaman's killer in no time."

"I certainly hope so." I smiled and rose. "But for now, I do have other duties to detain me and a great deal to think about."

"I'm so glad I was able to help," Mrs. Glassell cooed as she got up as well.

"I cannot thank you enough," I said.

Her eyes fell on something behind me and she started. I looked. There was nothing there but a writing desk littered with papers.

"Oh! How terribly careless of me," she said. "Mrs. Wilcox, you have not sent your response for Saturday night."

"Response?" I looked at her, completely puzzled.

"Our party," Mrs. Glassell said. "Surely you remember. We bought a cask of wine from you specifically to serve there."

"I remember that, but do not recall receiving an

invitation."

I knew very well that I had not received an invitation but was not nearly as put out as one might think. When Mr. and Mrs. Glassell gave a party, they usually invited the pueblo's elite citizens, most of whom were dreadful bores. I was occasionally invited, especially if the affair was to include dancing as opposed to a formal dinner. I liked dancing. However, most of the men in the pueblo were more likely to drag me about the room, stepping on my toes or my skirts in the process, than to actually dance.

"Good heavens, you didn't?" Mrs. Glassell looked shocked, and it appeared sincere. "Well, I must send one by this very afternoon. Do say you'll come."

"I'll do my best," I said. "Saturday nights are quite busy for me."

"Oh, let Dr. Skillen do the work for once. You deserve to amuse yourself for one night."

I did not point out that on Saturday nights, there was more than enough work for Dr. Skillen, Doc MacKenzie, and the other two doctors in the pueblo, in addition to myself.

"I will do my best," I said again. "And now, I must leave."

We made the usual good-byes and I was shortly on the street again. Alas, I was not in any good frame of mind. Mrs. Glassell's suspicions were of the usual sort. As I have noted, that did not mean they were all that trustworthy. Nonetheless, I could not dismiss them out of hand. It was most annoying.

I debated seeking out some of the people she had mentioned, but then thought better of it. If I had a chance to contemplate this new list of possible killers, I might stand a better chance of getting real answers from those I suspected rather than the usual dissembling. Therefore, I returned to my rancho and forced myself to work at the usual chores and tasks I performed at that time of year.

I felt quite guilty that I was not actively pursuing

Wei Li's killer. However, I knew that occasionally the best thing I could do in such situations was to put such ruminations aside, although knowing that did little to soothe my overwrought passions. Nor did the inattention reveal any new inspiration or insight. Thus, I spent the rest of the day and that night in a terribly sour mood and even excused myself from sharing supper with my household.

I was roused early the next morning by a summons from Mrs. Costa. Her husband had been mentioned by Mrs. Glassell as one who appeared to have more wealth than he had. And, as Mrs. Glassell intimated, he was often absent from his rancho.

Mrs. Costa had the sort of solid frame that bespoke years of hard labor tending to husband and children, which often meant tending to her husband's laborers, as well. The creases of worry had etched themselves deeply into her face and her mostly dark brown hair was sprinkled generously with gray. She had seldom looked happy, but she looked even worse that morning. I thought it might have been grief, as two of her children had died the previous summer from a very nasty fever and ague. Perhaps I should be more precise. It was the disease we now call malaria, rather than the family of diseases we thought were caused by pestilence in the air.

"He's this way," she said as she led me to the ranch house.

It was a long narrow room, filled with a variety of bunks next to the unpainted wall. Three of the hands had gathered around their fellow, who lay upon one of the bunks. He moaned as harsh spasms wracked his body.

"What's his name and how long has he been like this?" I asked.

"He's Leon Walters," Mrs. Costa said. She glared at the three men. "Don't you fellows have chores to do?"

"He's been like this since last week," one of them said as the other two shuffled off. The remaining hand was a fairly short fellow with broad shoulders and dark hair and beard. "Only it's lots worse today. It must be them Chinese herbs he got last month. Had the flux, he did."

Mr. Walters stiffened and shook. His eyes were wide open and it looked almost as if he were grinning. I put my hand on his forehead and it was quite warm.

"Mr. Walters, can you hear me?" I asked.

He groaned but could not move his mouth.

"There, there, Mr. Walters, I'll help you as best I can," I said as soothingly as I could.

Sadly, I strongly suspected that the only real help I had to offer would be to ease his pain as he left this world for the next. The spasms were too harsh for him to live much longer. I still managed to force some bromide of potassium through his stiff jaw.

"It must have been them herbs he got last month from that Chinese doctor," the ranch hand said again, this time bouncing on his toes. "You know, the fellow they hung."

"Efrem Smith, you've got work to do," Mrs. Costa growled.

Mr. Smith ignored her.

"When did he last take them?" I asked. Given the way Mr. Walters was flailing about, it seemed very unlikely, but I had to be sure. I also perused the shelf above Mr. Walter's bunk. There was a small box with Dr. Gene Wong's label on it.

"About a week after he got 'em," Mr. Smith said. "Said they worked right fine."

I opened the box. Whatever herbs there had been in the box were gone. Instead, the box held several nails.

Mrs. Costa snorted. I continued examining the ailing man.

"Say, isn't there some sort of herb that can make you dance around like that?" Mr. Smith demanded.

"I told him not to trust those Chinese," Mrs. Costa said, her derision making her voice flat and nasal.

"Yes, there is such an herb," I said to Mr. Smith. "But if Mr. Walters had taken any, he'd already be dead." I pulled up the ailing man's sleeve. "This is what's behind his illness. He has lockjaw."

There was a long, fresh scar along the top of his arm. I had seen it all too often, a wound that appeared to heal, then a week or two later, the dreaded disease would appear.

Mrs. Costa and Mr. Smith both swallowed. We'd all seen lockjaw, and as one of my later students would say, it was a very unpleasant way to go to the Beyond.

Still, I waited a few more minutes, hoping the bromide of potassium would take effect. I did inject some morphine into the poor man's arm. It calmed, but did not end, the spasms for a couple hours, during which time I was able to dose him again with the potassium.

While waiting to see if he would rally, I did take a look at the bottoms of the poor man's boots. They were whole and the boots, themselves, looked to be fairly new.

It proved to be a long morning. There was little I could do. As the morphine wore off, Mr. Walters became even worse than before. I gave him another injection, but it did little to stop the spasms. There was no dosing him with the bromide of potassium, either, as Mr. Walters' his jaws and neck had stiffened so, he could no longer swallow.

The spasms and flailing continued until the middle of the afternoon. His face had gone rigid and he had almost folded himself on top of his legs when he finally turned blue, trying to breathe through all the spasms, and failed. Falling backwards, he finally left this world for the next.

Mr. Smith had long since abandoned his friend's death bed, as had Mrs. Costa. I summoned her, however, once Mr. Walters had died. She came into the bunkhouse reluctantly.

"Is he gone yet?" She asked.

"I'm afraid he is. Do you want me to contact Mr.

Sutton's funeral parlor?"

"That'll be fine. I'll use his back wages to pay for the funeral." Mrs. Costa glared at the corpse. "Are you sure it wasn't them Chinese herbs that did this?"

"Very sure. If he'd been taking them and there was strychnine in the formula, he would have been dead long before this." I sighed, looking for a wash bowl to clean up in. "Lockjaw, on the other hand, takes a few days to get going and everything you have told me about when and how it happened is consistent with that."

"I don't trust them Chinamen," Mrs. Costa said.

"Then don't," I said rather acerbically. "That is your choice. However, what I have seen here does not support your suspicion, nor should it. Mr. Walters has, without question, succumbed to lockjaw and that is what I will testify to, no matter what you say."

I gathered my syringes and bottles together and put them in my leather bag. Mrs. Costa had a rather queer look on her face.

"I heard you like the Chinamen," she said.

"They are no worse, nor no better than any other person," I said. "At least, that has been my experience of them. Now, I will go and summon Mr. Sutton's people. Does Mr. Walter have any papers or other belongings that we should turn over to the courts for probate?"

Mrs. Costa shrugged. I left, fully expecting that my dear friend Angelina Sutton would see to getting the corpse and help sort out whatever will or other business Mr. Walter had left behind.

For myself, I left the ranch feeling quite out of sorts again. I had not made mention of it, nor should I have, nor did I really note it until I was on my way back to my rancho, but I did happen to notice Mrs. Costa's feet. They were not only quite large, but she also wore men's boots.

CHAPTER FIVE

The funeral for Mr. Walters was held the next afternoon. It was a simple graveside service, as Mr. Walters had not been much of a churchgoer. I had, with no little trouble, convinced the pastor of my church, Reverend Elmwood, to officiate.

I was surprised to see that the service was fairly well attended. Earlier that morning, Judge Sepulveda had convened the grand jury that would investigate the riot, and given the speculation about any impending indictments, I had fully expected that everyone would be elsewhere gossiping. But not only did most of the ranch hands from the Costa rancho show up, but several itinerant laborers from around the pueblo came, as well as Doc MacKenzie.

Doc MacKenzie was not, in fact, a medical doctor as he had no real training. But he did have a great deal of experience in the healing arts and was quite popular among the many workers in the pueblo.

He was a rather small man with gray hair and beard. But what one generally noticed first were his dark brown eyes, which looked over large, thanks to the spectacles that he wore.

The plain wood casket sat next to the open grave. Reverend Elmwood read from the Twenty-Third Psalm, noted that Mr. Walters had been a good and faithful hand, then asked if anyone had anything to say about Mr. Walters.

"I do!" cried Mr. Smith. "Leon Walters was my friend and he was murdered by that Chinese doctor that got hung. He was taking some of those strange herbs those fellows give out. And all of a sudden, he goes into spasms and dies. It had to be the herbs."

There was considerable grumbling among the other mourners.

"It was lockjaw," I blurted out. "For heaven's sake, even you said he hadn't taken any herbal remedies for several weeks. And poor Mr. Walters had cut his arm. Lockjaw often follows such injuries."

"Is that so?" Doc MacKenzie asked me.

"It most certainly is," I said, suddenly aware that I had made quite a scene.

"She likes them Chinamen," someone else cried out.

"Why shouldn't I?" I retorted, rather loudly, but it could not be helped. "Besides, if Mr. Walters had been helped to his reward by a bad batch of herbs, I would be the first to condemn it, no matter where the herbs had come from. And most of you know that."

"I certainly do," announced Doc MacKenzie. "Mrs. Wilcox is not only an able member of the medical profession, she is as honest as the day is long. Nor is she likely to hide malfeasance of any kind. You all know of her quests to find others who have killed in the pueblo, even though it cost her dearly. If she says Mr. Walters died of lockjaw, then I believe her."

I flushed a deep red. But Doc MacKenzie's words had stilled the fomenting anger for the time being.

A few other of Mr. Walters' fellows did step forward to speak of what a fine fellow he had been. Soon afterward, Reverend Elmwood led us in the Lord's Prayer, then dismissed us all so that the grave diggers could finish their work.

I left the cemetery with Juan and Damiano on my heels, as usual. Doc MacKenzie hastened to catch up to me.

"Mrs. Wilcox," he called, panting a little.

I waited until he caught up to me.

"Yes, Mr. MacKenzie?" I asked.

He looked around to be sure we were not overheard by the others from the gravesite.

"I am glad to offer you my support," he said, still breathing a little heavily. "But are you sure it was lockjaw?"

"It was not strychnine," I said. "Unless someone did not tell me the full truth of what Mr. Walters had consumed. Besides, are there any of the trees growing around here? I cannot imagine so, as I understand it requires a great deal of water to grow."

"I suppose so," Doc MacKenzie wavered for a moment. "It's just that I do have some herbs that Dr. Wong gave me to help with, well, a personal matter. But I have no idea what they are."

I sighed. "I do understand your confusion. Alas, it is the tradition among the Chinese doctors to mix herbs without specifying which herbs and in which strength they mix them. My own ranch hand, Mr. Wang, frequently does so and I have only recently convinced him that proper note taking is of the essence. Given that each concoction is made to meet a specific need of a specific patient, it is understandable that perhaps they do not see the same need to write it all down that we do."

"But the herbs that I was given..."

"I'm sure the late Dr. Wong knew what he was doing and that they are safe. I could ask my hand to consult, but I suspect he would be hesitant to cross what his forebear had done."

"No, no." Doc MacKenzie smiled nervously. "Frankly, I have nothing but respect for them Chinese doctors. They don't always get it right, but it sure seems they do at least as well as we do." He shuffled his feet nervously, and I could not help wondering what the bottoms of his boots looked like. "I do wish I could have gotten the same fancy training you got. I may have a knack for healing, but that doesn't always make much difference."

"Nor, alas, does training," I said with a deep sigh.

"Well, it's better than guessing, like I've been doing." He smiled haplessly. "Doc Skillen has been giving me his medical journals to read after he's done with them."

I couldn't help smiling. The reason Dr. Skillen had medical journals was because I shared mine with him. Doctors were not at all well-paid in those days and the only reason I could afford to pay for medical journals was that my winemaking business did very well for me. And because my sisters back in Boston were also well off and they were happy to send them to me.

"Then the three of us are considerably better off than most of the medical men in this county," I said. "And thank you so much for speaking up for me. I do appreciate it."

He shrugged. "It's no trouble and nothing but the truth."

"Well, it's nice to hear it for a change." I looked up, but the sky told me little. Gray clouds blanketed the area, looking oddly like a flat ceiling. I could barely make out a slightly brighter spot just past the meridian. "Time is getting on, I'm afraid."

"Of course. Good day, Mrs. Wilcox." Doc MacKenzie tipped his hat and moved up the road leading from the cemetery to his home on the western edge of the pueblo.

I debated my next course of action. I was wearing my indigo walking dress, so I did have some leeway as to where I could go next. I'm not sure what brought Mr. Shapiro's mercantile to mind, but it was as good an alternative as any.

I signaled Juan and Damiano and had them recite their geography lesson as we walked. The children on the rancho did not go to school as the Mexican children tended to get short shrift from the two school masters. So, we taught them ourselves, or rather, Anita Sanchez did. But we all helped out, and since Juan and Damiano were following me, I made it my business to make sure they didn't miss their lessons. The two boys complained bitterly but recited the capitals of the United States accurately.

Mr. Shapiro's mercantile was on the Calle Primavera, almost to Calle Tercero. I generally patronized the other mercantile on the Calle Principal, as they accepted the mail from the various trains that came in from Wilmington and the nearby bay, and the stagecoaches as well. Mr. Shapiro's establishment was noted, however, for the wide assortment of laces and other trims, as well as the many fine fabrics that he stocked. As I generally let Mrs. Washington, my dressmaker, purchase whatever fabrics she decided she needed, I had no idea if she patronized Mr. Shapiro's store or not.

The mercantile was fairly large, and there were many of the usual dry goods, neatly arranged on the many shelves. The fabric and other sewing supplies were at the back. Mr. Shapiro also arranged for tailoring and shirt making services, so one saw him taking orders for shirts and other garments as often as one saw him measuring out yardage from one of the many bolts of fabric on the nearby shelves.

I wandered among the bolts and saw the justice of Mrs. Glassell's complaint. However, the dusty bolts in question were stacked in a dark corner away from the main part of the store. As I wandered back toward the table where Mr. Shapiro held court, I was surprised to see Mrs. Judson running her hands along a lovely white fabric with Mr. Shapiro nodding as she did. It was silk and had been very cleverly woven so that it had shaded stripes running the length.

Mr. Shapiro was a thin man and seemed to be not quite thirty years of age. He was dressed in a neat black suit and wore his hat, even though he was indoors. It was, I'd been told, a tradition of the Jewish people.

"Did you want to order some more shirts for your husband?" he asked Mrs. Judson.

An average-sized woman with gray hair, there was little remarkable about her appearance. Yet her dresses were quite nice. That day she wore a walking suit made of a lovely ochre bombazine and trimmed in dark brown satin ruffles.

"I would dearly love to, but he has barely worn the ones from last year," she said with a sigh. "No, I only need a yard of this for some handkerchiefs."

"Very well," Mr. Shapiro said. He picked up his scissors and cut off the requested amount.

"Good day, Mrs. Judson," I said, smiling as if I had not already heard her speaking to Mr. Shapiro. "What a lovely fabric. It would make a fine shirt or two."

She flushed and glowered, then, apparently seeing no malice in me (as, indeed, there was none), she smiled.

"No shirts today," she said, then sighed in exasperation. "My darling husband is quite frugal in that he will wear his shirts and stockings until they are rags before he will wear a new one. He says there is no point in putting aside perfectly useful garments just because they have been mended."

"And yet his suits look perfectly respectable."

"That's because I was able to convince him that a banker wearing a threadbare suit would frighten his customers." She rolled her eyes heavenward. "But as long as it doesn't show, he will wear a shirt until it literally falls off of him." She tittered a little. "I suppose we all have our little quirks, and that is his."

I nodded. "Indeed. And what have you bought today? It looks quite nice."

"It is, isn't it?" Mrs. Judson ran her hand over the small piece of cloth that Mr. Shapiro had cut for her. "I make handkerchiefs as an amusement. Isn't this a wonderful bit of silk?"

"It's the best in the pueblo," said Mr. Shapiro with a grin.

I looked him over carefully, but could not see his feet, which were hidden under the counter.

"Undoubtedly," I said.

"It really is," said Mrs. Judson. "I have my dressmaker buy all of the silk for my dresses here. And most of the cottons for my tea gowns."

The silks were carefully stored behind Mr. Shapiro's table, including a lovely red one with the same woven stripes as the white bit Mrs. Judson had just had cut. I slipped my glove off my left hand and picked up some figured dark green cotton. It was lovely stuff. Alas, I had no idea how much would be needed for a tea dress. I made a mental note to speak to Mrs. Washington soon.

"And what brings you here today?" Mrs. Judson asked.

I found myself quite uncharacteristically at a loss for words. While I didn't doubt that Mrs. Glassell had spread it hither and yon that I was actively trying to find out who had murdered Wei Li, I also did not want to risk blackening Mr. Shapiro's good name should he prove to be innocent.

"I don't know," I finally said. "I have unexpectedly found myself at loose ends, and so took a stroll and landed here."

Mrs. Judson's eyes narrowed even as she smiled. She was exceptionally perspicacious, and I did not doubt she had guessed the true nature of my visit to the mercantile. However, unlike Mrs. Glassell, Mrs. Judson was genuinely discreet. Her eyes fell for the briefest of instants on Mr. Shapiro.

"I'm quite glad that you did," Mrs. Judson said. "How are you getting on? Poor thing. You've had to cope with more than any of us."

"Yes, it has been difficult," I said. "And poor Wei Li and his brother were just about to go home."

"They should all go home," Mr. Shapiro grumbled. "Thieving magpies."

Mrs. Judson looked at him. "I wasn't aware that you had any particular antipathy toward the Chinamen, Mr. Shapiro."

He shrugged. "Everyone knows they're thieves and scoundrels. I won't let them come in here. Something's always missing every time they do."

"That has not been my experience," I said. "My field hands have been perfectly trustworthy, and hard workers."

"As Mr. Judson often says, they are no better nor no worse than any other race," Mrs. Judson said. She shuddered. "And we've certainly seen the worst of what we, their supposed superiors, can do. At least, the ruffians among us. Actually, Mrs. Wilcox, that brings to my mind another campaign we might consider. Bringing more women to the pueblo. Then they can marry our lonely men and exert our best impulses toward civilizing them. What do you think?"

"It's not a bad idea," I said, desperately hoping that she did not intend for me to become one of those civilizing forces. "However, I am very much occupied with my campaign for better sanitation in the home."

"Oh, that is very important too," Mrs. Judson said with a smile that suggested that there was far more to be said on the subject of her idea.

"Indeed." I looked down at my hands and put my glove back on. "Mr. Shapiro, I'll have my dressmaker call on you soon. Mrs. Judson, it's been a pleasure speaking with you, but I must be on my way."

"Likewise, Mrs. Wilcox," said Mrs. Judson. "In fact, I'll walk with you."

We left the mercantile and headed back toward Calle Segundo, Juan and Damiano in tow.

"I hope I was able to help a little back there," Mrs. Judson said.

"Actually, you were quite helpful. Thank you."

Mrs. Judson glanced back at the mercantile. "It seems interesting that Mr. Shapiro would feel such antipathy toward the Chinamen."

"Perhaps, but sad to say, it's hardly an unusual sentiment."

"Sadly, it is not." Mrs. Judson said. "But you'll get to the bottom of it, no doubt."

"I appreciate your confidence."

We parted ways, she off in the direction of her house, I still wandering a bit aimlessly.

I finally made my way to the Sutton's funeral home. Angelina was not only in, her preparation room was unusually empty of bodies.

"I expect it shall be more than full by Sunday," she said cheerfully as she led me into her sitting room. "But

I'm glad for the respite. How are you?"

"Well enough, I suppose," I said, seating myself on the sofa.

Angelina's sitting room or study was a very comfortable place, with lace-curtained windows, two large armchairs, the sofa, and a large writing desk in one corner. Angelina also had a smaller writing table on wheels that she could move around to one of the armchairs as she wished.

"No luck finding the killer?"

"None whatsoever," I said. "The problem is that there's no easy way to look at the bottoms of boots. Almost everyone assumes the worst of the Chinese and thinks we should be rid of them. But why kill Wei Li? It makes no sense. Nor am I likely to find the guilty party by asking if he was near my rancho on Friday afternoon. All he would have to do is lie."

"It would depend on how good a liar he is," Angelina said, pulling her little table on wheels to her. "Most people are terrible liars." She pulled a pen from a little drawer in the table, opened up the inkwell affixed to the top, then turned over a piece of paper. "Maybe we should make a list."

Angelina loved lists and they had often proved useful.

"Well, Mrs. Glassell named several people who might be putting on appearances of looking well off," I said, taking off my gloves. "It is possible that our killer might be hiding the fact that his boots have holes in the bottoms."

"But why kill your Chinaman?"

I sighed. "That's the difficulty. There is no reason to kill him that way. At least not among those of us who are not Chinese. Wei Li didn't speak enough English to interact with anyone. It may have been another Chinaman who killed him, but I can't ask questions among them. Wang Fu is doing the asking there for me."

"So, the only reason to kill Mr. Li would be a general loathing of all Chinamen." Angelina tapped her pen against her teeth.

"It's Mr. Wei. The Chinese use their surnames first," I said absently.

"Oh."

We looked at each other and sighed at the same time.

"General loathing seems a rather thin reason to kill someone," Angelina said.

"It does, indeed."

"On the other hand, cutting off his queue and strangling him with it, that seems quite barbaric. Maybe it was actually one of the other Chinese."

I shrugged. "It could have been. After all, Wang Fu tells me his fellows keep their queues because they expect to go home at some point. All men in China wear their hair that way as a sign of unity, and if they cut it, they cannot go back home. They also send their fellows' bones back so that they can rest with their ancestors. That's especially important to them."

"Which would mean someone was very, very angry with Wei Li."

"But that does not necessarily mean it was another Chinaman," I said. "If he was killed by one of us, then that person could be very angry at the Chinese for some reason. I just haven't found anybody quite that angry."

"So, we're back to holes in boots," Angelina said. "A lot of the laborers do swear the Chinamen are taking their jobs."

"Who do you know that can't find a job?" I asked.

Angelina chuckled. "Just a couple drunks and one fellow who is well known as a thief."

"A thief?"

"That's what the rumor is," Angelina said. "Mr. Valdez has never been caught to my knowledge. But when I wanted someone last month to clear out the scrap wood from the coffins, I was warned against hiring him."

I thought. "If he has never been caught, is it possible that the rumors are false and he is angry enough to blame the Chinese?"

"That is possible. Why don't I find out? The scrap wood is building up again. Mr. Sutton will not lower himself to clear it. I'll see if Mr. Valdez wants to do it, and talk to him."

"Then please do so with all care," I said. "If he's that angry, it could be dangerous."

"As we both know too well." Angelina smiled. "I'll find a way to bring up the subject of the Chinamen with all due caution."

"His name is Mr. Valdez?" I asked, suddenly realizing it was important.

"Yes."

"I heard somebody speaking about a Mr. Valdez recently, and several other fellows." My brows knitted as I pulled the memory from the wool in my head. "Wait. Now I remember. It was Saturday night. Old Mr. Pugh mentioned a Valdez alongside several others who Mr. Pugh said had participated in the lynchings."

"Who did he say was there?" Angelina dipped her pen in the inkwell.

"Mr. Valdez. An Efrem Smith, Raymond Sanford, Leo Dillman and..." I shook my head. "There was one more. Mr. Pugh did not give him a first name. Worse yet, it seems to me that I'd already heard the name in connection with the riot, but I can't put my finger on it."

"Well, asking Mr. Pugh again won't help," Angelina said. "He'll probably give you a whole new list of names."

"Which also puts those names into doubt."

Angelina blew on the paper and held it out for me to see.

"Still, it's someplace to look," she said.

I pointed to one. "I've met Mr. Smith. It was his friend who died yesterday of lockjaw, and Mr. Smith insisted that some Chinese herbs were responsible. They worked together on the Costa rancho."

"We'll have to find a way to speak to him further," Angelina said, taking the list back.

"And let us not forget the several people that Mrs. Glassell posited are keeping up appearances they cannot support."

Angelina dipped her pen again. "Indeed, we should not."

"There was Mr. Montero, the tanner, and Mr. Gaines and Mr. Fletcher, who are both land agents, although Mr. Fletcher is also a lawyer, and there was another land agent." I paused. "And there was Mr. Handley, my insurance agent, and Mr. Shapiro of the mercantile. I've talked to Mr. Shapiro, however, and while he said the Chinese were all thieves, he did not seem particularly angry with them."

"We'll keep him on the list. It may be he holds more anger in his heart than appears."

"Good. And Mr. Costa, although I'd be just as suspicious of Mrs. Costa. She was quite vehement that the herbs had killed her ranch hand, and Mr. Smith does work for them."

"So noted. Anyone else?"

I thought. "Mr. Hewitt."

"But I'd heard Mr. Hewitt stood up to the lynchers."

"Only because it wasn't seemly to hang the men in front of his manufactory. There were ladies inside." I frowned. "At least, that's what Mr. Pugh said. Wait. That other land agent that Mr. Pugh mentioned was Mr. McKinley. And now that I think about it, he may have been part of the group that almost attacked me and Sebastiano and the Lees." I blinked my eyes trying once again to shut out the sights and sounds of that most terrible of nights. "Someone called him by name, but I doubt I would recognize him again."

Angelina looked at me, then shuddered. "I am amazed that you found the courage to go near the riot at all."

"One simply does," I said, my voice flat. I took a deep breath. "Nonetheless, we have other matters that we must focus on that may or may not be related to the riot. Therefore, let us focus on them."

"Very well," Angelina said and smiled. "Here is our list. I can speak to Mr. Valdez, and Mrs. Costa as I have business with her anyway, and perhaps Mr. Smith and Mr. Sanchez."

"I've already spoken with Mr. Dillman. It did not go well. But I can speak with the rest of them. How, I'm not sure."

"You'll find a way." Angelina found a second piece of paper and rapidly began copying our list down.

"At least, speaking with Mr. Montero and Mr. Handley should not be that difficult," I said. "I do business with both of them."

A grandfather clock in another room sonorously chimed the hour of five o'clock.

"Good heavens, is it that late?" I asked suddenly.

"Yes, and I must send you on your way so that I can be sure Mr. Sutton gets his supper on time."

I left quickly. I did not care for Mr. Sutton, who was a rather morose fellow, one of the reasons he had such an excellent reputation for kindness toward the families of the deceased. He had earned his sorrow, though, in that the three children Angelina had borne for him had all died quite young. How Angelina, who was equally grieved by their loss, managed to remain so cheerful, I never fully understood.

I hurried back to the rancho and got there in time to change to a work dress for supper with my household, then listen to the children's lessons, then to read my journals, and then to bed.

I had hoped to enjoy a peaceful rest, but instead woke up several times from the same nightmare that had troubled me before, of tombstones and accusing faces.

CHAPTER SIX

The next two and a half days left me with little opportunity to ask anything of anyone. The grapes for the angelica had finished fermenting and the wine needed to be poured away from the crushed grapes, or must, and the new wine moved to the barrels where it would settle, then be mixed with brandy from the year before and aged. We had to distill the new brandy from the must. It was a good thing neither task required my constant presence, as my skills as a physician became in high demand at about the same time.

According to my journal, there were five different households with the croup, one with whooping cough, and three different persons with broken bones. In the last of these cases, I had to amputate. I also had to check in on the four cases of consumption that were in the pueblo. A crew of ranch hands had all come down with the flux as well. Then we lost two infants to the measles and three other children came down with scarlet fever. The amputee unfortunately took sick from it, and we lost him Saturday morning.

As I was already out, after leaving the man's grieving family, I went on that morning to check the rest of my patients. The children with whooping cough seemed to be managing, although I was a little worried about the baby, and the other broken bones were mending.

I dosed the ranch hands again, hoping that they would manage, and found out they'd all drunk from a bad water barrel. The ranch owner wanted to dump the barrel into the nearest zanja, or irrigation ditch, but I convinced him that if the barrel was tainted, why taint the ditch as well?

I checked the children with scarlet fever and the younger two were sick but managing. The older boy had quite a high fever and I feared for him, so I offered to stay, but his mother and aunts agreed there was little more I could do for him and sent me on my way.

I left the house feeling quite down at heart, even though these were all the normal diseases and injuries that I saw day in and day out. There was just so little I could do.

I was walking back along the Calle Principal when I noted the building where Mr. Handley's office was. There was something I could do about Wei Li's death, and I decided to do it. I also had to pay my premium for my insurance, anyway, so I had an excuse to stop in.

Mr. Handley, who had a full blond beard, blond hair and wore spectacles on his nose, came out of his office the moment his clerk let him know I was there.

"Mrs. Wilcox!" he exclaimed, ushering me into his office. "What a pleasure to see you."

"Equally so, Mr. Handley." I sat in the chair in front of his desk and got out my coin purse. "I've come to pay my premium."

"Excellent." He got out a ledger. "All going well, I hope?"

"Not as such, I'm afraid," I said, flushing a little. "My field hand was murdered in a most terrible way a week before yesterday."

Mr. Handley looked up and blinked. "Oh, yes. I had heard that. One more terrible event."

"Yes. One would think the riot was bad enough." I said, handing over the coins for my premium.

"Indeed."

"Did you see much of it?"

"Eh, no." He smiled nervously.

"I hope all is going well with you," I said.

"Business has been quite good," he said, his usual friendly demeanor back in place.

"You didn't have any claims related to the riot?"

"Nary a one," he said, looking rather pleased with himself. "Most of those buildings were not insured, and I did not write the policies for the ones that were. I hope your business has been doing well in spite of the turmoil."

"Quite well," I said. "Aside from losing the field hand. That has been most perplexing. I'm trying to find out who was near my rancho that Friday afternoon."

He flushed, then stammered. "Me? I was here. Here all day."

"I was hoping someone had seen something," I said trying to sound soothing. After all, I had not asked him if he'd been near the ranch. Why had he reacted as if I'd accused him of killing Wei Li?

"I'm afraid not." He finished a slip of paper with a flourish and stood. "Here's your receipt, Mrs. Wilcox. Thank you for stopping by. I, eh, however, have a great deal of work to do."

"Yes, of course." I got up, took the receipt, and slipped out of the office.

The clerk let me out of the outer office, and I went on my way, wondering about the sudden change in Mr. Handley's demeanor. He had always been quite pleased to see me, even when I had filed a claim on my policy the year before. As Angelina had noted earlier that week, many people are terrible liars and it certainly seemed as if Mr. Handley was one such person. But how to prove it? And Mr. Handley was such a kind and mild fellow. I could not imagine him enraged enough to kill a Chinaman simply because of his race, nor had he mentioned any of the usual complaints about the Chinese.

The bell in the Clocktower Courthouse chimed the half hour and I could see that it was getting quite late. Juan and Damiano had been sent home earlier that day, and if Armando was shadowing my movements, he was being quite discreet about it. I decided that I would have to find some way to press Mr. Handley to tell the truth, but also decided that could wait for another time. And while I was not looking forward to it, I did have a party to dress for, as Mrs. Glassell's invitation had arrived the very afternoon we had spoken.

I got home in time for supper and ate heartily. It didn't matter how much food would be put out for the party, ladies were expected to eat daintily. So, it behooved me to eat well before I got there. As soon as we'd finished eating, Juanita shooed me into my adobe and went to work on my hair and the rest of my dress. My new evening dress had been recently delivered. It was a lovely dark yellow moire silk with bone-colored lace and pink silk roses and a full apron swept back over rows and rows of ruffles. Juanita added another silk rose to my swept-up hair. I had silk slippers to match the gown and my bone-colored kid gloves featured the exquisite embroidery done by Mrs. Montero, the wife of the tanner. Juanita draped my new black velvet cape over my shoulders and brought me out to the yard, where Daisy had been hitched to my buggy. Sebastiano's eldest, Ramon, was on the seat, ready to drive me. Ramon usually worked most nights at the Pico House Hotel, but he'd some-how gotten this night off.

Olivia and Magdalena stood next to the buggy.

"You be careful tonight," Olivia said.

"And don't eat too much," Magdalena added.

"And do not walk home," Juanita said. "You will ruin your shoes if you do."

"I will be good," I said. "And I'll have Ramon come for me at eleven p.m. sharp."

"If anyone calls you, you come home first and change clothes," Juanita said. "I do not want to try to get bloodstains out of silk."

Olivia and Magdalena added additional cautions about free-wheeling men and gossipy ladies and too much wine and several other cautions that I immediately put out of my mind. I was, after all, a grown woman, a widow, and mistress of my own rancho. Although I did have to wonder how much I was the mistress at times. Olivia, Magdalena, and Juanita only chided because they cared about me, and there was some justice in their complaints that I could not be trusted to take care of myself.

Ramon chuckled as he helped me to my seat. He clucked and shook the reins and Daisy led us away from the chorus of admonitions.

"They never give up," he said, once we had gone through the gate.

"No," I sighed. "I suppose I should be glad that they have such tender concern for my care."

"You should be glad you're not one of their children," Ramon said. "I am a man and Mama still reminds me every day to wash behind my ears and to put on a clean shirt."

I had to laugh at that.

The party was being held at the Bella Union Hotel, a common site for such occasions, as few in the pueblo had a house big enough for a party of any real size, let alone room for dancing. We waited in the line of buggies letting off various partygoers, then Ramon pulled up in front of the hotel and I got down onto the board sidewalk.

"I'll be back at eleven," he said.

"I'll see you then," I said.

Others would leave closer to midnight, but I anticipated a strong desire to leave earlier.

The room was quite splendid, with crystal chandeliers filled with candles above the wood floor, and wall sconces with real gas lighting on the walls. All in all, the room was quite brilliant, almost as if it were still daylight. But a wall of glass doors along one side of the room, looking like dark apertures, served as a reminder that it was night-time.

There was a table laid with all manner of delicious things to eat at the far end of the room, chairs scattered about the walls and a small orchestra at the end of the room. Mr. Glassell had spared no expense, having imported some Champagne from France. Waiters bore trays of glasses filled with both the Champagne and my own red wine (a blend of cabernet and merlot, if I remember correctly).

The Champagne being an unusual treat and one likely to run out sooner rather than later, I took a glass immediately and began to wander about the room. The orchestra, such as it was, was beginning to tune. Mrs. Glassell greeted me effusively, her husband with considerably more restraint. I thanked them quickly and moved on.

Mr. and Mrs. Judson were there, as were most of the notable couples in Los Angeles. Mr. and Mrs. Carson were present, which I fully expected, as Mrs. Carson and Mrs. Glassell were bosom friends. Even our former governor, Mr. Downey and his wife were there. Mrs. Downey and I had formed something of a friendship, as she was quite interested in astronomy and, while I was not, she was more interesting to talk to than many women in the pueblo. Mrs. Hewitt was there, scowling as her husband quickly drank a glass of Champagne. She and I were also friendly owing to the fact that we both worked in the world of men, Mrs. Hewitt being the one who saw to the management of the buggy manufactory as Mr. Hewitt was seldom sober enough to do so.

There were several unaccompanied men in the room, as well. Mr. Gaines I recognized, but others I did not. One gentleman stood out, being decidedly tall, with silver hair cut at his shoulders and a very neat beard and mustache. He was talking with another man, one who was not nearly as striking. The second man's hair was dark brown, cut short and slicked down, his beard long and seemingly untrimmed. He nodded in my direction. The tall man caught my eyes, nodded, then smiled, all the while continuing his conversation with the second man.

I made my way to the food table, got a small plate, and added a few bites to it. I would rather have filled my plate, but a lady did not do such things, and I was always a lady. I did, however, manage to slip by the food table several times. I chatted briefly with Mrs. Hewitt as the orchestra started the first dance. Three brave couples took to the floor. Mrs. Downey got a moment to greet me before she was pulled to the dance floor by her husband.

The dancing was decidedly deplorable. The orchestra had started with a lively jig and segued into an equally lively country dance. Couples bumped into each other relentlessly. Fortunately, they all laughed, but I saw more than one woman wincing and checking her skirts.

Sighing, I found myself next to the tall gentleman and his friend. Mrs. Judson happened to come up at just that moment.

"Mrs. Wilcox, how delightful to see you," she crowed. "Oh, and have you met these lovely gentlemen? Mr. Leighland, Mr. McKinley, may I present Mrs. Wilcox?"

Both men murmured their "how do you do's" as I murmured mine.

"Mrs. Wilcox is a widow," Mrs. Judson added, then suddenly seemed to spot a friend in the crowd and slipped away.

There was an awkward silence among us. My heart, however, was beating quite hard. I suddenly recognized Mr. McKinley from that most terrible of nights. He'd been the leader of the little gang that had stopped us and who had aimed his gun at me.

"I see that our glasses are empty," Mr. Leighland said. He was the tall man with the silver hair and beard, and his voice carried the soft purring accent of the gentry of the Deep South. "Shall I fetch us some new ones?"

"Yes, please," I said, handing him my glass, even though there was still a bit of Champagne in it.

Mr. McKinley, the dark-haired man, handed his glass to Mr. Leighland, as well.

"Mr. McKinley," I said smiling. "I have heard about you. You're a land agent?"

"Yes. Are you looking to acquire some land? I represent some exceptional acreage out in San Gabriel."

I couldn't help but wonder how exceptional it was. Most of the land in that direction was desert.

"I'm not looking for more land," I said. "But land agency, I hear that's a very difficult business."

"Not if you know what you're doing, and I do."

"Indubitably." I smiled again. "I'm so glad Mr. and Mrs. Glassell decided to put on this party. It's been so dreary since that terrible night."

Mr. McKinley glared at me. I realized then that he recognized me, but neither of us could acknowledge it in that moment.

Fortunately, Mr. Leighland returned with glasses of Champagne for all of us. I thanked him, then made my excuses and continued around the room, hoping I could find Mrs. Downey free, or Mrs. Hewitt.

I had made yet another circuit of the room (not forgetting the food table) and was standing near one of the glass doors to an outside courtyard, when my arm was pulled quite forcefully.

I almost yelped in surprise but had to give way and found myself outside in the chill air facing an enraged Mr. McKinley.

"I know about you," he said, in between all manner of foul words. "You don't know anything about being a true woman. You're unnatural, that's what you are."

"I don't understand, Mr. McKinley," I said, trying to keep my voice from quavering, and failing.

"You want to know about being a real woman. Here!"

The man proceeded to kiss me on the lips. It was disgusting, to say the least. I tried to push away, but he was quite strong.

"I'll show you how to be a real woman," he snarled.

He was taking liberties of the worst sort as I struggled and cried out.

Mr. Leighland appeared as if out of nowhere. He clapped Mr. McKinley on the shoulder and pulled the cur away.

"Come on, Jimbo. Let the lady be," he said, his voice purring and calm.

"But—"

"I know, but that's not the way to treat a lady and you know it."

He spun Mr. McKinley into the darkness, then gently took my arm.

I swallowed. "Thank you, Mr. Leighland."

"More than happy to oblige, Mrs. Wilcox," he replied as he gently led me back into the party. "I offer my apologies on Mr. McKinley's behalf. He is, unfortunately, not well at the moment."

"Regrettably," I said, trying to keep my voice calm even as I was still shaking.

I blinked at the brightness of the room and looked down at my dress to be sure all was where it should be, which fortunately it was.

"Then let us erase the memory of that ill-favored moment," Mr. Leighland said. "Would you do me the honor of this dance?"

The orchestra struck up a fine waltz at just that moment.

"Thank you, Mr. Leighland. I would love to."

Yes, I was lying. I had no reason to believe that Mr. Leighland would be any better at dancing than any of the other men who had done my toes such disservice. But I owed him some kindness for rescuing me when he had, and I was happy, at that moment, to offer it.

Ah, but he was the one who offered me the kindness. Mr. Leighland danced like a dream. He was firm, but gentle, in how he led me around the floor. My skirts were perfectly safe, let alone my toes. The waltz ended and all I wanted to do was dance some more.

So we did. In fact, we did several turns around the floor.

"Honestly, Mr. Leighland, I cannot remember a

time when I've danced so well," I told him, as we finally rested in a couple chairs next to the food table.

"You are as light as a feather, Mrs. Wilcox," Mr. Leighland said. He looked around. "Alas, it appears that the Champagne is gone."

"If you don't mind me being less than perfectly ladylike, I would love a glass of the red wine," I said.

Mr. Leighland fetched us each a glass of the red, and while I perhaps should have told him the origins of the wine, I did not. Instead, I actually giggled when I sipped it.

"I understand you are a widow?" Mr. Leighland asked.

"Yes, these eleven years now."

"How terribly lonely. I have only been a widower this past year and I'm having quite a bad time."

"I'm so sorry, Mr. Leighland. Being alone can be quite difficult."

"Yes, it is." He looked downcast for a moment, then smiled. "But one must go on. As you have." He looked up. "Another waltz. Have you rested enough?"

I hadn't, but I couldn't resist. We danced again. But by the end of the dance, both Mr. Leighland and I were quite winded.

"I dare say it is time I made my way home," I said, not quite conscious of what time it was.

"Are you sure?" Mr. Leighland pulled his watch from his vest. I thought I saw something glittering that dangled from the fob, but his hand covered it too quickly. "It's barely eleven."

"Oh," I said. I smiled at him as I headed for the cloak room. "Alas, my buggy should be here now."

"Then allow me to see you home," Mr. Leighland said.

"But what about my driver?"

"It should be no trouble for him to walk."

I thought for a moment. "No. We can ride in the back and Ramon can drive us."

Ramon's eyes lifted as he saw Mr. Leighland

join me in the back of the buggy. It was, admittedly, a bit unseemly to be riding in the back with a man I barely knew. But he had been exceptionally kind, and Ramon was there to see to my honor. Mr. Leighland did sit somewhat closer to me than was necessary, but I shifted away, and he then behaved as a gentleman should.

We chatted casually. He told me that he was from Savannah, Georgia, where he and his family had been involved in the shipping business. He had come to Los Angeles a year or so before to build that same business here. It would have been around the time he had lost his wife, I noted, but declined to mention it. Losing a family member to the journey here was far too familiar a story as it was.

He did stop talking about his life long enough to ask me about my rancho.

"My husband purchased it when we came here," I told him. "But I lost him shortly after and have had to make the best of it."

"How big is it?"

I smiled. "Why do you wish to know?"

"By way of conversation," he replied congenially.

"It's big enough," I replied.

That he laughed at my response was a point in his favor, but not much of one. I had met more than one gentleman who was more interested in taking my rancho than in being with me. Still, Mr. Leighland was quite charming and seemed to respect my reluctance to discuss how well I was or was not doing.

We pulled up to the ranch to the barking of Negrito and Beauty, the two ranch dogs. Beauty was a tan bitch, almost two feet tall at the shoulder, while Negrito was her shiny black mate. They slept in the barn. ChiChi barked from the inside of my adobe.

The barking roused Sebastiano and Enrique, who came to the gate bearing rifles. Pascual also ran up with his gun, followed closely by Wang Fu. When they saw it was us, Pascual hurried to open the gate and let us through.

Mr. Leighland laughed as Sebastiano helped me from the seat of the buggy.

"I hope I have been as good a guardian as you gentlemen," Mr. Leighland said, getting down behind me.

"You have been very kind," I replied. "Thank you for seeing me home."

"It was an honor, Mrs. Wilcox," Mr. Leighland said.

"Ramon, would you be so kind as to give Mr. Leighland a ride back to his home?" I asked.

"No, no, Mrs. Wilcox." Mr. Leighland breathed deeply. "It's a fine night. I think I would like to walk."

I thought it was a bit cool, even for me. But the air was dry, as it so often was, and refreshingly crisp, so I could understand his preference.

"Well, good night then," I said. "I enjoyed the dancing."

"It was my pleasure, Mrs. Wilcox." He looked as though he was about to take my hand and kiss it, but he caught Sebastiano, Enrique, and Wang Fu watching us and settled for tipping his hat instead. "Good night, Ma'am."

There was an awkward silence as Mr. Leighland left the rancho and Pascual saw to getting the gate closed.

"This is not something I expected," Sebastiano said somewhat darkly.

"Nor I, Sebastiano," I said. "However, while he is very charming and quite a gentleman, he is most certainly more interested in acquiring my property than me."

Sebastiano snorted. "He'll be happy to take you too."

"I stand warned. Thank you, Sebastiano."

I was used to his worry by then. Sebastiano's tender concern was as for a sister, as was Enrique's. Both of them were quite suspicious of any man who showed an interest in me, alas, usually with good reason. Given that I was already suspicious of Mr. Leighland's interests, I paid my fellows no mind.

If Sebastiano and Enrique were not terribly happy with how the evening had ended, Olivia, Magdalena, and Juanita were ecstatic.

"So, you have found a gentleman," Juanita crooned as she helped me from my dress.

"He seems quite handsome," Magdalena added as she and Olivia waited in the doorway.

"He was kind enough," I admitted. "However, I am not interested in acquiring a husband, as you all know quite well."

"You would still have your rancho," Olivia said.

It was true. While most women in the country were still forced to give up all their property to their husbands when they married, California had (and still has) an unusual law called community property that meant any property that a woman brought to a marriage remained hers and that husbands and wives owned everything together that they acquired as a couple. I'd been told that the law came from the Spanish era but had reason to appreciate it when my own husband passed from this world to the next. The reason I was able to keep the entirety of the rancho when Albert Wilcox died was the letter he'd written promising me all of his possessions.

"But I would be burdened with a husband," I said, quite tartly. "And I would strongly wager that this one has designs on my rancho more than he has on me."

Magdalena laughed loudly. "He has designs on you. We saw how he looked at you."

I smiled in spite of myself. "Well, he is destined to be disappointed either way."

Juanita giggled, and I shooed her and the others away so that I could finish my toilet in peace.

I spent the next hour or so writing in my journal, and even as I did, I couldn't help acknowledging that in spite of the satisfactions of my household and the friends I had, my life was somewhat lonely. I had heard many times of the solace and pleasant companionship that a husband could provide, and I must confess that I did sometimes wish for such a thing. But my late husband had certainly not been companionable in the least, and I had yet to meet a man who held much in the way of tender regard for me.

I couldn't help but wonder if Mr. Leighland could have such regard. He was rather confusing. He was quite courtly, and while he seemed to have the usual ideas held by his peers, he did not contradict me when I expressed my own preferences. And when I pulled away, he respected that.

I sighed, finally putting away my journal. My life was more than pleasant and I was quite happy to direct my own affairs. The last thing I wanted was a husband, who would have every right to insist that I put his interests and affairs first.

I was up with the sun, as usual, and decided to do a few small chores before dressing for church services. I fetched my own breakfast and started for the winery.

I was pulled up short by a young Chinese man, who came running up to the gate. He called out quite loudly in his own language and it was clear that he was terribly upset.

Wang Fu hurried up from the herb garden and listened. He suddenly gasped, then staggered backward.

"What is it, Wang Fu?" I asked, my heart beating hard in worry.

Wang Fu shut his eyes and gasped. "It is Wei Chin. He has been killed."

CHAPTER SEVEN

Rodolfo and Hernan had been feeding the animals when the young man had come on his sad errand. They came with Wang Fu and me as we hurried to the Plaza. Not far from the entrance to the Calle de los Negros we found a group of Chinese men gathered and wailing loudly around a body on the ground.

Wang Fu burst ahead of me, and the group pulled away to let him join them. He said something to the others, and they turned to look at me. Wang Fu nodded, and I joined the group, then bent down to look at Wei Chin, for indeed it was he. It was a ghastly sight, made the worse because in addition to having been strangled with his queue, he had been beaten quite severely.

One of his shoes was missing and there were small piles of dirt underneath his feet, as if he'd been dragged to that location. I stood and tried to discern from whence he'd been dragged. However, the men had trampled what tracks I could expect to find. I could hardly blame them. They would have had no idea of what to look for.

Wang Fu had his eyes clenched shut and when I touched his shoulder, he pulled back.

"I am so sorry, Wang Fu," I said quietly. "This is truly terrible."

He nodded. "Please. We must take him to Mrs. Sutton. We must know who is doing this to us."

"I was just about to suggest that," I said softly.

Wang Fu explained to his companions what we wanted to do. There was considerable chattering, but they apparently agreed that what I wanted to do was not going to harm Wei Chin's soul, and that my intentions were pure. I had Wang Fu also explain that the men should not touch Wei Chin, except as they needed to in order to carry him to the Sutton place. Rodolfo and Hernan led the way. I signaled to Wang Fu and we stayed behind.

"How long has he been here?" I asked, with Wang Fu translating.

It appeared that no one was sure. They had last seen Wei Chin sometime after eleven-thirty, when he left to go home.

"What was he doing here in the first place?" I asked Wang Fu, rather acerbically in spite of myself.

Wang Fu shrugged. "He want to be with friends."

A sharp, husky laugh startled both of us.

We turned and I recognized the small man who was responsible for the outburst. His name was Ah Chen, and he was head of one of the Chinese companies in the pueblo. Actually, it turned out, he was the victor in the war between the two companies that had set off the riot. Ah Chen owned several businesses on the Calle de los Negros, but he was best known for his brothel and opium den. He wore a traditional Chinese jacket in dark blue brocade, with blue pants in a familiar pattern of silk that I couldn't place just then.

"Wei Chin come to gamble," Mr. Ah declared. He was smiling but there was anger in his eyes. "And to cheat his fellows. He think he big man because he going home."

"What?" I asked, completely shocked.

"He and his brother cheat many people," Mr. Ah said. "No one know how. But nobody win like they do and not cheat. That how they get money to go home."

I looked at Wang Fu, who sighed and shuffled his feet. He had clearly been lying to me, and I was about to challenge him, but somehow could not, no matter how betrayed I felt.

"Then could one of your people have done this?" I asked Mr. Ah. "Maybe you were tired of being cheated."

"Wei Chin know better than to cheat me," Mr. Ah said, tossing his head. "And we not kill like that. We are not barbarians!"

His anger spread among the remaining men, but they did not move toward me.

"Did any of you see who did it?" I asked, standing my ground somehow.

Wang Fu translated and most of the men shook their heads. The young man who had come to get us from the rancho began waving one of the canvas shoes favored by the Chinese and pointing back toward the rancho with it.

"He says he found the shoe as we came back," Wang Fu said. "It was next to the turn to get to the rancho."

I looked back at the road. Alas, the shoe only confirmed my belief that Wei Chin had been killed elsewhere and dragged to where he had been found. It gave me no information as to who might have done the terrible deed.

I glanced at Mr. Ah, then looked at Wang Fu.

"No one else saw anything," Wang Fu said.

"Could one of them be lying?" I asked.

Wang Fu winced. He looked at Mr. Ah.

"None of us see anything," Mr. Ah said. "We only find body at dawn and Ning Yun go to find Wang Fu. We do not kill like that."

I swallowed. "Rest assured, Mr. Ah. I have no intention of accusing anyone until I have solid proof of who did it. And I will not assume that it was another of your people simply because of your race. However, if what you just told me is true, then it is quite possible that one of your countrymen is responsible and should be brought to justice."

"Justice? Here?" Mr. Ah spat into the dirt. "If one of us is responsible, we will see to justice."

"Then I will ask you to keep me informed of what you find," I said. "You, at least, owe Mr. Wang that much."

With that, I nodded at Wang Fu and together, we walked to the Sutton home in silence. Wang Fu must have been expecting some chastisement. I forbore to offer it, as we were out in public and I was not going to dress down a servant, no matter how deserving, in front of other people. Rodolfo and Hernan were waiting for us outside the Sutton place. I told them they could return to the rancho. Indeed, they needed to get home soon or be late for Mass. I insisted that Wang Fu stay with me.

We went around to the back, and, not surprisingly, Angelina was waiting for us. She was wearing her work dress and her hair, still in its night braid, had been hastily pinned up.

"Did you find anything?" I asked as she led us into the preparation room.

"Oh, yes," she said, nodding at the sheet-covered body on one of the preparation tables. Two more bodies shared another table not far away. "The body is just starting to stiffen, so he's been dead for several hours. How many, I cannot say. I've found that at this time of year, the stiffening often comes on more slowly. But, more importantly, he'd been beaten and was not shot."

"What do you mean?" I asked.

Angelina shrugged. "I don't know. I believe we surmised that his brother had been shot so that the villain could effectively get close enough to strangle him."

"Yes," I said. "Wei Li was in the vineyard, where there was no good cover."

"Then do you know where his brother was?"

I looked over at Wang Fu.

He sighed. "Wei Chin had business on the Calle de los Negros. So, he went under cover of darkness. The villain must have found him."

"One of the other Chinese found Wei Chin's shoe," I said. "It had been left near where the road turns toward my rancho, and there were signs that the body had been dragged to where it was found."

"He must have been beaten to get control of him, then strangled," Angelina said. "I also found this." She pulled back the sheet covering Wei Chin and pointed to his shirt. "It looks as though the killer stepped on him."

"What?" I bent closer.

There, on the faded dark cotton, was the imprint of a boot, an imprint I knew all too well. I pulled the paper from my bag.

"Is it the same?" Angelina asked.

"It is." I said.

"I found one other thing,"

Angelina held out her hand. Lying in her palm was a small gold anchor, about the size of my thumbnail, with several tiny diamonds set along the length of it.

"It looks like a watch fob ornament," I said, then frowned. "I've seen this before." I closed my eyes. Unbidden, visions of the riot filled my head. "Oh dear. I do believe I know where I saw it, assuming it's the same ornament."

"Where?" asked Angelina.

I took the small ornament. "The night of the riot. One of the fellows who wanted to kill us if we did not give up our Chinese friends wore an ornament like this. How did you find it?"

"It was caught in the queue," said Angelina. "But how many men have ornaments like this?"

"I have no idea." I thought. "Would it make sense to let people know that we have it?"

"It would not," said Wang Fu. "The villain would know why we are asking."

"That does seem reasonable to assume," I said. "Unfortunately, this means we are probably looking for one of the eight men who challenged us that night."

"It is possible someone else found the anchor," said Wang Fu.

"Nor will it be easy to find the men who challenged you," Angelina said. "Not with the grand jury looking for men to indict, and everyone hiding from the grand jury."

"I do know one of them," I said and shuddered. "The land agent Mr. McKinley. But the ornament does not belong to him. It was another fellow who was wearing it. However, I seriously doubt we will be able to convince Mr. McKinley to tell us who his friends were that night."

Angelina shook her head. "Given what I've heard about those ruffians, he may not even know who was with him."

"Indeed." I looked again at the tiny anchor. "I suppose the villain would have to assume it was either lost on the street, buried with Wei Chin or that you have it. Perhaps I should keep it at the rancho. It should be safe there."

"Safer than it would be with me," Angelina said. She frowned and looked at me. "With both of these men dead and in such a similar way, it seems as though the attacks were of a more personal nature than general anger at the Chinese."

I nodded. "It would seem so. And I have learned that they were prone to cheating their fellows at games of chance. Alas, I have no way of questioning those men."

Wang Fu had the decency to keep his face neutral.

"It's still possible that they offended someone among our own," Angelina said. "Perhaps while they were making a delivery for you."

"That is possible," I said, shaking my head. "But they only sometimes helped with deliveries, and never went alone. They didn't speak enough English, which makes it even less likely that they offended someone."

"Alas, it's all too easy to draw someone's ire around here," Angelina grumbled. "I've seen far too many bodies that became that way because someone took umbrage at a mere look, let alone the grave wrong of being a Chinaman."

"Indeed." I sighed and shrugged.

We left shortly after, as Angelina had to get dressed for Mass and I had to get dressed for services.

Wang Fu hurried on ahead of me, clearly trying to avoid the coming storm. I went on to church, where Reverend Elmwood's sermon on a Christian home was possibly the most piously mundane thing I had ever heard. It is only after I have gone over my journals that I realized he gave it every year or so, and I noted it in almost the exact same way each time he did.

We held the funeral for Wei Chin that afternoon, after dinner, never mind that it was Sunday. The Chinese did not find such a thing amiss and there were no Christians but my household to mourn our field hand. Alas, there were not even that many of the Chinese. The Lee family was kind enough to attend, but it was clear that they were afraid that Wei Chin's murder would not be the last. However, they were not so afraid that they accepted my offer to stay on the rancho until we found the villain.

When my household and I arrived back at the rancho, everyone scattered to their respective housing. Except Wang Fu, who stood in the yard, watching me.

"You want explanation," he said calmly.

"I most certainly do," I replied. "Come into my parlor."

Juanita was in the house, so there was no impropriety.

"What did you know about the Wei brothers' activities?" I demanded the moment we were inside.

"I know they gamble," Wang Fu said.

He stood in the center of the room as I placed my bag on the chair next to the door, then crossed to the other side.

"But the cheating?"

"That, I do not know. They very lucky, true. And maybe they did. But I do not know how or how many times."

"Were they doing anything else that would have made someone angry with them?"

"I do not think so." Wang Fu shrugged.

I glared at him. "Can I believe that?"

Wang Fu sighed deeply. "I have earned your anger. I am sorry. I was afraid."

"After all this time, you do not trust me?" I turned away, blinking back my tears.

"We are hated by everyone," Wang Fu said, his calm dissolving into hurt. "Do you know what that is like? Just because we are Chinese. They do not hate the Negroes as much as they hate us. And, yes, you have good heart. But you are not Chinese. You do not understand. You call gambling evil. We do not. It is an amusement only, and we do not have much else here. I do not want you to think Wei Li and Wei Chin are evil because they gamble."

"I wasn't going to think that. And you could have explained. I would have heard you."

"Yes. You would hear, but not understand. Maybe you tell Mrs. Sutton. Maybe you tell Mr. Sebastiano. They do not understand. And they do not try, like you. Then we have more angry Americans and we not need that now."

I looked at him, then away again. In my deepest heart, I knew that Wang Fu's cause was just. It did not matter that I was trustworthy. He and his fellows were still in peril. Just because the lynchings had been quelled and denounced, clearly there was another in the pueblo who was still bent on killing Chinamen, whether it was the Wei brothers specifically, or the Chinese, in general.

I swallowed my pride. "Wang Fu, if we are to find who is doing this, then we must work together. You must tell me everything you know, and I will tell you everything I know. If I do not understand, then you must make me understand." I looked at him, sadly. "I call you my friend."

"You are friend, too. But we are different. You must remember that."

He turned and left my adobe, the door shutting silently behind him.

I debated following him, then realized he probably

needed some time to himself after such an emotional encounter. I did, however, seek him out the next morning and found him in the herb garden, as usual. I told him everything I had learned, and he recounted what little he had found, namely the rumors that the Wei brothers had cheated at their games of chance. The problem was, they hadn't ruined anybody financially by winning so often, and there didn't seem to be anyone so angry that they would kill them.

"I think I can understand why one of us would cut off their queues," Wang Fu said, finally. "It would keep them from going home. But once they are dead, their bones will be sent back so that they can rest with their ancestors. There is no queue then. If someone want to keep them from going home by cutting off their queue, why would they kill them?"

"So, it would be nastier to let them live and not be able to return to China than to simply kill them?" I asked.

Wang Fu nodded.

There was still some coolness between us, and I found it very frustrating. I had not realized until that point how much I treasured Wang Fu's friendship. There had to be some way to mend the rift, but I did not know what it was.

"Well," I said after an uncomfortable pause. "I shall call upon Mr. Hewitt to see what I can find out, and perhaps Mr. Fletcher and Mr. Gaines."

"I would like to go to the Calle to talk to more of my fellows," Wang Fu said.

"Oh dear," I said. "Yes, you must, I suppose. How are we to keep you protected?"

Wang Fu shook his head. "I know to watch. I will be safe."

I nodded and went to put on my indigo walking dress. For all we were different, I couldn't help but think that when it came to male stubbornness, the Chinese men were not all that different than American men.

I made my way into town with Juan and Damiano in tow, as always. Given the likelihood that no one would admit that they had participated in the riots, I decided to focus on finding the boot I needed, or perhaps someone who might have seen something the night that Wei Chin was killed. The first stop on my list was the Hewitts'.

As it turned out, when I got to the buggy manufactory, Mr. Hewitt was indisposed. I thought it was a bit early for such things, but Mrs. Hewitt, a lovely woman the size of a mouse but with the temper of a lion when roused, confided in me that Mr. Hewitt's indisposition had more to do with the night before.

"I simply cannot believe it," she complained. I was one of the few who knew the details of her true situation and thus she occasionally bared her soul to me. "He did not come home from the saloon last night until after midnight. And worse yet, he continued ranting and drinking for another hour or so. Which is why he is still in bed, sleeping it off. My poor daughters were terrified. They thought the riots had started again."

We were sitting in her office, which was more like a comfortable sitting room above the manufactory floor, with a large desk at one end.

"How terrible," I said. "That must have been very frightening for them, what with some of the lynchings happening so close."

"They have yet to get over the trauma of it," Mrs. Hewitt said.

Mrs. Hewitt spent most of her time running the buggy manufactory, as her husband could not. Therefore, her three daughters were left in the care of Mrs. Hewitt's mother and the Negro maid. They were still rather young at the time, and I could well imagine that they had, indeed, been frightened by the lynchings across the way.

"And those poor Chinamen," Mrs. Hewitt sighed. "I wouldn't hire any, myself, but they do seem mostly harmless. Mrs. Fletcher has one for her gardener and to help build things, and she says he is quite reliable and a good, steady worker."

"They are, at that," I said. "In fact, I shall have to see to hiring some new field hands to replace them. I don't know if you've heard."

"Well, I heard about the one," Mrs. Hewitt said.

"That was Wei Li," I said. "His brother Wei Chin was slaughtered Saturday night. We found him yesterday morning."

"Oh, how terrible!"

"It is," I sighed. "The problem is, in order to stop this horrible person from wreaking more havoc, I have to ask all manner of unseemly questions of everyone."

Mrs. Hewitt rolled her eyes but did not become aroused. "And I suppose you have reason to question Mr. Hewitt, though about what, I have no idea. He did challenge those terrible men, you know."

"I do indeed, and while I think it unlikely that he is the one I seek, I must be thorough. I am looking for someone who presents himself as better off than he is. Mr. Hewitt is not without means, and I know that is from how admirably well you have kept this business. But even so, it is possible that he forgets to have his clothes mended or his boots repaired."

"Of course, he forgets," Mrs. Hewitt growled. "That is yet another thing I must see to. And I assure you, his appointments are in perfect repair. I insist upon it. Otherwise, people might suspect that he is not capable of running a business, and I cannot afford even the least hint that he isn't."

"No, you cannot," I said. "Yours is quite the heavy burden, Mrs. Hewitt."

She sighed deeply. "I suppose it could be worse. He may not be sober, but at least he is companionable. Nor is he the type to be mean when he is indisposed. And I have free rein to see to our interests."

"It could, indeed, be a great deal worse," I said.

We had both seen the worst that a drunken husband could do. Mrs. Hewitt was unusually fortunate in that she not only had her husband's tacit permission to manage their interests, but also had secured the loyalty of their employees, who were almost as determined to keep the family secret as she was. But it was still a difficult row to hoe, being a woman doing a man's work, which is why I let her air the rest of her complaints in spite of me being anxious to move on to my next interview.

I decided to visit Mr. Fletcher next. I knew his wife well enough to make an uninvited call at their home, which is what I did. I was quite fortunate to find Mr. Fletcher in and left the boys on the front porch with their slates and several arithmetic problems to solve.

"I'm so glad you're here," Mr. Fletcher said, upon my admission to his front parlor.

It was a comfortable and tasteful room, with some excellent art on the walls, including a lovely still life by Raphaelle Peale.

"I did not know I was wanted," I said.

"We need someone," Mr. Fletcher said, his voice hoarse. "Mrs. Fletcher has the worst grippe. She cannot stop coughing."

He was a thin, wiry fellow, unlike his wife, who was rather stout. His hair and beard were brown, and the latter was neatly trimmed.

The only thing marring the loveliness of the front parlor was the omnipresent stench of tobacco. It was not unusual. Many men in the pueblo smoked, though many did not do so in their homes, unless they had a private study or smoking room, because it was considered very shameful for a lady to smoke and most would have nothing to do with it. However, I happened to know that Mrs. Fletcher did smoke. To the best of my knowledge, she kept her secret from her husband, mostly because he smoked his cigarettes in the house and thus could not smell hers.

"That does sound terrible." I looked around. "Where is she?"

"Upstairs, in her chamber." Mr. Fletcher smiled

wanly at me. "Do you think you can help?"

"I can't say until I've seen her. Will you show me the way?"

Mr. Fletcher eagerly showed me upstairs. I could hear the ragged cough even as I crested the staircase, and Mr. Fletcher was quite correct that it did not seem to stop. However, Mrs. Fletcher did not appear to have whooping cough or the consumption, so I was left to conclude that she merely had a bad cough, probably from a catarrh. I was able to give her an elixir that usually worked well with coughs. It contained some rather potent spirits, along with honey and lemon peel. I also had some lozenges made with pine oil and suggested that she suck on them as needed.

Mrs. Fletcher did not have much to say, but after dosing her with the elixir, I waited until she fell asleep, which fortunately, did not take long. Mr. Fletcher seemed delighted.

"She hasn't been able to sleep for coughing," he whispered to me as we left the chamber.

"That's often how it is," I said. "It may take a while for the cough to fully abate. In the meantime, I have plenty of lozenges that she can suck on."

"I am so glad you came to call," Mr. Fletcher said. "I was beside myself with worry."

"Well, I did come with another purpose," I said, suddenly realizing that both Mr. and Mrs. Fletcher had been at the party the previous Saturday night. "As you may have heard, one of my field hands was slaughtered the night of the Glassells' party. I was hoping that perhaps you had seen something as you left the hotel. Perhaps you had to go by the Calle de los Negros to fetch your buggy."

"I don't go near that place," Mr. Fletcher said so quickly I was fairly certain that he was lying. "My buggy was hitched nearby in any case, and I certainly didn't see anything."

"Oh. I was hoping someone did," I said. "It's been so dreadful, what with the riots and now my two field hands.”

“Serves you right for hiring one of those nasty Chinamen.” He made a face and began fidgeting with his watch chain.

“But I was given to understand that you have a Chinese servant.”

“He’s all right.” Mr. Fletcher shrugged. “It was my wife’s idea. But the rest of them. Pah.”

“That has not been my experience,” I said, my voice growing colder in spite of myself. I knew lecturing the man would do little good and would make it harder to get the information I needed. “When I heard that your wife had spoken highly of your servant, I got the impression that you disapproved of the lynching.”

“Of course, I did!” Mr. Fletcher’s fidgeting became even more pronounced and he started pacing about the room. “Just because most of those rogues deserved what they got doesn’t mean I do not believe in the rule of law.”

“So, you did not participate.”

“Never.” He coughed loudly and would not look at me. “It was all the lower element in town. Like that teamster Sanford. I know for a fact that he was there.”

“And how do you know that?” I asked.

“I, eh, eh, heard him bragging about it the other week.”

“Ah. Interesting. From what I’ve heard, most of those involved are desperately trying to hide it, for fear of being indicted.”

Mr. Fletcher pulled himself up straight. “Yes, most of them are. But I have nothing to worry about. I was not there.”

“How very interesting, Mr. Fletcher.” I replaced my bag over my shoulder. “Thank you for speaking with me and please keep me informed as to your wife’s condition.”

“I will. I will, indeed. Thank you for coming.”

He handed me a dollar and all but pushed me out the front door. I sighed. I was fairly sure he’d lied to me about where he'd been that Saturday night, but had no way to prove it. I looked at the coin in my hand. At least, I was not going to have to send him a remittance letter for my services.

CHAPTER EIGHT

I left the Fletcher house feeling out of sorts. That was the second time Mr. Sanford had been cited as having participated in the riot. But he was a teamster. How was I, a woman, to speak with him unless he or a fellow fell ill or came to some sort of grief? I knew many of the teamsters seemed to prefer the Uribe saloon. But even if I were not prohibited from venturing into the front because of my gender, there was good reason to believe that Mr. Sanford would be off driving someone's team of horses or mules to deliver or retrieve a load of goods.

I made my way to the saloon, nonetheless. Mr. Sedonez was tending bar but was happy to come to the back room to speak with me.

"I need to contrive a way to speak with Mr. Sanford, and perhaps some of the other laborers who come here," I said. "I, obviously, cannot simply walk into the bar and strike up a conversation."

"You mean about your field hand?" Mr. Sedonez asked. His full hair and mustache were bright white, but his face was unlined, and he carried himself with the strength of a younger man.

"Yes. It's quite a ticklish situation. There are many who could have done the evil deed. However, if I can talk to Mr. Sanford and perhaps a few others, then I might be able to exonerate them and narrow down the list of those who might have done it."

Mr. Sedonez nodded. "Well, Sanford is gone with a load and the only fellows here right now just came in with a mule train from San Francisco. I've never seen them before, so I don't think they were here for the riot.

Everyone else is working. Wait. Old Man Pugh is here."

I sighed. "He has been helpful, but I would guess that he is already indisposed for the day."

"He's been telling a few tales and the fellows from San Francisco have bought him some rounds."

"In other words, he won't be much help at the present."

"He can hold his liquor better than most."

"Or he's merely so confused generally that one hardly knows the difference when he's the worse off for drink."

Mr. Sedonez laughed. "I would not dismiss him so quickly. He's a lot stronger than you would think. I would be happy if I were as spry as he is when I get to his age."

I could hear the Clocktower Courthouse strike the hour of eleven and the clock on the desk chimed along. I didn't have a lot of time before needing to return to my rancho for my lunch. I took leave of Mr. Sedonez and started back to the rancho.

However, as I walked down the Calle Principal, I noted an office that made me stop. Mr. Gaines had been named by Mrs. Glassell as one who was not as well off as he appeared and I recalled Miss Gaines' worries over her father marrying her off to the highest bidder to ensure that she would be well cared for. Perhaps his business was not doing as well as might be.

I sent Damiano back to the rancho, offering my regrets to Olivia that I might be delayed, but saying I would try to return in time for lunch. It would not appease her entirely, however I had to make the effort.

Leaving Juan outside with a reminder to work on his history lesson, I entered the building, then climbed the long, narrow staircase that led upstairs. The hall was lit by windows at one end of the building and by the glass windows of the various office doors. I paused outside the Gaines' office, as I could hear voices within that suggested that some business was being concluded and I did not care to interrupt.

"It was a pleasure seeing you, Robert," Mr. Gaines was saying as I waited.

"It was, indeed," came Mr. Leighland's elegant Southern drawl. "And please be sure to give my fondest regards to that lovely daughter of yours."

I didn't know if I was miffed or relieved that Mr. Leighland seemed to be courting Miss Gaines. He had certainly been paying his attentions to me on Saturday night, but that could have been mere flirting. I did not have time to consider the matter, however, as Mr. Leighland left the office at just that moment.

He smiled and tipped his hat. "Mrs. Wilcox, what a pleasure to see you."

"The pleasure is mine, Mr. Leighland," I said, smiling.

I looked to enter the office and Mr. Leighland stepped aside.

"Good day," he said.

"Good day," I returned, then went into the office.

Mr. Gaines, a tall man with a florid complexion who was usually angry with someone or something, appeared to be quite pleased with himself that morning.

"Good day, Mrs. Wilcox," he said. "And how might I help you? Are you finally interested in that bit of land north of your property?"

I decided to let him think so in the hopes of gaining his confidence.

"It's under consideration," I replied, realizing that the purchase could be quite beneficial. "At the moment, though, I'm looking for people who were near the Calle de los Negros on Saturday night. As you know, my field hand came to grief there and I'm hoping to find someone who might have seen something."

"I'm afraid I didn't see anything," Mr. Gaines said. "Maybe my son did." He opened the door to the inner office. "Timothy? You were at Mahoney's Saturday, weren't you?"

Timothy Gaines, a younger, somewhat paler version of his father, with a darker beard, appeared in the doorway.

"I told you, father, it was a necessary meeting with some of the Common Council," he said.

The senior Mr. Gaines did not approve of drinking in saloons. At least, that is what he claimed. He was fairly well known at Mr. Mahoney's place. In fairness, however, it was a common meeting spot for the wealthier and more influential citizens of the pueblo.

"Yes, yes, I know," Mr. Gaines said, his usual irritability rising to the fore. "Mrs. Wilcox is here, asking about her field hand who was killed Saturday night. She's trying to find out if anyone saw anything near the Calle de los Negros."

The younger Mr. Gaines glared at me.

"I saw nothing of note," he said. "Have you tried asking those of the Chinamen still there?"

"We are pursuing that avenue of inquiry, yes," I said. "However, there seems to be good reason to believe that the murder was not committed by one of the Chinese."

"I saw nothing." The younger Mr. Gaines shrugged and returned to the inner office, shutting the door.

"I'm so sorry we couldn't be more helpful," his father said. "Do think about that property. It would be in your best interests to buy it."

"I will definitely think about it," I said, and left the office wondering whether the piece of land was such a good value after all.

Damiano had returned by that point with the news that Olivia would keep some soup warm for me. I signaled the boys, but then decided to stop at the mercantile where I generally picked up my mail. It would only take a few minutes to post a notice that I was in want of two field hands. Which is what I did, and it took even less time than I'd thought.

The weather was still somewhat cool, and I must confess I was quite glad of the steaming bowl of soup that Olivia placed before me, with fresh bread alongside it. She'd also made some coffee, and I added a bit of cream and some more sugar. It was quite a comfortable lunch and I was even happier that it hadn't waited more than a few minutes after all.

I tried to think of who else I should talk to that day. However, Sebastiano wanted me to check the new distillate and there were several other chores that could not wait. Wang Fu came back from the Calle de los Negros late that afternoon, and we were able to talk.

"I have found the men that Wei Chin gamble with that night," Wang Fu said after I had recounted my day. "But they did not know anything. He lost, too, so why would they be angry enough to kill him?"

"You're right. It makes no sense," I said. "But then neither of the killings make much sense. What do you plan to do next?"

"I will talk to Ah Chen," Wang Fu said. "He was most angry at Wei Chin. You?"

"I'm not sure." I frowned. "The men I am most suspicious of I am least able to talk to. I do want to visit my dressmaker tomorrow, in any case. With luck I will find somebody along the way."

The next morning, Sebastiano announced that the wine for the angelica had settled and was probably ready to be blended with the previous year's brandy. We usually evenly mixed the wine with the brandy, but we both had to taste the wine first, then the brandy, and then test blends with different proportions. We spat out a great many of our tastes more to avoid the inebriating effects of the wine than because we didn't like what we tasted. I still made a point of chewing on some mint leaves at lunch in the hopes that my breath would not betray my occupation.

Once we decided that the usual even mix was the best, and as there had been no responses to the notice I'd posted the previous day, I was left with my afternoon free enough that I could visit Mrs. Washington. Mr. Shapiro's beautiful figured green cotton had stayed in the back of my mind, and it happened that I could use a second tea dress.

On the surface of it, it seems that ordering a new dress in the midst of needing to find a killer before he struck again might be considered quite frivolous. I certainly considered it so at the time and spent quite a few minutes of the walk to Mrs. Washington's assuaging my guilty feelings by reminding myself that sometimes such a treat helped to soothe the turbulence of my mind enough to return to rational thought. However, if I understand Dr. Freud's recent work correctly, it may have actually been my subconscious mind at work.

Of course, at that time, we had no idea Dr. Freud existed, let alone the world of psychology. I merely assumed that I was trying to excuse some rather selfish behavior on my part. Still, when I arrived at the adobe on Wine Street, I felt the same delicious release of worry as when I settle down to an excellent meal and take my first sip of wine.

Mrs. Bella Washington served her customers in the tiny parlor of her adobe. There was a large mirror at one end, with a small platform in front of it. Rolls of different fabrics in all the colors of the rainbow were stacked on their ends against the walls. There were two small settees, one of which was piled high with books of fashion plates and piles of scrap fabrics. Mrs. Washington, herself, was a Negress and stout, with amber eyes and graying hair. Her posture was stooped from years of work over a needle.

She was easily the best dressmaker in the pueblo, and there were not one, but two sewing machines in her little parlor as testament to her excellence. I had heard rumors that Mrs. Washington could be "difficult," but I had never found her so. I eventually came to notice that the ladies most likely to complain about Mrs. Washington were those who treated with disdain their servants and anyone else they considered their lesser. I did not doubt that Mrs. Washington had found them equally as difficult and had found a way to quietly and politely deny them her services.

I was admitted by Mrs. Washington's granddaughter, a pretty young girl with very dark skin, who was going to take up her grandmother's trade, apparently. At least, she wore a measuring tape about her neck and had three threaded needles stuck in the cuff of her work dress. I was offered the empty settee and a cup of tea, which the young woman hurried off to fetch.

Then Mrs. Washington, herself, came in, her gait slow and measured.

I stood. "I apologize for coming by without an appointment."

"Oh, always happy to see you, Mrs. Wilcox." Mrs. Washington smiled at me. "Now, what can I help you with today?"

"I would like to order a tea dress," I said. "I saw the loveliest dark green figured cotton at Mr. Shapiro's mercantile and thought it would be perfect."

"Hmph," Mrs. Washington snorted. "Might be at that, but it'll be expensive if you want that exact fabric."

"How so?"

"That dad-blamed fellow see me coming, he charges me three times what he charges the other dressmakers in town."

Mrs. Washington was also noted for her salty tongue.

"That's dreadful," I said, although why I was shocked, I do not know. "Do you have something similar?"

"I might," Mrs. Washington moved over to the rolls of fabric piled along the wall in her parlor. "If not, I can get some." She looked over at me. "Do you need it right away?"

"No, although it would be nice to have for Christmas tea," I said.

Almost wheezing, she pulled roll after roll away from the wall.

"Here, allow me to help," I said, suiting action to

my words.

"That be kind of you, Mrs. Wilcox," she said. She put her hands on a roll. "Now, this be silk, but it's figured and it's a good color, I think."

It was a dark green silk with figured stripes. I suddenly realized that I had seen its like in two different places. The first was the white figured silk that Mrs. Judson had purchased from Mr. Shapiro the day I had visited there. The second time I saw the fabric, it had been blue and I'd seen it the day we'd found Wei Chin's body.

"Ah Chen," I said suddenly.

"I didn't say nothing about a Chinaman," Mrs. Washington grumbled, looking a little guilty.

"No," I said. "Forgive me, Mrs. Washington. I've seen this fabric before, in different colors. Mr. Shapiro had some in white, and Mr. Ah Chen was wearing some trousers made of it in blue."

"And what of it?" Mrs. Washington looked at me with a guarded expression.

"It would be very interesting to know the source of this fabric," I said. "I don't know how, but it might help me find the miscreant who killed my field hands."

Mrs. Washington sighed. "I don't tell no one where I get my silk."

"Obviously, you need to protect your source so that others don't buy the same fabrics."

"T'ain't that," she said. She shrugged. "I buy my fabrics from all over, mind. Most of the cottons, I get from mills in the South. They don't know what I look like, so I get the best. Same with the mills in the North, where I get good wool, linen, and bombazine. I can tell folks that I get the best fabrics, which I do. But the silk. That I buy direct from the Chinese. That Mr. Ah, he brings it in from his homeland. Now, I can't tell anybody that."

"I understand," I said, looking again at the striped green silk. "But if you got this from Mr. Ah, then it's entirely possible that Mr. Shapiro gets his silk from the same place."

"Don't see how knowing that is going to help you find out who killed your field hands," she said.

I sighed. "I'm afraid I don't see how, either. However, I have found that sometimes it's the smallest detail that reveals everything, whether I am trying to make a diagnosis or find a killer."

"That most certainly be the truth of it, Mrs. Wilcox," Mrs. Washington said. "Same as in dressmaking. The smallest detail makes all the difference between a dress that fits and one that is always catching at you." Her brow creased as she thought something over. "I do declare, Mrs. Wilcox, I have had an idea. Perhaps I can go to Mr. Shapiro and buy that figured cotton you got your heart set on. It would cost you a might more, but maybe I can get him to 'fess up about where he gets his silk from."

I thought it over. "That does sound like an excellent plan." I suddenly frowned. "Except that I would like to be there to see how he reacts. Perhaps I can buy the fabric, myself. How much would I need?"

"That depends on the dress you want," Mrs. Washington said.

We looked over several fashion plates at that point. The granddaughter, Maisie was her name, came in with the tea, then silently returned to the back of the adobe. We settled on a design and Mrs. Washington said that I would need about 30 yards of fabric.

Sometime later, Regina told me, with no end of amusement, that the dressmaker had requested at least twice as much fabric as would have been needed. However, I did not begrudge Mrs. Washington the deception. As Mr. Shapiro was charging her three times what he charged me, I thought it fair. Furthermore, the gown she eventually made was exquisite. I won't say I was the envy of the pueblo that winter. After all, that sort of vanity is counter to all I hold dear. But I must confess that I did spot the occasional glare of jealousy, and it was most unbecomingly gratifying.

After Mrs. Washington had told me how much fabric to buy, we discussed shoes, hats, and gloves. I decided that I already had appropriate boots and slippers, but a visit to the milliner for a new hat was definitely in order, as was an order for new gloves.

The gloves were not, in fact, in any way needed. However, I remembered that Mr. Montero, the tanner, was one of the people Mrs. Glassell had suggested as looking better off than he was, and it was his wife who made the most beautiful gloves I'd ever seen. Since the dress was to be ready for Christmas, I decided that some red gloves would add an extra cheery note to the ensemble, even if they were rather impractical.

So, instead of visiting Mr. Shapiro, I went to the tannery, on the outskirts of the city's southern border. There is a very good reason why the tannery was on the edge of the city. The work of tanning hides creates the most appalling odors. On my way there, I noted that at least two new houses were being built nearby. The pueblo was growing, and I wondered how much longer Mr. Montero would be able to keep his tannery at that location.

Mr. Montero was in the yard, watching as several Chinamen went about their work, pulling skins from various vats and replacing the skins with others. I hailed him and asked after Mrs. Montero. He sent me to the small house on the edge of the property, where Mrs. Montero invited me inside.

Both Mr. and Mrs. Montero were Negroes, although Mr. Montero's skin was light enough that others sometimes thought he was a Mexican. Mrs. Montero, a small woman with a pleasant demeanor, had skin as dark as night. Both had always been free, Mr. Montero having been born and raised in Mexico proper and Mrs. Montero having been raised in one of the island countries in the ocean between the southern U.S. and South America.

I placed my order for my gloves with Mrs. Montero, who was delighted and even produced a bit of kidskin which had been dyed several shades of red, so that I could pick which hue I wanted. All the while, I looked around, trying to surreptitiously determine whether all was as it should be.

"And how is your business these days?" I asked as Mrs. Montero made her notes on my order.

"Oh, it is very good," Mrs. Montero said in her soft island accent. "And with no little thanks to you. Because you have worn my gloves, other of the ladies in the pueblo have noticed. And because they cannot abide it that you have something better than they do, they come to me to get their gloves. Or their dressmakers do."

"Such as Mrs. Washington."

Mrs. Montero laughed and nodded. "She, herself, cannot come out here so far, so she insists that her ladies come, themselves. Sometimes they send for me. Either way, I shall soon be able to leave the teamsters' gloves to my assistant and only make good ladies' gloves."

"I'm glad to hear it," I said. "Your husband seems well."

She laughed again. "He is quite busy. The pueblo is growing, which means more saddles and bags and shoes and belts and gloves."

"I hope he's not so busy that he forgets to see to his own needs," I said.

"I see to them well enough." Her eyes twinkled as if she suddenly realized what I was asking, there being no doubt that she'd heard about the boot I was seeking. "The soles of his boots are in good repair, I assure you. And he is a good man, who eats at my table every night and does not leave to go to saloons and other disreputable places."

"Well, thank you, Mrs. Montero."

We concluded our business and I returned to the yard to thank Mr. Montero.

"I take it business is going well?" I asked.

"Well enough," he said in a low voice.

"You have quite a few Chinese working for you."

"No one else wants to," he grumbled.

Something gaseous burst through a bubble in one of the vats near us and we both bent over coughing from the fumes.

I wiped my eyes. "I can understand why."

Mr. Montero laughed. "One gets accustomed to it. You see my fellows. They do not know the difference."

Indeed, the men did not appear to.

"You seem to have quite the regard for the Chinamen you have hired," I said.

"These men, yes." He shrugged. "Others, I have not heard such good things."

I watched the men a moment more, then realized at least two of them looked familiar.

"Who are those two?" I asked, pointing at a nearby vat where the two I was curious about were stirring the contents with two long posts.

"Say Chan and Yu Quon," said Mr. Montero.

"I would like to speak with them, if I may," I said.

"Hey, Chan, Quon, come over here."

The two men left their poles in the vat and hurried over.

"Mrs. Wilcox would like to speak with you," Mr. Montero said, then headed over to another part of the yard.

The two were dressed in the usual Chinese shirt and pants, with the fronts of their head shaved and long queues hanging from the napes of their necks.

"I am Chan Tse," said one, a somewhat taller fellow with a long, thin face. "Quon Yu not speak much English."

Quon Yu was quite round and smiled as he bobbed and nodded.

"I saw you when we found Wei Chin," I said. "Were you with him that night?"

"No," said Chan Tse. "I go to bed early. Must come here to work."

"Surely Mr. Montero doesn't make you work on

the Lord's Day."

Mr. Chan shifted while Mr. Quon nodded enthusiastically.

"I go to bed early," Mr. Chan said again. He looked over his shoulder. "Must go back to work. Ask Ah Chen about Wei Chin. He know."

The two men went back to the vat and commenced stirring the contents as if it were the most important thing in the world.

There was nothing for me to do but leave.

CHAPTER NINE

We were riding that day, I on Daisy, and Juan and Damiano on one of the mules. As we left the tannery, it was my purpose to go to Mr. Shapiro's mercantile, but one of the boys from Mr. Uribe's saloon found us first and told us that Mr. Sedonez wanted to see me right away.

We hurried to the saloon and tied the horse and mule up behind the building. I brought the boys inside with me, as I did not find the alley a particularly sanitary place. They had a grammar lesson to study, so they got their books and slates and went to work.

When Mr. Sedonez appeared, it turned out that he merely had an emergency order.

"There was a party last night," he explained. "And the men drank all of the angelica for some reason."

"I'll see to it that you get a fresh cask right away," I said.

I was about to ask him if Mr. Sanford had returned to town, when the man in question began swearing loudly from the front. I, initially, had no idea it was he, but Mr. Sedonez hurried from the back room and immediately began yelling at Mr. Sanford, and from there I was able to draw that conclusion.

The swearing did not entirely stop. Apparently, Mr. Sanford was quite annoyed at mules, Chinamen, owners, Indians, Chinamen, barkeeps, Chinamen, and any number of other people as well. Mr. Sedonez returned, dragging Mr. Smith with him.

"I know you want to speak with Mr. Sanford," Mr. Sedonez said. "But he's not in a fit state to talk."

"That much I surmised," I said, grimly. I looked at Mr. Smith. "It's good to see you again, Mr. Smith."

Mr. Smith adjusted the wad of chewing tobacco packed in his cheek and let loose a noxious stream onto the floor.

"Dagnabbit!" Mr. Sedonez yelled. He grabbed a rag off of a desk and threw it at Mr. Smith. "How many times do I have to tell you people to use the spittoons? Now, swab that up if you want to keep drinking here."

Mr. Smith shifted his wad, then bent slowly to do Mr. Sedonez' bidding.

"It's bad enough you had to rile Sanford up," Mr. Sedonez continued. "What, in Heaven's name, did you have to do that for?"

Mr. Smith stood up and glared. "He was saying I was part of that riot. I weren't there. I swear it. He's just trying to cover it up that he was. He and Mr. McKinley were roaming the streets looking for loose Chinamen to grab."

"And how do you know that?" I asked.

"Uh, he was bragging about it that night," Mr. Smith said. "He and McKinley and that Fletcher fellow were in here, laughing up about how they even scared that lady doctor." He stopped and looked abashed. "I mean you, ma'am. Begging your pardon."

"Granted," I said, somewhat automatically as I tried to hide the shudder I felt. Alas, I remembered that part all too well. "So, Mr. McKinley, Mr. Sanford, and Mr. Fletcher were all part of that group. I seem to remember there were eight men in total. Do you know who the others were?"

"No, ma'am. Just that they weren't me." Mr. Smith shifted the wad in his cheek again as he shuffled his feet. "I mean it. I was not there."

"And yet, you bear considerable antipathy toward the Chinese."

Mr. Smith looked around anxiously, then hurried to the side of the desk and used the spittoon. He wiped his mouth, then looked nervously up at me.

"They're taking our jobs," he grumbled, finally.

"Has Mrs. Costa hired a Chinaman and put you out?" I asked.

He shuffled his feet again. "No, but I know fellows that have been."

"Well, would you tell these fellows of yours to please contact me?" I said. "I have need of two more field hands and would be grateful to have them. Indeed, given that there are so many poor men who have been unjustly robbed of their jobs, I would think I would have received several responses to my notice already."

Mr. Smith expectorated again and remained silent. I reassured Mr. Sedonez that I would have the cask sent promptly, called the boys, then left.

Once again, I could feel my temper flaring, which is why I decided to walk rather than ride. I took Daisy's reins in my hands and let the boys ride on ahead.

We were walking down the Calle Principal when Mr. Leighland sauntered up and tipped his hat to me.

"Good day, Mr. Leighland," I said, smiling in spite of my pique.

"Good day, Mrs. Wilcox," he replied. "What good fortune to come across you at this moment."

"Are you not feeling well?" I asked, touching my ever-present bag.

"I am as fit as a fiddle," he said with a chuckle. "I only meant that I am happy to have this opportunity to see you."

I smiled even though he was spreading the butter on a bit thick, so to speak.

"I'm glad you're happy to see me," I replied. "I am, however, on the way back to my rancho. I have some business to take care of once there and after that it will be supper time."

"Then will you do me the honor of allowing me to walk you home?"

There was nothing I could say to that except yes, so we continued on our way. Mr. Leighland attempted to take my arm, but I managed to wriggle away.

"Come now, Mrs. Wilcox," he said laughing. He reached for me again. "You would not bruise my fragile heart by disallowing a basic courtesy, would you?"

I avoided him again. "I do not wish to bruise anybody's feelings, but I do prefer to walk by myself, especially since we are not on terms of that kind of intimacy."

"Perhaps not yet," Mr. Leighland said.

My heart froze. It did seem as though he was trying to court me. But I had good reason to believe that Mr. Leighland was, in fact, trying to court Miss Gaines. After all, he had spoken of her quite tenderly when he asked Mr. Gaines to send on his fondest regards. Had I misinterpreted his intent so very badly?

I was both annoyed that I possibly had, and somewhat pleased. He was very charming, and one cannot help but be flattered when such a gentleman pays her his attentions. On the other hand, I did not want a husband and Mr. Leighland did seem to be the type who would expect me to obey him.

"Mr. Leighland, I had gotten the impression that your attentions were focused elsewhere," I said. "I did accidentally overhear you asking Miss Gaines' father to give her your fondest regards, if I recall correctly."

"Oh, I'm just being friendly is all," Mr. Leighland said.

"I'm sure you are, Mr. Leighland," I replied, not at all sure what he meant by that and rendered unable to ask by the customs of polite society. "One can always use another friend."

"I'm glad you think so, Mrs. Wilcox."

"I seem to remember that you are in the shipping business. I trust it is going well?"

"Well enough. But I can't imagine a lady like you would find it interesting to hear about ships and bills of lading and manufacturers agents."

"Actually, I find it quite interesting, and it's a good thing I do, since I ship a good third of my wine to San Francisco."

That seemed to flummox him for a moment. He coughed lightly, then recovered his usual aplomb.

"Indeed."

"Yes. The angelica is quite popular. They are starting to make some respectable wines in the region north of San Francisco. But the angelica is unique to our region, and hence we get considerable call for it from there. Mr. Wiley is my usual agent. Are you familiar with him?"

His smile became rather forced, then eased. "He's a good man. A very good man. You are fortunate to work with him."

"That I am."

We walked through the plaza and I could not help but wince when I saw the spot where we had found Wei Chin.

"Something wrong, Mrs. Wilcox?" Mr. Leighland asked.

"My field hand," I replied, then something occurred to me. "Mr. Leighland, is it possible you came this way Saturday evening after leaving me? Perhaps you saw something."

"I regret, Mrs. Wilcox, that I did not."

We arrived at the rancho gate shortly after.

"Well, good day, Mr. Leighland. It was pleasant walking with you. Oh, one other thing. I am looking to hire two new field hands to replace the ones I recently lost."

"A terrible thing," he said. He looked over the gate and his glance hardened for a second. "Do you plan to hire more Chinamen?"

"I might. They are good workers."

"They are, at that. Well, good day, Mrs. Wilcox."

He tipped his hat again and headed back toward town.

I entered the gate feeling somewhat unsettled. It is a good thing, in general, that the early stages of courting are customarily left rather vague. It allows a lady to dissuade a suitor with the fewest hurt feelings.

Indeed, the way girls lead their beaux on these days is fraught with peril for tender young hearts. However, such vagueness could cause all manner of confusion. Not being able to tell if Mr. Leighland was courting me or Miss Gaines was annoying enough. Not knowing my own mind well enough to know if I wanted him to court me or not, that was aggravating.

Nonetheless, Juan and Damiano were waiting for their grammar lesson, so I shook off the feeling, sent the boys to Anita, then went to get the cask of angelica sent to Mr. Sedonez.

The evening passed in the normal way, with discussion over dinner about the impending indictments to come over the riot. The general consensus of my household was that a week seemed like far too long a time to be deliberating about something that everyone knew had happened. I sincerely hoped the grand jury would turn in any indictments at all. There had been a lynching the year before and the jury had failed to indict anyone connected.

After dinner, I listened to the children's lessons, along with Anita. I took some time to write in my journal, then went off to a largely unrestful sleep. I woke twice and managed to fall back asleep somewhat promptly. The third time I woke, it was thanks to the horrible nightmare, and there would be no sleep after that. I was glad when a couple hours before dawn I was summoned to the bedside of an elderly man who was having difficulty breathing. For once, I was left alone to do my duty, as the boys were still asleep when I left.

There wasn't much I could do. After all, Mr. Fuentes was quite old and had been ill for at least two months already. The blessing was that he was surrounded by his family and his priest and passed away as comfortably as one can.

I waited with the family as Mr. Sutton's men were summoned. They arrived promptly and one mentioned that Mrs. Sutton wanted a word with me as soon as I was able. Sighing, I followed the men to the funeral home. Angelina was, indeed, waiting, and impatiently directed the men to put Mr. Fuentes' body on one of the tables and waited until they had left.

"Come outside," she said, urgently.

Outside, a young Mexican man dispiritedly placed various bits of planking into a wheelbarrow.

"Hello, Mr. Valdez," Angelina said. "Mrs. Wilcox can see to that cut of yours."

He was broad in the shoulders with a square face that suggested that he was at least part Indian. Sighing, he held out his hand.

"It's just a cut," he grumbled.

I pulled my bag from over my shoulder. "Well, it's my job to see that it remains so."

The bandage he had tied around his hand was very dirty and I despaired of what I would find underneath it. Fortunately, what I found was a poultice of herbs and, underneath that, what looked like a knife cut across his palm. The edges were still fiery red, but it had scabbed over well enough. I gently pressed it.

"Does that hurt?"

Mr. Valdez shrugged.

"When did you cut yourself?"

"Last night."

"How?"

He shrugged again.

I sighed as I rummaged through my bag. "You were fighting, weren't you? You don't have to say. I know a knife cut when I see one. It looks like you've managed the contagion well enough. Who dressed this?"

"Mama Jane," he said.

Mama Jane was an Indian woman known for her cures. She made some excellent poultices, the ingredients of which she refused to share with anyone else.

It was clearly time to replace that particular one, so I did, adding some of my own herbs that I had soaked in wine. It was part of the gunpowder poultice that I had gotten from Dr. Skillen.

As I have noted earlier in this account, Dr. Skillen's poultice relied on herbs soaked in wine, to which had been added a bit of gunpowder. Dr. Skillen had been trained as a homeopath, and certainly his remedies were as effective as anything else our colleagues were trying. It is utterly ironic to me that the homeopaths, at the time, were almost more invested in scientific inquiry than most other doctors. Until, alas, science disproved their philosophies.

I re-bandaged Mr. Valdez' hand, lecturing him on the importance of keeping the wound clean and sanitary.

"Now, I have heard that you participated in the riots," I said, slowly.

He crumbled. "I didn't! I didn't! I was nearby, yes, but I didn't do anything to the Chinamen. I didn't even cheer."

"But did you want to?"

"Of course! They have taken all the jobs. I can hardly get hired."

"Rumor has it that you are a thief."

He drew himself up. "I am no thief. If they say that, it is because I am an Indian, and they say that about all Indians. We are no more thieves than you are."

I nodded. "It would seem that you have been falsely accused."

"They tried to say that I hurt the Chinamen, but I didn't," he said almost sobbing. "They even made me testify. I swore I didn't hurt the Chinamen. But they said they would arrest me if I didn't say who else was there. So I did. And they will not let me leave here until they are finished with their jury. If my friends find out that I told what I'd seen, they will kill me."

"Oh dear," I said. I looked over at Angelina.

"There, there, Mr. Valdez," she said. "We won't say anything. Just do a good job and I'll see what other work I can find for you."

"I also need a new field hand," I said.

"I could be a good field hand," he said.

"As long as you don't get into any more fights," I said. "Finish your work here, then get your belongings. My field hands live in the bunkhouse on my rancho. We'll see how you get on for a month or so. Will that suit you?"

"It will, Mrs. Wilcox. Thank you. Thank you."

He fell to his work with considerably more vigor than before, and Angelina and I left him to it.

"I do hope that I have not invited a killer into our midst," I said as we entered her little parlor.

"I think you are safe. He was kind to Chin Tai."

"That speaks well of him, at least. I haven't had much luck elsewhere." I stopped. "I did tell you that I knew one of the eight from the riot, Mr. McKinley. But I don't think I told you the whole of it. We were both at the Glassell's party. He recognized me too and attacked me."

"How awful," Angelina said, then a sly grin spread across her face. "Was this before or after you spent your time dancing with Mr. Leighland?"

"Oh. You've heard about that." I shrugged. "I haven't said so, but he is the one who rescued me from Mr. McKinley. That's why I agreed to dance with him, only to find he is a most excellent dancer. However, I feel somewhat unquiet in my mind about him. He seems to be paying me attentions and I believe that he may also be courting Miss Lavina Gaines. But when I asked him about it, he didn't really answer me one way or another."

"Hm. He arrived here last January, as far as I know, and has been trying to buy some land or something. I understand his business is shipping, but why isn't he living in Wilmington or closer to the ocean?"

"That is an excellent question," I said. "Perhaps he hopes to find a manufacturer to represent."

"So, you are not charmed by him?"

I shook my head. "He is charming enough. But I also suspect he has designs on my rancho and I have no interest in letting him have it. Now what do we do about Mr. McKinley?"

"He's a land agent, is he not?"

"Yes."

Angelina picked up the morning newspaper and perused it. "Yes, here he is. McKinley and Associates. It lists an office on Calle Primavera. Do you think he has employed any clerks?"

"I have no idea," I said. "Why should that make a difference?"

"If he has clerks in his office, it will make it harder for him to behave badly, thus making it safer for you to accost him."

"I have no intention of accosting him," I said. "I would merely like to ask him about the night of the riot and his activities since."

"And he will immediately fall prostrate and confess all," Angelina said with a wry smile.

I tried to glare at her but fell prey to the humor of the situation.

"That may, in fact, be a bit optimistic," I finally said. "Why don't you come with me? It will be a great deal harder for him to force his affections, such as they are, on one of us if there is a second to scream for help."

Angelina laughed loudly. "Let me get my hat and gloves. I will be but a moment."

If I am to be completely honest, as I hope I always am, I was particularly glad that Angelina had consented to accompany me. I found Mr. McKinley quite frightening. Angelina, being rather small of stature, did not appear to be much of a threat. But I trusted her to be as fierce as I would need, and indeed, she did not fail me in that regard.

The two of us made our way to the office on Calle Primavera. Mr. McKinley had his office on the second floor, as was the usual. We knocked and were invited to enter the small room. Three clerks sat behind desks set so closely together that Angelina and I were hard pressed to move, given the hoops under our skirts.

"We wish to see Mr. McKinley," I said.

One of the clerks opened the door to an inner office, then asked us to go in. We squeezed past the desk, narrowly avoiding a most immodest display.

Mr. McKinley scrambled to his feet as he saw us.

"What do you two want?" he demanded from behind his large oak wood desk, littered with papers, inkwells, and pens.

"To know what you were doing last Saturday night and into dawn," I said, foregoing asking him about his role in the riot as I already knew it all too well. "And the afternoon of Friday, November third."

My plan was to frighten him enough to give reasonably honest answers regarding his fellows. It was, regrettably, not my best thinking.

"What in tarnation do you want to know that for?"

Angelina glared at him. "Mr. McKinley! We are ladies!"

Mr. McKinley pointed at me. "She is an abomination. And no lady would want to be seen with her."

I could see Angelina getting ready to let him know what she thought of that.

"Be that as it may," I said firmly before she could. "You have not answered my question. And given that I know how you were involved in the riot, I would think that it would serve you well to avoid insulting me and my friend, lest I turn you over to the grand jury."

Mr. McKinley turned pale. "You wouldn't. No one would believe you."

"But they will believe Mr. Ortiz and his nephew, who were with me that night."

"You know where I was Saturday night," Mr. McKinley snarled.

"I know where you were earlier in the evening. What I want to know is where you were later."

Mr. McKinley glared at both Angelina and me. It looked for a moment as if he wanted to attack both of us. However, he was still behind his desk. I also caught sight of Angelina's face just then. Her eyes were blazing, but there was just a hint of a smile on her face. Mr. McKinley backed down.

"I went home," he mumbled.

"And the afternoon of Friday, November third?"

"How am I supposed to know where I am every day?"

I could have pointed out that he did have a diary in front of him, and it would be possible to check it. But even were he to do so, I seriously doubted that he'd say anything truthful.

"Very well, then," I said. "Good day, Mr. McKinley."

Angelina glared at him one more time and we swept out of the inner office, then picked our way around the desks of the outer office.

"What a completely odious man," Angelina said as soon as we were on the street. "He is utterly vile."

"He is at that," I said. I looked at her. "But I do believe I saw you smiling at him when it looked as though he was going to attack."

"I was," said Angelina. I saw that same daring smirk cross her face yet again. "I was hoping he would."

"Good Heavens, Angelina! He's very strong. I can attest to that." I shuddered at the memory of him grabbing me at the party.

"And I carry around dead bodies all day. Besides, horrible men such as him don't expect a woman to fight back. It surprises them and you can use that against them. You saw how quickly Mr. McKinley thought better of attacking us."

"Indeed." I sighed, then looked up and saw yet another office I wished to visit. "My wine agent, Mr. Wiley."

"Yes?"

"I need to check someone's bona fides. Mr. Wiley might know something."

I forbore to say whose bona fides I wished to check, although from the mischievous look in Angelina's eyes, I could tell she'd already guessed.

"Well, I've an errand, myself," Angelina said. "Thank you for reminding me."

She headed off toward the corner of the Calle Primavera and Calle Primero. I entered the building and found Mr. Wiley's office. I did not get to speak with him, however, because he had not yet returned from his latest trip. He was expected to arrive home soon, but there was no way of knowing exactly when. I left the office feeling somewhat annoyed, never mind that my pique was completely unjust.

As I stepped onto the street, I heard a terrible shrieking. It came from an alley shrouded in shadows nearby. I ran in that direction and was bowled over by a man, I did not see whom, running from the alley. The shrieking stopped and Angelina ran out of the alley, breathing heavily.

"Oh, thanks be!" she gasped when she saw me. "Hurry!"

I got to my feet as fast as I could and ran after her. Just inside the alley was another man lying on the ground. He was on his face, and he wore a long, braided queue that had been partially severed. With Angelina's help, I gently rolled him over onto his back. It was Wang Fu.

CHAPTER TEN

Fortunately, Wang Fu's injuries, though bad enough, turned out not to be immediately life-threatening. His nose and his left arm were broken, and he had a nasty goose egg on the back of his head. It was his good fortune that Angelina had come across the alley when she had and was still feeling angry enough from our encounter with Mr. McKinley that she was ready to wreak some havoc.

"Did you see who it was?" I asked both of them as I tried to staunch the flow of blood from Wang Fu's nose.

"No," gasped Wang Fu through my handkerchief.

I felt his chest to see if there was another wound there. Angelina had sent a street urchin after the men from her funeral parlor and was looking down the alley for their arrival.

"He was wearing a kerchief over his face," Angelina said. "And he was bent over Wang Fu, so I couldn't even tell you how short or tall he was. I just saw him, started shrieking and ran at him as hard as I could. I didn't even know it was Wang Fu that he was hitting."

"And you simply rushed in?" I glared at her and her gaze shifted to the ground. "Goodness gracious, Angelina. You could have been hurt, or worse, and it wouldn't have done anything to save Wang Fu."

"I am grateful," Wang Fu said.

"As I must be also," I said, shuddering. "And what were you doing in this part of the pueblo, anyway, Wang Fu?"

"You left this morning without escort," he said simply. "I hide, but follow to help keep you safe."

I groaned in utter exasperation. "I am not an infant that needs constant minding! And look what good it did you. It could have been much worse. What if you'd run into the same fellow who killed Wei Li and Wei Chin?"

"He may have," said Angelina, opening the chatelaine bag that hung from her waist. "Oh, these ridiculous little bags! Maddie, do you have any paper?"

With one hand still on Wang Fu's nose, I dug through my bag.

"Yes," I said, pulling out a slim blank diary. "Have you found something?"

"I think so." Angelina took the journal and her own small pencil and walked slowly toward the alley's entrance onto the Calle Primavera, watching the ground. "One here, here, and here. Yes, they're the same."

"What?" I asked.

Angelina was sketching furiously. "Boot prints. Here. Does this heel look familiar?"

I looked at the drawing. "Yes. The boot we're looking for. But there's no hole."

"He's had it repaired." Angelina pointed to a track that was reasonably close to me and Wang Fu. "Look. There's a tiny little line under where the hole would have been. He must be quite poor if he didn't have enough money to mend his heel, as well."

"But he would have to repair the hole, as he knew we were looking for it," I said. "That much has gotten around."

Wang Fu coughed, and I gently turned him so that he would not choke. The coughing stilled and Wang Fu nodded at me and he rolled onto his back.

"It's broad daylight," I continued. "Our villain must be getting bolder."

"Or he was looking for me," Wang Fu said. "He grab my hat and laugh, as if he found what he wanted."

"Have any of your fellows also been attacked?" I asked.

"No." Wang Fu coughed again, but it wasn't dire.

"How often do you leave the rancho, Wang Fu?" Angelina asked.

"No leave much. Today I leave to help Maddie."

"Which would account for the attack during daylight hours," I said. "Assuming our killer is after my field hands, specifically. He couldn't get to Wang Fu any other way. But why would he kill my field hands and not someone else's?"

Angelina looked at me helplessly as her employees arrived with the litter.

Back at the rancho, I set Wang Fu's arm and insisted on putting on a plaster cast. I also gave him some morphine, although he protested and wanted me to get his needles for the needle cure he liked to use. We also had a mild debate over which herbs he would need for his headache, as well as the best way to set his broken nose. But he trusted me enough to give me my way, and I decided to compromise by giving him willow bark tea for his headache rather than the laudanum I often used in such cases.

I was greatly heartened in that it was our usual banter and disparaging of each other's methods. It did not mean that we did not respect them. However, I have yet to meet another physician who, when sick or injured, will not try to direct his own treatment. In addition, Wang Fu and I often teased each other, even though he was confident that I was better at setting bones and stitching up cuts, and I was happy to concede that he was a much better herbalist.

He finally drifted off to sleep. Magdalena insisted on watching him so that I could eat my supper. It was a most generous offer, as Magdalena had always been somewhat afraid of the Chinese.

We ate supper downstairs in the bunkhouse, the great room there being the only inside place that could hold everyone. Mr. Valdez had arrived and settled his belongings. The others seemed to like him well enough, even if he sat at the far end of the table and said little during supper.

Needless to say, the topic of the afternoon was the attack on Wang Fu and what that meant in light of everything else that had happened. His courage in attempting to protect me in spite of the peril to his own life ignited the fervor of the others as few things could. But it was when Juan and Damiano began to go on about how they would have handled the mysterious attacker that I put my foot down.

"I can no longer allow the children to accompany me," I said.

The boys groaned and protested very loudly, even as their fathers shushed them.

"What do you mean, Maddie?" Sebastiano asked, worry filling his eyes.

"I can no longer risk their lives," I said simply. Then, to quell the storm of youthful protest, "It is no reflection on anyone's abilities. It is simply that I can no longer put children of such tender years at risk of attack."

"But how do we keep you safe?" Enrique asked.

Olivia rolled her eyes. "As usual, she does not worry about us. She will risk her own life without a thought for the people who care for her."

"Oh, for Heaven's sake!" I snarled. "I am an adult woman. At what point am I to be allowed to move about the world as I see fit?"

"We are partners," Sebastiano said, his eyes getting round and full.

"Yes, we are," I replied. "And you are the very people who will benefit the most from my demise. Furthermore, as equal partners, I should have equal say about how I choose to move about the pueblo."

"Then we'll teach you how to shoot," said Enrique.

"Absolutely not. I have seen enough of what a gun can do," I said, feeling quite outraged.

"But if you can shoot, you can defend yourself," Enrique said. "Then you are safe."

I must confess, I was not entirely reassured. But if learning how to shoot was going to give me the freedom

I needed, then I decided I would learn.

"Until then, I can go with Mrs. Wilcox," Mr. Valdez said. "My years are not so tender."

I suppose I should have had more regard for their loving concern, and in truth, the concern was valid, given what a horribly violent place Los Angeles was in those days. But it irked me not to be able to move about freely.

After supper and listening to the children's lessons, I went to relieve Magdalena and found that Olivia had already relieved her at Wang Fu's bedside. Wang Fu was still asleep. Fortunately, he was breathing quite well, his color apart from his bruises was good, and his fever was relatively light.

"I'll watch for now," I said.

"Very well," Olivia said, getting up. "Maria will watch next, so call her when you can no longer stay awake. She says she will be up with the baby anyway." She looked at Wang Fu tenderly. "He is a good man. Why do we say the Chinese are rogues? Wei Li and Wei Chin may have gotten into some mischief, but they were not rogues."

I sighed as I took the chair next to the bed.

"Why do we say that women cannot learn and are only good for civilizing men?" I asked. "Why do we say that Indians are merely drunkards and Negroes only fit for servitude? Or Mexicans, for that matter? I do not understand these things, Olivia. Why do we fear that which is different from us? It seems to me that there is much more to be learned than to be despised."

Olivia nodded. "I do believe you are right, Maddie. Remember to call Maria."

"I will," I said.

I was not sure how late I would watch. I was a little surprised that Maria's baby, who was a little over a year old at that point, was not sleeping through the night. It's not unheard of, by any means, and it is not usually a reason to be worried. But it is not entirely common, either.

But Maria's littlest boy was the least of my concerns at that moment. I did make a point of rousing Wang Fu every hour or so, as head injuries such as his can lead to a coma. However, shortly after the clock struck midnight, Wang Fu awoke on his own.

"You watch," he muttered.

"Of course."

He let out a weak chuckle. "You have good heart."

"Thank you."

He remained silent for several minutes more and I even thought he'd gone back to sleep.

"This was not done by Chinese," Wang Fu said, surprising me out of my torpor.

"No, I don't think it was," I said, even though I had been fairly sure the villain behind these killings was an American since Wang Fu and I had concluded that the cut off queues were not likely to have been the act of a Chinaman. "There is that anchor ornament to consider, in addition to your conclusion about why the Wei brothers' queues were cut off. No, I think we are looking for one among the fellows who challenged us that night."

"How do we find the Americans?" he asked.

"I do not know. I will ask questions, but that does not necessarily reveal the villain."

"No. It does not. But it does help to eliminate others."

"Yes. It can." I remained silent.

I could understand that the group of men from the riot would have strong feelings of antipathy toward the Chinese, but I could not understand why they would target my field hands and not others. There were others on the Calle de los Negros who could be said to pose a greater threat. However, the vast majority of the Chinese in our fair pueblo worked hard and kept to themselves.

I looked at Wang Fu. "Why did you come to America?"

He sighed. "In my village, people are very poor.

We come to the Golden Mountain so that our families can have money and live easily."

"But it's very hard to make money here," I said. "I know the Wei brothers managed to."

"They work very hard and save." Wang Fu blinked. "And are lucky gambling. I am not so lucky."

"You were today," I said. "Do you want to go home?"

"Yes. I like my village."

"Do you know where Wei Chin hid their money?"

"Yes."

"Would you like to take it?"

"No. Not honorable. It is for their family."

"Can I pay you to take the money to them? I can give you enough that you can go home and your family can live comfortably."

He looked confused. "Why would you do that?"

I sighed. "Wei Li and Wei Chin were so close to achieving their purpose and dream in coming here. They were going to go home. They were only waiting until after pruning season for my sake. And look what happened. Then today..." I blinked back tears. "I treasure our friendship, Wang Fu. But you are going to go home at some point. That's why you're here. Why take the chance that you won't make it?"

He grunted sadly. "I want to go home, but I cannot."

"Your queue is still mostly whole. Only part of it was cut."

His face went blank. "My family is dishonored."

"But if you have money..."

"Not enough money," Wang Fu said with a weak smile. "Is not important. The company will find someone to take the money to the Wei family. You do not have to worry."

"I suppose not."

We fell silent again and shortly after, Wang Fu slept. I called for Maria and then went to my own rest.

The next morning, Wang Fu wanted to get up, but I insisted that he stay in bed, and he eventually agreed that the injury to his head warranted it.

I left the rancho with Mr. Valdez walking next to me. He told me as we walked that he had been born in San Gabriel, but had traveled all over the state, going from job to job. This was his third time in Los Angeles, and he hadn't liked it much until I had hired him.

I found his chatter unaccountably soothing, so I let the words wash over me without really paying them much attention. I was bent on speaking with as many people as I could find, Mr. Shapiro being the first on my list.

I entered the mercantile and went straight to the back. Mr. Shapiro looked up as we walked up to his counter. He smiled, at first, then seeing something in me, suddenly quailed.

"I haven't done anything," he whimpered.

"I didn't say you had," I said, sternly. "But I do need the truth from you. I am trying to find the man who killed my field hands. You are someone who has expressed great antipathy toward the Chinese. Therefore, you might know something and not realize it. I know you have been getting your silk from Ah Chen."

"I have not! I get it direct from the finest mills in China."

"Then why does Ah Chen have that very fabric over there? The one with the figured stripes?"

"No, he doesn't."

"Yes, he does. He has blue pants made from it and someone else has it, too, and got it from Mr. Ah."

"It's from China." Mr. Shapiro backed away.

"Imported by Mr. Ah Chen," I insisted. "Honestly, Mr. Shapiro, there is no crime in buying fabric from a local man."

"But if the ladies of the pueblo knew it, they would no longer buy from me," Mr. Shapiro gulped.

"Perhaps you are overcharging them," I said.

"It doesn't matter. I would be ruined."

"If you fear ruin so much, why did you participate

in the riot?"

He turned completely pale. "But I didn't! I was in the saloon when it started, and I did follow outside to see what was going on. But it was too frightening. So, I went back to the saloon."

"Why didn't you just go home?"

"I would have had to go around the mob. They were too terrible!"

"I am looking for a group of about eight men who accosted me and my friends that night. Did any return to the saloon?"

"Yes. Mr. Gluck did. And that clerk from the county court, Mr. Alverno." Mr. Shapiro seemed to recover some of his confidence. "And many others. That land agent, er..."

"Mr. McKinley. I know about him."

"No. Mr. Fletcher. He's the land agent."

"I'm familiar with him. He says he wasn't there."

Mr. Shapiro snorted. "Everyone is saying that."

"Including you."

"No!" Mr. Shapiro groaned. "I saw what was happening, yes, but I swear I hid in the saloon."

I was not entirely convinced of his honesty, but could find no guile, nor foot shuffling or other signs that he was lying. Nor could I find any discrepancies in his statement. I debated only briefly making my order for my yardage. After all, it did seem somewhat impolitic to not do so after asking so many difficult questions. In addition, I thought a good order might also assuage him and I did want my new dress.

He cut the order very efficiently, and if he tried any chicanery, I did not see it. He even charged quite a reasonable amount of money for the order. Thus, I had even less reason to be suspicious of his honesty than I had before. I had the fabric sent to Mrs. Washington, then returned to the street and headed back toward the center of the pueblo. Mr. Valdez walked alongside me, alert, but seemingly relaxed.

"Mr. Valdez," I said suddenly. "What do you

remember of the riot? You said you were nearby but did not do anything.”

I had been hesitating to ask him about what he’d seen as he’d already seemingly had quite the time of it with the grand jury.

“It was a terrible night,” he said, shuddering. “My friends were so taken up. It’s as if they were at a very loud ranch party, right before everybody starts fighting and shooting.”

“Something I am all too familiar with,” I grumbled. “And who were your friends?”

He sighed. “Mrs. Wilcox, I cannot tell you. The judge, he was very clear that I am not to say anything about what I told the jury. And I am happy not to. My friends, they can be dangerous people when they get riled.”

“I’m sure they are, and I cannot ask you to break a court order,” I said. “But if we do not catch this killer, we do not know who he will kill next. And I do not doubt that he will kill again.”

Mr. Valdez winced. “That is terrible.” He thought. “I cannot say who I saw, but I can say this. I did not see any of the men you are seeking. Nor did I hear any of them bragging about scaring a lady and her friends, let alone a doctor.”

“Then you couldn’t help me even without your silence being secured.”

“That is correct, Mrs. Wilcox.” Mr. Valdez smiled haplessly.

At that moment, Mr. Wiley, my wine agent, saw me and hurried over.

“Mrs. Wilcox, how good to see you,” he said. He was a small, rather gaunt man with sandy hair and beard, and blue eyes. “I only just returned this morning and have some money for you. Will you come with me to my office so that I can give it to you?”

“Yes, thank you, Mr. Wiley.” I said, falling into step with him. “I also wanted to ask you some questions about a possible mutual acquaintance.”

"Oh?"

Mr. Valdez waited outside the building while I went upstairs to Mr. Wiley's office. I sat in front of his desk and we took care of our business promptly.

"Now, that mutual acquaintance?" he asked, his eyes glittering almost as if he'd heard something already.

"Yes. I seem to have attracted the attentions of a Mr. Leighland."

"I'm not surprised you're asking," Mr. Wiley replied. "My wife mentioned that he had spent the larger part of the Glassells' party dancing with you."

"He did, indeed." I shifted. "However, as a woman of property, I cannot be too careful."

"No, indeed you cannot," Mr. Wiley said with a chuckle. He paused and thought. "I would not question his affections. I'm sure that any kind feelings he has toward you are probably genuine."

"But what about his motives?" I asked. "I am not known for my gentle temper and womanly ways. And I do have some impressive acreage and a thriving business."

"If you are asking if he wants your rancho, I'm sure he does. That does not mean, however, that he would not be a kind and tender husband." Mr. Wiley sighed. "If I can trust your confidence?"

"Of course."

"I must be particularly circumspect in that I would be loath to hurt Mr. Leighland, as I find him a very fine fellow. And he would be deeply embarrassed if anyone thought the least bit ill of him. But, alas, he is not doing well."

"Is it his health?"

"Oh, no. He is quite hale and hearty in that respect. It is his personal fortunes that are at a low ebb."

"I have heard that he is in the shipping business."

"Well, yes." Mr. Wiley fidgeted with a pen that was lying on his desk. "His story is, alas, a sad one, and also all too common these days. He's from Savannah,

Georgia, where his family had a successful shipping business. I do not know them personally but had occasion to arrange for their services and found the company fair, efficient, and honest. However, there was the war, and they lost just about everything. I think they were down to one ship when Mr. Leighland decided to seek his fortunes here in California. He brought a load overland with his son, while his wife and two daughters were to come on that last ship of theirs. That ship went down with all aboard somewhere just past Cape Horn. Mr. Leighland and his son arrived in Wilmington with their load, got paid for it, but then the son got in trouble and was killed."

"My goodness," I said. "No wonder he is not having an easy time of it."

"It has been difficult," Mr. Wiley said. "I invited him to come up here when I heard of his son's death. As I said, I did not know him or his family, but had done business with them."

"And you have every reason to believe he has not assumed the name to his own gain?"

Mr. Wiley chuckled. "I did make some inquiries, and he does seem to be the man he names himself as. He has been a perfect gentleman, as well, so as I said, he may have a decided interest in your fortune, but he would be kind and tender."

I smiled even though I was not sure what to make of it. So, I stood, and Mr. Wiley rose to his feet.

"Well, I thank you very much for your candor, Mr. Wiley," I said. "I shall, of course, make no mention of this conversation, least of all to Mr. Leighland."

We made the usual parting pleasantries and I soon found myself out on the street again with no idea of which avenue to pursue next. I was not, as some would have you believe, insensible to the pleasures of having a suitor. And if Mr. Leighland's means were as straightened as Mr. Wiley implied, then I could well understand seeking out a wife who had property. Indeed, it was a rather sensible undertaking, as long as one was willing to be kind about it. Ultimately, I thought it was rather flattering that Mr. Leighland seemed to be paying me attentions.

The problem was that suitors eventually want to become husbands, and I had (and still have) little use for one. Yes, I have occasionally been lonely in my widowed state, and I think that during this time I was wondering if my sham of a marriage was truly representative of what the marital state had to offer. Nor did I want to close myself off from a truly satisfying union out of sheer stubbornness.

Mr. Leighland was charming, and I did not doubt that he would be a kind and loving husband, in so far as that went. He did not, however, seem to have the full appreciation of my independence, and that would cause rancor on both our parts as time went on. It was not easy to simply say no. I did not, in fact, know him that well, and his attentions were mostly pleasant, not to mention the fact that he could dance.

However, I knew that at some point, I was going to have to let Mr. Leighland know that there was little hope for his suit. And I also knew, somehow, that he was not going to take it well.

CHAPTER ELEVEN

Once on the street, I quickly located Mr. Valdez, and since we were relatively close to the Clocktower Courthouse, I directed us thither to speak to Mr. Alverno. I had come across the court clerk before and had found him to be rather difficult. I was not alone in my experience.

I will concede that perhaps it would have been better to try to find a place to speak to Mr. Alverno apart from his place of employment. But in my defense, I had no other place in which to find him.

Mr. Alverno was small and balding with dark strands of hair scraped across his scalp. One of his front teeth was missing and his clothes were dingy. One assumed they were clean, but they were yellowed as if they had not been cleaned properly. Nonetheless, what made Mr. Alverno particularly stand out was his entire mien, which was that of the long-suffering, as if the people he had been hired to serve were there to utterly inconvenience him, rather than it being his duty to serve them.

He was at his desk, writing something, when I approached. I waited until I believed he had finished a sentence or other thought before greeting him.

"Just a minute," he said, continuing to write.

I waited several more, by the eight-day clock on the wall behind him.

"Mr. Alverno," I began.

"Just a minute," he said again.

"I apologize for interrupting, Mr. Alverno, but I would like to ask you a question or two."

He sighed deeply. "Yes?"

"I need some information pertaining to the riots."

He sucked his teeth and rolled his eyes.

"I know," he said. "Everyone does and they all expect me to know what the status of the grand jury is. Can you imagine?"

Actually, I could well imagine, insofar as he was one of the clerks attached to the grand jury.

"I was more interested in your personal participation," I said calmly.

"I am an officer of the court," he replied with great disdain. "Can you imagine the uproar if I had done something like that?"

"And yet I have witnesses who will swear that you were among those collecting and lynching the Chinamen."

He rolled his eyes again and shook his head. "Then your witnesses are lying. They do that quite frequently. You'd think they'd understand the meaning of swearing under oath, but that doesn't stop them."

"Where were you that night?"

"I believe I was in the saloon."

"Which one?"

"Mr. Mahoney's." He glared at me. "And what business is it of yours to ask me these questions?"

"My two field hands were ruthlessly murdered and a third has been beaten very badly. Which means there is a killer loose among our populace, and he is not just a ruffian caught up in a mob. I don't suppose you would like to meet up with this fellow."

"I seriously doubt he's going to come after me," Mr. Alverno said.

"And what makes you so certain of that?"

"I'm not Chinese." He rolled his eyes again, as if I should have known that he would not become the victim of this villain.

I could feel the ire rising inside me like the waves of a great storm tide, threatening to surge out and flatten everything in their path. Somehow, I managed to bite back the worst of the angry words.

"I am glad you can be so certain," I said through tight lips. "I, for one, would not be, were I in your shoes."

I left the courthouse thinking that I was not going to be able to do much for anyone if I were to become enraged every time someone said something unkind about the Chinese. It is at such times of deep provocation that I find myself reflecting on my late mother's wisdom, and as I stood on the street, I turned my mind to her loving presence.

My mother was a firm believer in not letting the sun go down on one's anger. I remember one instance when I was a young girl, in which I had been sorely tried by one of my classmates. The wretched girl had falsely accused me before the entire class of ruining her slate. Our teacher had rapped my knuckles and made me stand in front of the class for the rest of the afternoon.

Needless to say, I was furious. But my mother insisted that I find a way to put aside my anger. I had thought this dreadfully unfair, as this had hardly been the first time my accuser had found a way to humiliate and torture me.

"I did not say it would be easy," Mother said. "But, my darling Maddie, you must look at your anger, then put it aside, or else you will not be able to think clearly. And whenever there is an injustice, if you are to help, then you must be able to think clearly."

I somehow managed to take her advice on that occasion and once my ire had cooled, I realized that I could not have ruined the slate in question as I was not even in the room at the time and the teacher should have known so. Fortunately, before I pointed this out to him, I did consult my mother, who, in turn, convinced my Grandmother Franklin to let me have lessons at home. Grandmother Franklin, my father's mother, often despaired of me but was not going to let her granddaughter be humiliated by a mere schoolteacher.

Back on the street in Los Angeles, I took a few

deep breaths. My anger was fully justified, but letting it hold sway with me was not going to help me find the killer I sought. I signaled Mr. Valdez and together we headed toward the hospital, where I hoped to find Mr. Gluck.

It was past time I removed his stitches, anyway. I concede that I had been avoiding him since our last encounter, which had so filled me with rage. Yet, he alone, of all those I'd spoken with had not only admitted his role but had shown considerable contrition for his evil deeds. It was time to speak with him again.

He was sitting up in bed when I got there. I listened to his lungs, then checked over his several wounds, all of which were healing satisfactorily, and removed the stitches. He endured all with patience. I sat down on the chair next to him. Mr. Valdez stood nearby.

"Mr. Gluck," I said as kindly as I could. "I truly regret it, but since I have last spoken with you, another of my field hands has been murdered, and a third has been grievously attacked. We have reason to believe that the killer was among a group of fellows who challenged me and my companions the night of the riot. There were eight of them, led by Mr. McKinley, and they were trying to round up Chinamen to lynch."

Mr. Gluck nodded and frowned. "They found a few too, I think. At least, I heard some of them laughing about it in Uribe's saloon that night. There was a group. They were laughing about how they scared the lady doctor. That must have been you."

"Do you know the names of the men in that group?"

"I think I heard one of them call the other McKinley." Mr. Gluck's frown deepened. "And Sanford. He's that teamster. He was fighting with another fellow. That one coughed a lot. Then there were a pair of ranch hands. I think one's name was Walters."

"Leon Walters," I said softly.

Mr. Gluck shrugged. "I do not know. There was a carpenter, too. I see the ranch hands at the saloon fairly often, but I do not know their names since they do not talk to me."

"Well, if Mr. Walters was among those you saw, then he won't be talking to you again, as he has died."

"That is sad," Mr. Gluck said. He wiggled his toes under the blankets, then looked at Mr. Valdez curiously. "I saw you that night. But I did not see you do anything."

"I didn't," Mr. Valdez said. "I only watched. The men were crazy. It was very frightening."

"It was," Mr. Gluck said sadly. "And I did something terrible. Father says that I can be absolved, but I must also confess to the grand jury."

"They will want you to tell them what everyone did," Mr. Valdez said. "They made me talk to them. I was terrified."

"If you like, Mr. Gluck, I can find an attorney for you," I said.

He shook his head and shrugged. "I did something terrible. I should pay for it. It is my penance. Then my soul will be healed. That's what Father said."

"Then let us trust that to God," I said, getting up. "Come along, Mr. Valdez, we have more people to visit."

I did feel better for having spoken with Mr. Gluck, but that also meant that I sorely needed Angelina to help me make another list. When we arrived at the funeral parlor, I left Mr. Valdez on the porch, and went inside. Angelina, it turned out, had a little surprise for me. Regina was in her little sitting room having tea.

"I am so glad to see you, Regina," I said. "I hope all is well?"

"Quite well for the boots in this town," Regina said with a chuckle. "Not one of my girls has found one that isn't intact."

"What about Mr. Dillman?" I asked.

"Annie swears his boots are whole." Regina shifted. "I have an odd feeling there is something else on her mind than his boots. You wouldn't think it, but the silly things do sometimes fall in love, and I'm afraid she has."

"I'm glad you came by," Angelina said to me. "Regina and I have been talking to shoemakers in the pueblo this morning, to see if we could find the fellow who repaired our villain's boot."

"And you have found him?"

Angelina and Regina each looked at each other and sighed.

"Alas, no," said Regina. "But we each, in turn, spoke with one fellow in particular, Mr. Johnson. The gambling gentlemen in my house seem to think that he will be the one the jury points to as the ringleader behind the riot. He is also a shoemaker."

"The difficulty is that he won't say if he's repaired the boot we want," Angelina said. "I spoke to him first, and at first, he denied repairing any boots at all, which is ridiculous. He's a shoemaker. He must be repairing boots every day. When I pointed that out, he claimed he couldn't remember."

"When I went there a little later, I tried to be more convincing," Regina said. "He still wouldn't remember. However, before I spoke with him, I saw him finish a repair, and then he wrote something down in his ledger. In short, he keeps decent records. Which might prove useful if we need a judge to see things our way."

"I'm less worried about the judge than finding this villain," I said. "I wonder how we can get that ledger."

"Maddie," Regina purred. "You can't seriously be considering doing something illegal, are you?"

"No," I sighed. "I suppose the end does not justify the means."

"It does not," said Angelina staunchly.

"Besides illegal is my stock in trade," said Regina. "Nonetheless, perhaps we should wait until it becomes absolutely necessary to go fetch that ledger. After all, we do not know who we are looking for yet."

"We know it must be one of the men who were with Mr. McKinley's group that night," I said.

"Ah, yes," said Regina. "The little trinket."

"It's not certain that the man that Maddie saw that

night is the same one who is our villain," Angelina said. "After all, the villain could have stolen the ornament, then left it in Wei Chin's queue by accident."

"But it seems more than likely that the villain and the man in the group are the same," I said. "At the very least, we'll have some way to narrow down the possibilities. If we do not find our villain among that group of rogues, then we'll have to assume that the ornament was stolen. Until then, who do we know were part of that group?"

"Mr. McKinley," Angelina said.

"Mr. Gluck said that Mr. Sanford was part of it," I added. "And Mr. Shapiro said that he saw Mr. Fletcher, and then Mr. Gluck added that there was one man who was part of the group who coughed a lot. Mr. Fletcher does have quite a bad cough. As his wife does, too, it will make it easier for me to visit them. However, Mr. Fletcher was quite adamant that he had nothing to with the riot."

Regina laughed out loud at that. "That poor little man. He tries to act as though he's a pillar of society, and yet he is no better than the worst of us. Do you know why he is mostly working as a land agent these days? A certain judge, whose name I cannot disclose, came very close to censuring him for less than honest dealings."

"That doesn't mean he was part of the group that challenged me," I said. I frowned. "I would think I would have recognized him. But the only man I saw clearly was Mr. McKinley."

"Oh, Maddie," said Angelina. "It was such a horrible event. I'm surprised you remembered Mr. McKinley."

"That is neither here nor there," I said, trying to banish the horrible images that flashed across my mind. "Then there is the teamster, Mr. Sanford. His name seems to come up fairly often in connection with the riots."

Angelina and Regina looked at each other and

shrugged.

"A teamster?" Regina asked. "He seems unlikely to have crossed my doorstep."

"I don't know him," Angelina said.

"Apparently, he frequents Mr. Uribe's saloon, where he gets obstreperous," I said. "I have told Mr. Sedonez that I would like to talk to Mr. Sanford, but that has yet to come to pass." I paused. "I just thought. One of the men was quite probably a ranch hand named Leon Walters."

Angelina's eyebrows rose. "If it's the same Mr. Walters as I'm thinking, there's a problem in that he's dead."

"I'm guessing the same thing," I said. "More importantly, Mr. Walters died before Wei Chin was killed. But his friend Mr. Smith could have easily been involved, especially since Mr. Smith was quite outspoken regarding his dislike of the Chinese. He even went so far as to blame Dr. Wong for his friend's death."

Angelina scrambled for her little desk that had the wheels on it. She got settled and got out her inkwell, pen, and a bit of paper.

"Very well," she said, dipping her pen, then writing. "We know that Mr. McKinley did not have the anchor ornament, and thus, is less likely to be our villain. However, among his companions on the night of the riot, we have reason to believe that Mr. Sanford, possibly Mr. Fletcher and Mr. Walters are included. And maybe Mr. Smith. Does that sound right?"

"So far, yes," I said. "But there were eight men. We have, at best, five. How are we to make sure of these and find the others, then find out which one had the ornament?"

"And find out which one had recently repaired his boots," Regina said.

The obstacles we faced could not have seemed more insurmountable. Bless them, Angelina and Regina tried so hard to console me and otherwise restore my confidence. In the end, we decided that the best thing I could do was go home and get some rest. I had not been sleeping well, and the night before, watching Wang Fu, had been quite long indeed. If nothing else, the lack of sleep was wreaking havoc with my ability to keep my temper, and as I have noted earlier in these pages, I could not afford to let my anger overwhelm me.

But rest was not to be mine, at least not right away. When I arrived back at the rancho, Mr. Montero was in the yard, waiting for me.

"Is someone ill?" I asked, reaching for my bag.

"No. We are all well," he said. "I just wanted to talk to you."

"Please, sit down," I said, gesturing at the bench next to the door to my adobe.

He sat down and I joined him.

"I am worried that you think I killed your Chinamen," he said, once we were settled.

"If you were among a certain group of men during the night of the riot, I might be," I said. "However, your wife has told me that you eat dinner at home in the evenings and stay there."

Mr. Montero smiled softly. "Yes, I do."

"Then I am curious as to why you felt the need to come here and tell me something that I had no reason to doubt?"

He shook his head. "My wife, she says I worry too much about what others think of me. Perhaps I do. But so many people have wanted to know about where I was that night. I tell them I was at home, but they do not believe me. We did not even know what had happened until the next morning when we found our yard men hiding behind the vats. One was missing, but we did not find out until that afternoon that he was among those who had been lynched."

"How terrible," I said.

"It was." He shrugged. "But then the day after you visited, that teamster, Sanford, he came to pick up a load of leather for the buggy maker. He asked me about where I was the night of the riot. When I said I was at home, he laughed and said he didn't believe me, and that he was going to tell the grand jury that I was right there with him. That was bad enough. Then he started telling me I'd better have my boots fixed, since you were asking after boots with holes in them."

"Oh, no."

"I might not have worried, but then Mrs. Montero mentioned that you had asked after my boots."

"Mr. Montero, I did not want to unduly cause you alarm," I said. I suddenly felt horribly guilty. It took a great deal of effort not to burst into tears. "I did accept your wife's word without question."

"I know. But the way he joked about the grand jury…" Mr. Montero winced.

"How preposterous!" I let out what I hoped was a lady-like snort, then blinked my eyes several times, and took a deep breath. "I assure you, Mr. Montero, Mr. Sanford is even more eager than you to avoid talking to the grand jury, and furthermore, from what I have learned, he has good reason not to want to do so. What nonsense!"

"But you are looking for boots with holes in them. I know because every shoemaker in the pueblo is calling for more leather."

"I knew I shouldn't have told Mrs. Glassell about that," I grumbled.

Mr. Montero's face grew worried again, so I hastened to explain.

"We did find a rather singular boot print and we are hoping that it will identify the villain."

"But if he has gotten his boot fixed, then how will you know which is the right boot?"

"That has made it harder," I conceded. "And we do know that he did indeed get the boot fixed. But we have other things to look for, as well. We may even know which shoemaker fixed the villain's boot. The problem will be in getting him to tell us whose boots he fixed and what they looked like before he fixed them."

Mr. Montero suddenly smiled. "I can help with that."

"How?"

"Shoemakers love to gossip, like everyone else. I talk to them all the time. They won't think anything of it if I ask about the boots. And I can usually tell who mended a boot or slipper."

"Really?"

"Of course. Each shoemaker does things a little bit differently and I know them all. I have to, since Mr. Mendoza likes his leather one way and Mr. Simon likes his another way."

"What about Mr. Johnson?"

"He likes his sole leather extra smooth. And he cuts the old piece off at an angle. He says it doesn't break again as easily."

I thought of the drawing that Angelina had made. I did trust Mr. Montero but given what he'd told me about the sudden increase in boot repairs in the pueblo, I was, perhaps, a bit more cautious than need be.

Mr. Montero was looking at me again. "Do you think Mr. Johnson fixed your villain's boot?"

I shrugged. "It's possible. We think he lied to us when he said he didn't remember whose boots he fixed."

"Actually, he may not have remembered, with everyone rushing to have their boots fixed so that they are not accused."

"Which does not help me in the least."

"But I have an idea." Mr. Montero got up.

"Please, Mr. Montero, do not do anything that would get you hurt," I said. "The villain is very vicious. I would hate to see you get hurt because you were trying to help me."

"I know what I can do. Don't worry."

I rose with him and bade him good-bye just in time for Olivia to come looking for me.

"It's time you ate your lunch," she said, sounding quite peevish, although her glare was actually directed at Mr. Montero's retreating form.

The lunch was quite nice with mole and chicken, and a glass of angelica. Feeling particularly sated, I retired to my chamber and had a good, solid nap, only to be aroused not even an hour later by someone needing help.

CHAPTER TWELVE

The Miller family, whose children had whooping cough, were quite worried, and rightfully so. The baby, who was almost two, was having a terrible time and one of the other children appeared to have cracked a rib. There was little I could do, sadly. I bandaged the one child's chest and tried a couple different plasters for the baby. I made a strong tea of eucalyptus leaves and had the children breathe the steam, which helped a little. The baby, however, was so restless, it was hard to get him to stay over the steaming bowl long enough to get the steam into his lungs. The tincture of belladonna that I had been giving all of them was almost gone. I sent Mr. Valdez to the apothecary to get some more.

The problem with whooping cough is that once it gets started, it is relentless, as any of us who have had it well know. Most children do survive it quite well. So, I was mostly worried about the baby. Mr. Valdez came back with the belladonna and I gave the little boy as strong a dose as I dared. The shrill whooping as he gasped for air between the harsh, hacking coughs continued into the night. The older boy, whose rib had cracked, cried in between coughing spells because he hurt so badly, and I gave him a small dose of laudanum. There was little else I could do. The cough would eventually pass, although the older children would be coughing for the next month or so.

Sadly, as the evening slid into deep night, the baby gasped, choked, and stilled. His mother wailed over the tiny body and I blinked back my own tears. I knew I had done everything that could have been done, but that did not ease my heartache in the least. I checked the older children one last time, then made my way home with Mr. Valdez close by.

I was surprised to see Mr. Leighland coming down the street as I headed back to my rancho.

"I'm so glad to have caught up with you," he said, his stride joining mine. "It's terribly late for a lady like you to be out."

Indeed, it was well past the time that merchants were required to keep the gas lamps lit. Nonetheless, it was a clear night, with the moon waning, but not yet halfway gone, and the stars adding to the light.

"I appreciate your concern, Mr. Leighland," I said, not slowing my pace. "But it is to be expected in my vocation and I have Mr. Valdez here to defend me."

"He seems quite capable," Mr. Leighland said, tipping his hat to Mr. Valdez, who likewise tipped his. "You are quite a saintly woman to brave these streets to come to the aid of the stricken."

"I'm glad you think so highly of me, Mr. Leighland, but it is merely my job."

"You must long for the day when you no longer must rush out in the dead of night."

"I don't know that I do," I said.

That brought him up short. "Pardon me, but I do not understand."

"I mean that I am not a doctor to support myself in my bereavement," I said, guessing that had been the meaning behind his observation on my longings. "Which is a very good thing, as it is almost impossible to support one's self as a doctor. Fortunately, I have my rancho and winery."

If my tone was more curt than I would have liked, one could hardly fault me, given my state of exhaustion and what had just happened at the Miller household.

"Oh," said Mr. Leighland.

I stopped walking and sighed. "Mr. Leighland, is it possible that you were hoping to take me away from this terrible burden of healing people to make my way?"

"Well, I... Er..."

"Oh, dear." I looked out over the silver and deep blue landscape. Somewhere in the distance, a coyote howled. "Mr. Leighland, I do not know what your intentions are, and I had hoped I would not have to make this speech quite so soon. I do not wish to be harsh. However, I have just watched a baby die of whooping cough and held his mother in her grief. I am very tired. If your intentions are only that of a pleasant friendship, then I most humbly beg your pardon. Let us, indeed, be friends. I would treasure it. But if you are hoping to ply a more serious suit, then I cannot in all fairness encourage you. I am more than content as a widow and am not at all interested in marrying again. If it makes you feel better, I am still grieving my long-departed husband." I looked behind me at my other companion. "Mr. Valdez, let us move on. Our evening couches await."

I will give Mr. Leighland credit. He did not carry on. But he did not take my speech at all well, and stalked off back toward the pueblo, his back rigid and I could see that he was in a considerably bad temper.

My temper was not much better. Visions of Mr. Leighland stalking back toward the pueblo haunted my dreams that night to the point that I slept far longer than I wanted to the next morning. Usually, I am awake at the first crack of dawn, and even earlier in the autumn and winter. If I am not, Juanita comes to wake me. However, the clock in my chamber was chiming nine when I finally opened my eyes. I could see bright sunlight leaking through the curtains on my window.

I sighed. Juanita had obviously decided that I needed to sleep. Worse yet, I knew she was right.

Once she saw that I was awake, she helped me put on my indigo walking dress. A breakfast of sweet bread and coffee was waiting for me, then Sebastiano assured me that everything at the winery was in good order.

Fortunately, I did not have to tell him my intentions for the day. He had already surmised them and completely supported my plans.

"I wish I could join you," he told me as I finished eating. "I want to know who is attacking our field hands almost as badly as you do. After all, will this fellow stop with the Chinamen?"

We both looked out over the yard, where several of the children were playing as a break from their studies. It was too frightening to contemplate what the villain had in mind.

"I agree," I said. "Which is why I want to make all possible haste."

Sebastiano winced. "Mr. Valdez cannot ride."

"Then we shall walk. Is he ready?"

"I think so."

Mr. Valdez was waiting as I left the adobe. I looked wistfully toward the stable and my mare. But Mr. Valdez was not accustomed to riding, and the mules could be difficult with new riders. I had good reason to believe that I could keep most of my stops within the nucleus of the town center.

However, I did first have to venture somewhat beyond the center of town to get to the Fletcher home. Both Mr. and Mrs. Fletcher were in. Mrs. Fletcher's cough had improved considerably. It was neither as frequent nor as harsh. But it was still there, and as it turned out, she never would shed it.

After checking on her, I went again to the front parlor to speak to Mr. Fletcher.

"I am sorry to have to press you," I began.

He sniffed and coughed. "I assure you, the bottoms of my boots are completely whole and have been for over a month."

"I am not here to make accusations," I said. "But you do have information and I need it. By all accounts, you were among the men who accosted me and my friends the night of the riot. I need to know who the others were."

"I was not there!" He advanced on me, angrily.

"I have witnesses who say you were." I folded my arms across my chest and stood my ground.

"Then they lied to you."

"No, you are lying to me. And the worst of it is, I knew it when I first spoke to you about this issue. Since then, others have made mention of you. Now, I know that in addition to you, Mr. McKinley was part of that group, as was Mr. Sanford. But that leaves five others whose names I either need to certify or need to learn outright. Who was with you?"

"I was not there. I did not participate." He glared fiercely at me. "You can say what you want, Mrs. Wilcox. I will say nothing else."

"Even to the grand jury? They like being lied to even less than I do. If they can confirm that you were there and you insist you weren't, then you will have committed perjury and for that, alone, you could be put in jail."

"I have nothing to fear from the grand jury," he said. "I tell you, I was not there. You cannot prove otherwise."

"Maybe not at this time. However, if there is another killing on my rancho before I can find this villain, then it will be on your head."

I turned and left. Outside, I had to blink back my tears and then take several deep breaths to control the shaking in my hands.

"He made you angry," Mr. Valdez observed from where he waited near the street.

"I am afraid so, Mr. Valdez." I closed my eyes and took one last breath. "I apologize for making you witness that."

He chuckled. "If I were that angry, there would be a fight with fists and maybe even knives."

I glanced back at the house as we started down the street. "Mr. Valdez, I am a lady and I do my best to behave as one at all times. As a woman of property and as a doctor, I have no other option, as there are those who like to think that any outbursts on my part prove that my so-called delicate sensibilities make me unfit for what I do. Finally, I like to think that I am in better control of my passions."

Mr. Valdez shrugged. "Perhaps."

I heard a cough behind me, and I turned. Mrs. Fletcher was slowly coming down the front walk of the house toward me.

"Mrs. Wilcox," she called out as best she could, then put a handkerchief to her face and coughed.

"Mrs. Fletcher, you are not fully healed yet," I admonished her.

She was normally quite a fierce creature, easily capable of inspiring fear in anyone upon whom she looked with disdain. I had been the target of her ire more than once. So, I was surprised to see her step back from me, before once again gathering her strength.

"But I must talk to you," she said, and swallowed. "I tried to tell Mr. Fletcher that you are an honorable woman and that he would not be the worse for telling you the truth, as you were sure to find it out anyway."

"I do my best."

She coughed again and shook her head. "He would not listen." She took a deep breath. "To be honest, I do not know where he was that terrible night. It is entirely possible that he wasn't there. He has not been himself of late." She looked down at the sidewalk, then wiped her eyes. "We lost our son and his family last summer, you know."

"Yes. A cholera break-out."

She nodded. "It was at a stage stop on the way to Sacramento. No one knew until it was too late. My son was to take up a prestigious clerkship in the Legislature. But the entire family was wiped out."

"I am so sorry."

And indeed, I was. Cholera was yet another relentless killer that I was powerless to stop. Nowadays, we prevent it with clean water systems, and even then, it still takes more lives than it should.

Mrs. Fletcher recovered herself. "The problem is that Mr. Fletcher has not been himself. Since last summer, he is spending ever more time in saloons. Then the week before the riot, we had a reversal of fortune. I do not know the whole of it. Merely that my husband had lost some money involving some speculation in a property on the Calle de los Negros. He blamed the Chinamen for some reason. Do not ask me what. I do not know. I've only been able to piece together bits that he has been ranting about. I do not know if he was abroad the night of the riot. I do know he went to lunch at one of the saloons and did not come back to work. Then, in the dead of night, some lads brought him home, completely insensible. Since then, he has sworn that he did not participate in the lynchings." She blinked and dabbed her eyes with her handkerchief. "But others have hinted that he was seen doing just that. Our reputation is suffering quite badly as a result. And yet, there is more to make it worse. He may be swearing that he did not participate because he cannot remember that he did." The tears that she so tried to keep back finally spilt upon her cheek. "It happens sometimes when he is the worse for drink. We have had entire conversations that he did not remember the next day."

"I am familiar with the malady," I said. "But there is nothing I can do for it. The only cure I know is to forswear drink."

"Then we are lost!" She broke down in weeping and coughing.

I reached over and patted her arm. "Perhaps not. Yes, it is a terrible thing when men become enslaved to drink. But some men do overcome it. Others manage their businesses quite well in spite of it. Or their wives do. You will manage."

"But what about the riot?"

"I cannot help you in that respect." I smiled softly. "I will, however, be very sure before I make any accusations and will not involve your husband unless

I must."

Mrs. Fletcher wiped her eyes and nodded. "You are kind to say so. Ah, Mrs. Wilcox, the trials we must endure as women."

"Yes, Mrs. Fletcher," I said. "Now, I am afraid I must go about my business. Get some rest and try not to talk for a few more days. That should ease your throat."

"Yes, Mrs. Wilcox. Thank you."

I waited as she made her way up the walk and back inside her house. I did not want to fulminate on the injustices faced by women, especially when their husbands choose to leave the straight and narrow path. Those who know me understand that it is a favorite theme of mine. However, I was determined to keep my head free of the cloud of anger that surrounded me. It was a decidedly good thing that I had chosen to walk that day, and Mr. Valdez scrambled after me as I headed back to the center of the pueblo.

We made our way to the Uribe saloon, where I hoped to find Mr. Sanford and perhaps some of his companions. As it happened, we were in luck. Mr. Sanford was there eating lunch. Mr. Sedonez was happy to bring him in to the back room.

"Oh, it's you," Mr. Sanford grumbled when he saw me.

He was a tall man, with broad shoulders, red hair and scruffy beard, and bright blue eyes.

"Mr. Sanford, I am not here to accuse you," I said.

"I don't care what you're here to do. I got nothing to say to you," he said and started to turn back to the main room of the saloon.

"Sanford," Mr. Sedonez said. "Give the lady a chance. She is trying to find a killer."

Mr. Sanford turned and glared at me again. "He didn't kill anybody important."

"My field hands were important to me," I said, trying to keep my temper. "Furthermore, it has been my experience that when a villain like this kills, he does so again and again until he is stopped. It does not matter how important or unimportant the victims were. If this killer is allowed to roam free, you may eventually become one of his victims as well."

He snorted.

I sighed. "Mr. Sanford, I have learned that you were among the group of men who accosted me and my friends the night of the riot." I held up my hands as a sign of peace. "I do not accuse in that respect. I am merely looking for your companions. One of them is the worst of villains who has killed two of my field hands. Now, I understand..."

"You don't understand," Mr. Sanford said, adding a particularly vile epithet. "That dagnabbed grand jury is looking for all of us."

"I have no intention of turning you over to the grand jury." I may have been less than honest in that point, but I felt that it was more important to get the information I needed.

Mr. Sanford's language grew even more vile.

"Sanford!" Mr. Sedonez snapped. "Mrs. Wilcox is a lady. Comport yourself as such."

"She's trying to get me hung!" Mr. Sanford said, failing utterly in moderating his language.

"No, I am not!" I said. I must concede my voice had risen to more than what was ladylike. In my defense, I was sorely tried at that moment.

"Then leave it alone!" Mr. Sanford cried. "It was just a couple of Chinamen."

"They are human beings," I shouted back. "They have feelings. They have mothers that love them. They are no better nor no worse than you and I. And in the case of my field hands, these were decent, hard-working men who only wanted to make enough money to help their families live in comfort. Do you care that much about your family? Are you trying to set them up in comfort?"

"You don't know nothing about my family!" Mr. Sanford raged. "Who do you think you are? You would stand up for Chinamen ahead of your own kind? You are unnatural!"

"And you are a heartless beast!"

In truth, that may not have been the best retort I could have offered. It certainly aroused Mr. Sanford to the point that he lunged at me. Both Mr. Sedonez and Mr. Valdez leapt forward to pull the huge man back from me.

Mr. Sanford continued to harangue me with all manner of obscene epithets. I decided that it would not serve any of us well to ask him any more questions, and waved at Mr. Sedonez that I was taking my leave. Mr. Sedonez, still grappling with Mr. Sanford, nodded vigorously.

I hurried out of the saloon and made my way to the Calle Primavera. I wanted to get to either Aliso Street or the Plaza, from which I could get down to Alameda and the road that headed to my rancho. I trusted that Mr. Valdez would not be far behind.

What many of us nowadays forget is that the Calle Primavera (which we now call by its English name, Spring Street) is actually on a decent slope. I was heading uphill and was just a touch winded when I walked past the alley just under Mr. McKinley's office.

It would have been impossible to have foreseen what happened next, let alone have forestalled it. Nonetheless, there is that part of me that keeps wondering how it might have been different if I had only been more alert. If I had only waited but a minute to leave the saloon. If only I had been stronger.

As I walked past the opening of the alley, I was grabbed and pulled even deeper into the shadows between the buildings. My attacker did not say anything but made free with his hands about my person. I was, initially, too startled to cry out, but that did not last long. Remembering Angelina's wise words about most men being surprised by women who fight back, I started by screaming as loudly as I could.

His arms had bound mine and I could do little

more than struggle. But then he put his gloved hand over my mouth. A finger slipped in and I bit down as hard as I could.

He howled. I tried to kick back at his legs, but my skirts got in the way. He boxed my ear, once, twice, and I saw stars float before my eyes. And then I felt someone knock both myself and my attacker to ground. I scrambled away as fast as I could and screamed again. Then I heard the crack of two gunshots very nearby. A man wearing a kerchief over his face rolled out from underneath another. The kerchiefed man then shot the body on the ground again and ran off.

I blinked to clear my eyes. I heard footsteps and Mr. Lomax came running up.

"Mrs. Wilcox, are you all right?" he asked.

I pointed at the body. "He saved me."

"What?"

"Mr. Valdez. He's dead, but he saved me."

CHAPTER THIRTEEN

I was still in a considerable daze when Angelina came running up and enfolded me in her arms.

"Oh, Maddie, you poor thing? What happened?"

"He saved me," I stammered.

"Who? Mr. Lomax?"

"No. Mr. Valdez." I sniffed and the tears began falling. "I was attacked."

"Mr. Valdez attacked you?"

"No!" I screamed. I choked and tried to get control of myself. "I was grabbed from behind. I could not see the villain. Then Mr. Valdez must have knocked us over. I got away but heard gun shots. The man crawled out from under Mr. Valdez, stood, and shot him again. Then he ran."

"Did you see who it was?"

I pushed away from Angelina. "Boot prints! We must look for the boot prints."

Angelina pulled me back and pinned me in her arms. She really was quite strong.

"You are not doing anything," she snapped. "Mr. Lomax is looking for the prints."

I could see Mr. Lomax look at her and nod. Then he began scanning the ground heading deeper into the alley.

"It's all right," Angelina crooned, still holding me. "You're safe now."

"But the man."

"Did you see who he was?"

"No." I frowned, then realized why I hadn't. "He was wearing a kerchief over his face. I couldn't even see his hair."

Mr. Lomax approached. "It sure looks like that boot you told me about, Mrs. Sutton. You can even see the mend."

"Why would he attack me?" I heard myself ask.

I was truly in a dazed and stunned state. I knew very well that it was possible that the killer would start attacking others than the Chinese. I had been telling people that all morning. In addition, it was then obvious that I was the killer's target.

"We'll explore that question later," Angelina said. "Please, Maddie. You've just been accosted in the worst way. You cannot possibly be as clear and rational as you normally are."

"But why attack me? We must answer that question."

"We will after you get some rest and recover." Angelina looked at me, obviously very worried. I say obviously because the next thing she did was to put to use one of the few levers that would have moved me. "Do you want me to tell Olivia, Magdalena, and Juanita that you are not taking care of yourself again?"

I groaned and bent to Angelina's will.

I may not have found the good and loving husband that my mother wished for me, but I somehow managed to find the warmth of a happy family in my friends and especially my household. Moments after this, Sebastiano, Enrique, and Pascual pulled up in my buggy and gently helped me into the seat, where Juanita waited with a blanket and soft words. Pascual drove us home, where Olivia had soup waiting and Magdalena had a warming pan in my bed.

I was immediately sent right to that same bed. Apart from the shock, my actual injuries were not severe, mostly bruising to my limbs and torso. However, such was the tender concern of my household that as soon as Juanita had gotten me into my nightclothes and under the covers, everyone, including the children, gathered around me, and watched me eat soup from a tray.

"I'm not dying," I protested. "I was not even seriously injured."

Rodolfo muttered something to Hernan, who nodded and waved at his cousins, Pascual and Emilio. They all left the room. Then Anita let each of the children offer me a kiss, shooing them out once they had done so.

Sebastiano's daughter Elena elected to help nurse me. She was about sixteen at the time and already quite talented in the healing arts. She was also quite a beauty, with dark hair and fair skin. I had high hopes of getting her into a medical college, but worried that some young swain would marry her first. Fortunately, she wanted to go to medical college even more than I wanted it for her. She took the soup bowl from Olivia and presumably brought it back to the kitchen.

Some minutes later, Elena returned carrying a cup and saucer, with Wang Fu behind her, walking carefully.

"Drink this," he ordered me, pointing at the cup.

"You should still be in bed," I retorted, taking the cup, nonetheless.

"I feel better. You should drink," he said.

Elena giggled.

I sniffed. "Is this another one of your miserable nostrums?"

Wang Fu chuckled, and I could tell that he was glad to hear me tease him. The spring before, I had caught the grippe. He had put together one of his herb brews, which had turned out to be quite effective. However, it tasted absolutely vile.

"It is willow bark tea," Wang Fu said. "And one or two other herbs. Good for shock."

He took my pulse with his good hand. I waited until he had released my wrist.

"Wang Fu, you are supposed to be resting," I protested.

"So are you," he said.

"I'm not that seriously injured," I said, sipping my brew. Fortunately, it did not taste nearly as bitter as the stuff from the spring before.

I am afraid it is indeed true that physicians make the worst patients. Elena laughed softly, then shooed Magdalena and Maria out of the room.

"Both of you need to rest," she said, pulling the curtains closed over my window. "And you had both best do so right now, or I will let Mama scold you."

Olivia grumbled something under her breath, and I strongly suspected she would have dearly loved the opportunity. Elena pushed both her mother and Wang Fu out of the room, and I finally closed my eyes.

What I did not know at that moment was that the men of my rancho had joined Mr. Lomax and two of his fellows to search for the villain. Several men of the pueblo joined them also.

"Including that nice Mr. Leighland," Juanita told me later the next afternoon as she tucked me in for another nap.

"Oh, dear," I sighed. "He can't be holding out hope, can he?"

"Maddie!" Juanita sat back on the edge of the bed. "Did you send another gentleman away?"

"He was about to ply his suit," I said. "I cannot possibly encourage that sort of thing, and you know very well that I can't."

Juanita made a face. "You could. You just don't want to, and I cannot blame you for that. They told me he did show the most tender concern for your condition."

"Bah! My condition is hardly worth worrying about." Tears sprang to my eyes. "What of Mr. Valdez?"

Juanita bowed her head. "We had a mass for him this morning, then buried him. I told them you would have liked to have been there. But it was better to get it over and done with."

I sniffed. "He was very brave."

Juanita nodded and sniffed, too. "He admired you

greatly, Maddie. You were willing to give him a chance. Not many people were. It meant a lot to him."

"He certainly proved himself worthy," I said. "I know there was nothing I could have done, but I do feel as though it was my fault that he was killed."

"I know." Juanita tried to glare at me. "One can't help it sometimes. Whenever you leave here, I worry that something bad will happen and it will be my fault because I did not take good enough care of you."

I put my hand on hers. "Juanita, this was not your fault."

"It wasn't yours, either. But we still feel that way. It's because we care about each other." She shrugged. "It's part of life."

"Yes, I suppose it is." I smiled at her.

She was so very, very dear to me. I thought once again of my mother's desire to see me happily wedded and in a loving family. I was often glad that my mother had died before my father made his cruel decision to marry me off to Albert Wilcox. Although, as I've come to think about it, it could have been my mother's death that drove my father to his cruelty. I shook my head gently to clear it.

"Now, you rest," Juanita said, getting up. "If you are good, maybe you can have some visitors tomorrow."

I remembered something. "Juanita, did they find him?"

"Who?"

"The villain who attacked me, and most likely also attacked Wang Fu and killed the Wei brothers."

"Oh, him." She opened the door. "No, they did not. It's as though he vanished."

She slipped outside the room. I wondered at her words, but still being bedridden, thanks to my several bruises, there was little I could do but wonder.

I did try to sleep, but my slumber was disturbed yet again by the nightmare of the tombstones. This time, Wei Chin had joined my accusers, as had Mr. Valdez.

I did get guests the next day. First, the reverend's wife, Mrs. Elmwood came for several very uncomfortable minutes. I knew how much she hated visiting, so I was actually rather touched. Then Mrs. Carson and Mrs. Glassell came by. They were two of a kind, both stout and of an age. They were all atwitter and enraged.

"It's utterly terrible," Mrs. Carson said. "It's getting so that a lady can't walk the streets in broad daylight without being afraid."

I avoided looking at Mrs. Glassell, who was not afraid of walking the streets of the pueblo even at night, largely thanks to the exceptionally large gun that she carried.

"It is dreadful," Mrs. Glassell said demurely. "Something must be done and done promptly, I say."

"Although, I must confess, Mr. Carson was wondering what you'd done now that had gotten someone angry enough to attack you."

"It's still a disgrace," Mrs. Glassell said. "We shall have to make another petition to the Council. We need more police and that's all there is to it."

I let their words wash over me. That was the good thing about encounters with Mrs. Carson and Mrs. Glassell together. One seldom needed to add to the conversation. Indeed, one would have been hard pressed to do so.

While I knew that Mr. Carson's complaint had more to do with wondering how I'd gotten myself into trouble again, I did begin to question again why I and my field hands had been attacked. Was it more than mere chance?

"Pray forgive me for interrupting, Mrs. Carson," I said suddenly. "What you said about Mr. Carson's wondering what I'd done to make someone angry. Do you know of anyone who is angry at me? I mean apart from trying to expose him?"

"Oh, it's simply more of Mr. Carson's nonsense," Mrs. Glassell said, sending a mild glare toward her friend.

"Exactly," said Mrs. Carson. "It's his idea of a joke. I'm sure you don't have a thing to worry about."

"Except for ruffians on the streets with no decent morals or kind sensibilities," said Mrs. Glassell. "Not to mention there being not nearly as many policemen as we need. Perhaps we should form a committee. What do you think, Mrs. Wilcox?"

"A committee is exactly what we need," said Mrs. Carson. "Perhaps we can get Mrs. Judson to chair it. Her husband was on the council last year."

They nattered on for some time, then finally excused themselves and left. Fortunately, I did not have much time to brood over the thought that someone wanted to kill me and my household specifically. There was dinner to eat, then I received two other guests, Regina and Angelina.

Olivia left us in my study with sweet breads, a decanter of angelica, and firm instructions not let me drink too much of it.

"We never let you drink too much," Regina said, quickly pouring the wine into small glasses for each of us.

"Then why do I feel as though my ears have been boxed every time you pour?" Angelina teased.

We settled and Angelina opened her wooden travel desk.

"We don't think you have that much to worry about," Angelina said, finally.

"Will you forgive me if I beg to differ?" I said, rather more acerbically than I'd intended.

"No!" Angelina groaned. "What we mean is that it will be harder for the villain to attack you again."

"I don't understand," I said.

"The whole pueblo is up in arms," Regina said. "They are looking for this villain everywhere."

"The mayor even went so far as to swear that he was going to strictly enforce the masquerade ordinance," Angelina said.

The ordinance specifically forbade anyone from

wearing a mask or otherwise pretending to be other than he was. Angelina and I looked sadly at Regina, who was forced to be other than her true self to protect her secret.

"I seriously doubt they will want to enforce the ordinance against me," she said with a small shrug.

It was true that her business was extremely popular among the wealthiest of the pueblo. There were even a few righteous fellows who often bemoaned that one could scarcely get any business done without patronizing Regina Medina's house.

"In short," Angelina continued. "Thanks to all the hue and cry, the villain will not be able to easily attack without risking being seen."

"And thus, caught," I said. "That makes sense. But there is one other aspect to this latest attack that makes me think that perhaps we are looking at this from the wrong perspective."

"In what way?" asked Regina.

"Well, initially, based on how Wei Li and Wei Chin were left, we thought that the villain had killed them just out of a hatred for the Chinese. That was reinforced by the way he beat Wang Fu." I frowned. "But what if it wasn't simply a general hatred, but a specific one? What if the villain wanted to attack me?"

"But then why attack your field hands?" Angelina asked.

"That's the part that I don't understand." I sighed. "But the night of the riot, when Mr. McKinley's party demanded our Chinese friends and I said no, one of the men said to shoot me. I was the lady doctor and I would finally get what was coming to me."

"Surely that was just the heat of the moment," Regina said.

"Perhaps it wasn't," I said, my throat closing off. "I am considered an abomination by some."

Regina chuckled. "You are considered a nuisance. That I have definitely heard. But what that also means is that you are not worth the gunpowder needed to send you to your reward."

"Mr. McKinley called me an abomination when he attacked me at the Glassell's party."

"Hmmm." Regina glared at her glass, then reached over and poured some more. "Based on what I have heard, if he called you an abomination, then he is a hypocrite of the worst sort."

"Nonetheless," Angelina said. "This latest attack happened just under Mr. McKinley's office."

"That's interesting," Regina said. "I guess it's time you and Angelina had another discussion with Mr. McKinley. One I would dearly love to see."

I was startled by the anger in Regina's voice, but not surprised. She despised hypocrisy above all else. It often frustrated her that she could not come to my rescue more directly. She was exceedingly careful of Angelina's and my reputations, with some justice, alas. Thus, she did as much as she could from the shadows where she lived most of her life.

Having agreed to seek out Mr. McKinley, we went on to make a list of several other people to speak to the next day. Angelina said that she would accompany me, as well, which did me no end of good. I was only sad that Regina would not be there.

The next morning, Sebastiano drove me to the Calle Primavera near Mr. McKinley's office. He let me off there, then took the buggy further back along the street. Angelina hurried up a minute later.

"You're alone," she observed after we had greeted each other.

"Not quite," I replied, trying to hide a yawn. My sleep the night before had, once again, been usurped by the nightmare. "Sebastiano has the buggy tethered somewhere near here and will be watching me. I fear he is hoping the villain will attack."

"If the villain does, then I pity the villain."

To be honest, I pitied the villain as well. It had been rather startling to see the anger in Sebastiano's eyes that morning, though I suppose it shouldn't have been. We had all been sorely tried by the deaths of our dear fellows and the subsequent attacks on Wang Fu and myself. I began to feel guilty that I had not been as attentive to my household and their feelings as I should have been. However, I was forced to put my own shame aside to meet with Angelina. I was determined not to succumb to that, and my anger, so that I could think clearly.

Angelina and I went up to the second floor and the land agent's too-crowded office. We fully expected to find that Mr. McKinley had told his clerks not to admit us, but he hadn't. We were admitted to his office immediately. He was behind his desk again, and not only scrambled to his feet when he saw us but backed away.

"What... Why..." he jabbered.

I suppose he was caught between the foul language he preferred and the tongue lashing he'd gotten from Angelina the week before.

"We need answers, Mr. McKinley," I said, my voice far calmer than I had any right to expect. "Honest ones. We know you were involved in the riot. You are perfectly aware that we know that. Now, there were eight men in your group. Some of them I know. Some of them I do not. I need their names, as at least one of them was the man who attacked me last Friday."

Mr. McKinley gulped and looked frantically about the room. "But I don't know. I really don't. It was utter madness that night. And there was drink. Who knows what happened and who did it?"

"Mr. McKinley," Angelina purred. "Do you really expect us to believe that you wish to harbor a malevolent killer? One the entire pueblo is looking for?"

"No, but I am telling you the truth." He blinked his eyes. "I do not remember everyone that came with us."

"Then why not some of them?" I asked, glaring at him.

"Well..." He blinked again. "There was that Walters fellow. Works for Mrs. Costa. You can ask her about him. And a fellow named Dillman. And... And... Er... Mr. Handley. Yes. Mr. Handley was most certainly there. I remember him quite clearly."

"Perhaps there was someone else you remember," Angelina said with a coy smile. "We're here to find a particular killer and keep peace in our beloved pueblo."

"Of course." Mr. McKinley swallowed. "I remember no one else."

I glanced at Angelina. She did not appear to believe him any more than I did. However, neither of us had any idea of how to press him for more.

We left the office in silence, waiting until we were on the street to converse.

"He was lying," Angelina said. "I am fairly certain that he remembers a great deal more about who was with him that night than he says he does."

"As am I," I said. "But he is not going to part with any more names unless he is duly forced to. Do you think you can force him?"

She shook her head. "No. Not any more than you can."

She suddenly let loose with quite a vile epithet.

"Angelina!"

"I know," she said, rolling her eyes. "We are supposed to behave as ladies. But I swear to you, Maddie, some days it is simply not worth it."

I had to chuckle at that. Still, there was more to be considered.

"I am surprised about Mr. Handley," I said. "I have always found him to be rather mild and kind."

"He is surely more upstanding and honest than most insurance agents I know," Angelina said. "And Mr. Walters is dead and far too soon to have been our villain."

I felt my brows knit together as I realized something. "Mrs. Costa, oddly enough, is big enough to have worn the boots we seek. However, how would she have gotten the anchor ornament? I can't imagine she was among the fellows that accosted us."

"Would she scruple to wear men's clothing?" Angelina thought. "You know that I have seen it several times before, a woman feigning the appearance of a man. Alas, I am not able to ask the reasons, as they are already dead."

"I can think of many reasons why it would be useful to be thought of as a man," I replied. "However, that does not answer our questions about Mrs. Costa."

"And who is this Mr. Dillman?"

I groaned. "He is a carpenter in Regina's employ. I had him over to my home and found him quite aggravating. However, if he had any holes in his boots, I don't doubt Regina or one of her ladies would have found them by now."

"We shall have to ask, although I seriously doubt Regina would have forgotten to tell us something so important."

"I agree." I looked at her. "Mr. Handley is closest. Shall we speak to him next?"

"Let us do so."

It was not a long walk. Still, walking along the Calle Primavera, I got an odd sensation. It was not unusual for men to tip their hats to me as I went by. It was, after all, common courtesy. Yet I got the strange feeling that they were also looking around me, as if some villain were about to spring out. I hoped that we were not to have any confrontations with Sebastiano hiding in the shadows to protect me. Either it was common knowledge that he was there, or else Sebastiano knew his business well enough to avoid being seen. I do not know for sure which it was, but if I were prone to gambling, I would have been willing to wager a sizable amount on the latter.

In any case, Angelina and I arrived at Mr. Handley's office in good time and without confrontations, and found the insurance agent in. He did not seem as happy to see me that morning as he had on many earlier occasions. As a result, I could not help but feel quite cross.

"For Heaven's sake, Mr. Handley," I told him as Angelina and I stood across his desk from him. "I am not here to make baseless accusations. I merely need information."

"But I lied to you," he whimpered in a most unseemly way for a man of his stature. His blond beard quivered as he blinked.

"I know that. But about what and why?" I asked.

"You knew?"

I rolled my eyes. Angelina smirked.

"Of course, I did," I said. "You are, in fact, a decidedly terrible liar. But people lie about all manner of things, most of which are of no consequence whatsoever. So, what was your business the night of the riot?"

Mr. Handley gulped. "You will please keep this quiet?"

"If I can."

"I was trying to stop the lynchings." He got out his handkerchief and dabbed at his eyes. "I yelled at the men. I even tried to pull one of the poor unfortunates away, all to no avail. Mrs. Wilcox, I tell you in all earnestness, it was the most terrible thing I have ever witnessed in my life. The men, they were such beasts. And the cries of the Chinamen." He shook his head. "Even now, I can still hear them." He closed his eyes, took a deep breath, then looked at me. "I don't know why I didn't simply say so. I suppose it is because I am so deeply ashamed that I could not do more."

"You stood up when no one else would," I said, knowing full well the depth of his shame, as it mirrored my own. "Good Heavens, Mr. Handley, you have nothing to be ashamed of."

"I am honored that you think so." He shifted his spectacles and blinked again. "However, you will not think so highly of me when I tell you where I was when your first field hand was killed." He sighed. "I was at Mrs. Medina's house of ill-repute."

I happened to catch Angelina's face out of the corner of my eye and realized that she was trying just as hard as I was not to laugh.

"I was not there to avail myself of the offerings," he protested.

"Mr. Handley," I groaned. "Any man of substance in this pueblo visits Mrs. Medina's house. It is a matter of doing business, whether or not you seek what she offers. As for whether or not you do, I do not care to know, let alone make any judgments. I am simply grateful that you have told me."

Mr. Handley looked at me oddly, then smiled gratefully.

"Mrs. Wilcox, you are the very personification of kindness and mercy," he said, dabbing at his eyes again.

"I am glad you think so, Mr. Handley," I said. "Thank you for your honesty. Now, I'm afraid Mrs. Sutton and I must be on our way."

"Thank you again, Mrs. Wilcox. Thank you!"

Angelina and I left quickly. Angelina found the encounter quite amusing. I, however, was less than amused, but then I never did appreciate fulsomeness.

CHAPTER FOURTEEN

When Angelina and I returned to the street, we determined that our next visit should be to the Costa rancho.

"After all," Angelina said, consulting one of her lists. "Not only did Mr. McKinley mention her and her employee, Mr. Walters, someone else has named Mr. Smith as being among Mr. McKinley's companions."

"And he works there as well," I said. I looked around for my buggy.

Sebastiano had apparently already seen us, as I had barely lifted my head when I saw the buggy, with Daisy hitched to it, approaching from down the street.

"Thank you, Sebastiano," I said as he pulled up. "We need to visit the Costa rancho, please."

Nodding, he hopped down from the seat and helped Angelina and me into the back. He was about to get back up to the seat when we were hailed from the doorway of a nearby saloon.

"Mrs. Wilcox," wheezed Mr. Pugh, as he stumbled up to the back of the buggy.

I held my breath and Sebastiano hurried to catch Daisy's head. Daisy was very calm for a horse, but no horse likes to be approached from the rear, especially when hitched to a buggy.

Mr. Pugh wheezed again as he leaned on the buggy's small door.

"Mrs. Wilcox, I have news for you," Mr. Pugh said.

"You do?" I said, trying to swallow my skepticism.

Given the state of his breath, which had fumes strong enough to induce intoxication, my skepticism seemed well-placed. However, I remembered that both Mr. Lomax and Mr. Sedonez trusted Mr. Pugh's eyes to some degree.

"I saw that feller attack you," he said. "I watched your friend knock him over, then how that feller shot him."

I winced at the memory. "Do you know the villain?"

Mr. Pugh coughed and expectorated into the street.

"Nope," he said. "But I did see him later. You know how it is. You hear gunplay, you get going. I hid on the Calle Principal. He had taken the kerchief off his face and was using it to wipe the dust and dirt off his clothes. I figure he's one of them high-falutin' fellows, which is why I don't know him. He sure was tall, though."

"Do you remember anything else about him? His hair color, perhaps?" I asked.

"He was light-haired." Mr. Pugh's face wrinkled as he tried to remember. "Least I think he was. Something about his beard, too. It was real neat."

I looked at Angelina, then back at Mr. Pugh.

"Well, thank you, Mr. Pugh," I said and smiled.

"Any time, Mrs. Wilcox," he said.

He seemed to be waiting for something, then with a profound sigh, shuffled back to the saloon. Sebastiano, assured that Daisy was not going to feel threatened, got onto the buggy's seat and chucked the reins.

"That was interesting," Angelina said over the buggy's creaking.

"He was trying to tell Mr. Lomax something that Friday," Sebastiano said. "Maybe we should ask Mr. Lomax."

"Mr. Sedonez says that Mr. Pugh is of sounder mind than one might think," I said. "And Mr. Lomax does trust him to make an early identification when a fight breaks out."

"If Mr. Lomax trusts him, and he's spoken to Mr. Lomax, then his information must not have been very useful," Angelina said. "A tall man with possibly light hair and a neat beard."

"A neat beard might be very distinguishing," I said. Almost every man in the pueblo wore a full beard of some sort, most of them untrimmed and quite wild. "However, a lot depends on what Mr. Pugh considers a neat beard."

"Which could mean anything that's trimmed at all," Angelina said, with a sigh. "How would he define high-faluting?"

"Sebastiano, do you have any idea?" I asked.

"I have no idea," Sebastiano said. "I don't know Mr. Pugh well, I'm afraid. Most of the other men see him as a nuisance, especially when he's talking up a fight to Mr. Lomax. But I don't know any that wish the old man ill. Some of the richer men, they'll just ignore Mr. Pugh and a couple have been known to treat him roughly."

"Come to think of it, I saw Mr. Carson kick the old man once," I said. "Mr. Pugh was making a pest of himself, as he does at times. But he hardly deserved to be kicked."

"Well, let us hope that no one saw him talking to you, Maddie," Angelina said. "I don't doubt that our villain wouldn't hesitate to kill an old drunk."

"I don't doubt it, either," I said, wincing. "However, most people consider Mr. Pugh quite daft."

"I don't care," said Sebastiano. "The first chance I get, I will have Enrique follow the old man. In fact, here is our chance now."

He pulled up the buggy and signaled a group of boys playing in a nearby yard. While Sebastiano arranged for them to carry a message, I got out a piece of paper and a pencil and wrote the note in question. I had Sebastiano look the note over before he dispatched it to the rancho in the care of a lively-looking fellow about Damiano's age. We sent another note to Mr. Lomax, as well.

Once the messages were sent, we went on to the Costa place. One of Mrs. Costa's several children saw us coming and hailed us excitedly. The dark-haired lad was about ten, and he ran alongside the buggy, far enough away not to spook Daisy, but close enough to welcome us.

His mother was not so welcoming. We found her in the yard, doing laundry next to the zanja that irrigated the rancho. She chided her son as Sebastiano helped Angelina and me to the ground. The boy ran off and Mrs. Costa turned to face us.

"Why are you here?" she demanded.

"We are trying to learn the names of the men that accosted Sebastiano and me the night of the riot," I said. "One of those men killed my two field hands, hurt another and then attacked me most foully this past Friday."

"Why would I know any of them?" Mrs. Costa asked, eyeing me suspiciously. "I was here the night of the riot."

"But some of your men were there," I said calmly.

She shrugged. "Then go ask them."

"I am asking you first as I am hardly likely to get honest answers out of men who have reason to fear just retribution from the law for their activities," I said.

"I don't know who was there and who wasn't." She returned to scrubbing a shirt on her washboard with a brush that looked very new.

"Surely, you may have heard someone speaking out of turn, overheard a conversation or two?"

She shuddered, then shook her head. "I don't pay them any mind. They are nothing but a flock of unruly fools, all too often the worse for drink. They are best left to themselves and that's what I do. It is bad enough that I must feed them, wash their clothes and take care of them when they come down sick or hurt themselves."

I sighed. "Perhaps Mr. Costa would know more."

"He's not here," she said, her voice tinged with anger. "He left last month to sell a load of hides up north."

"He's been gone a while," I said. "You must be very

worried about him."

Mrs. Costa's lips tightened. It was barely perceptible. If Angelina and I had not been looking for just such a sign, it would have escaped both of us.

"Not so long," she said, worrying at a spot on the shirt with the brush. "He's often gone longer."

Something I'd heard some days before suddenly sprang to mind.

"Yes. I have heard that he is away a great deal," I said.

"Not much I can do about it," she said.

"Couldn't he hire an agent?" I asked.

"Yes." She dropped the shirt she'd been washing into the rinse tub next to her. "But he won't. He once got skinned by one, so now he believes they are all rogues and will not trust any of them."

"You are a very brave woman," I said.

She slapped the next shirt onto her washboard and began scrubbing. Her jaw tightened.

"I do what I must do." She sent me a glare as if to say that if what she must do included doing me harm, she would not mind.

It chilled me to my marrow.

Fortunately, Angelina spoke up.

"It seems terribly unfair of your husband to leave you here like this," she said. "I know he must. But how unfortunate that he is gone, with all the trouble in the pueblo, and you left to take care of unruly ranch hands."

She looked up at Angelina and her face softened a little.

"Aren't you worried about the grand jury carting away one of your men?" Angelina continued.

"Might suit them," she said. I could see her considering something. She looked at Angelina. "Is there a reason I should be worried about the grand jury?"

Angelina looked at me.

I took a deep breath. "We have recently learned

that Mr. Walters, the hand that just died, was among those who participated in the riot. He, obviously, is innocent of the attacks on my field hands and myself. However, we are hoping that one or more of his companions may know something and that perhaps you happened to hear it."

Her eyes flicked between Angelina and me for a minute or so. She dropped the shirt she'd been scrubbing into the rinse bucket, then felt around the washtub, pulled up a third shirt and spread it on the washboard.

"As I said, I don't pay those fools no mind," she said slowly as she worked on the shirt. "But Mr. Smith may have something to tell you. He and Mr. Walters were friends, you know. I did not hear anything for certain, mind you."

"No, of course not," Angelina said. "Where is he?"

"In the tool shed. Or he should be." She scrubbed at another spot. "I told him to get it cleaned out." She eyed me again. "Don't need any more lockjaw around here."

"To be sure," I said.

"You better take your man with you," Mrs. Costa said. "Mr. Smith can be mean."

I was already well aware of how mean Mr. Smith could be. With a glance, I indicated to Angelina that we should wait to discuss our conclusions regarding Mrs. Costa until we had left her rancho. Angelina nodded. I signaled Sebastiano, who was waiting with the buggy. He checked to see that Daisy was securely hitched to a fence railing, then ambled over as we made our way to the tool shed.

Mr. Smith was just outside, leaning on the side and stretching his shoulders. His cheek was distended by a wad of chewing tobacco, and he expectorated as we walked up. He cursed when he saw me.

"Goodness gracious, Mr. Smith," Angelina snapped.

Mr. Smith expectorated again and shook his head.

"What do you want with me?"

I sighed. "We need to know the names of the party that accosted me on the night of the riot. We know your friend Mr. Walters was among the men. There were eight, however."

"I told you I wasn't there," Mr. Smith snapped. He looked nervously about the yard.

"That does not mean that what you told me was the truth," I said.

"Why do you have to pick on me?"

"I am not picking on anyone," I groaned. "But I am getting very tired of being lied to. I need information. After all, two men have died, another seriously injured and I, myself, was attacked three days ago!"

"But I do not have any information." He choked a little, then expectorated.

"You are lying!" I cried, more loudly than I intended.

He glanced over at Sebastiano, who was behind me.

"I'm not lying," Mr. Smith said. He was just beginning to sound frightened.

"You are too." I felt my temper flaring but was helpless to stop it. "Your friend Mr. Walters was part of the group and yet you failed to mention him when you told me that you'd heard Mr. McKinley, Mr. Fletcher, and Mr. Sanford laughing in the saloon. You had to have known Mr. Walters was part of the group, since he's your friend. So why didn't you mention him? He is certainly beyond human judgment now."

"I don't know." Mr. Smith bent over and spat out the entire wad he'd been chewing. He choked again, then stood. "I don't know. I truly don't."

"You don't know what?" I asked.

He looked at me and sniffed. "Anything."

"I think you do know who was part of that group."

"I don't! I didn't even know that Fletcher fellow, or even McKinley. They don't drink with fellows like me. I just heard their names later. I swear."

"Then did you know any of the others?"

He blinked his eyes and began weeping. "I can't say. I really can't. You don't know what it was like, Mrs. Wilcox. Well, you know partly. But it's different for me. You don't have to be mean to survive. I do. You don't know these fellows. They're like chickens on a sick hen. If they think you're weak, they'll knock you toothless." He sank back against the shed. "That night, it scared me like nothing else. Those men were crazy. I never saw bloodlust like that before. It was Leon's idea to go looking for the Chinamen. He met up with Sanford and said I was coming, too. Sanford found Mr. McKinley and that carpenter, Mr. Dillman. And Mr. Fletcher was there. Next thing I know there were two other fellows that I had never seen before. One knew Mr. Fletcher and the other knew Mr. McKinley."

"Do you remember what they looked like?"

"One was pretty tall." He shook his head. "I think he had a kerchief on his face, too. I don't know why."

"Perhaps he realized that what he was doing was wrong and did not want to be recognized," I said.

Mr. Smith wept all the harder. Alas, I must confess that it did not soften my heart any.

"Are you sure you did not recognize anyone else?" Sebastiano asked, his voice low, but powerful.

I looked back. Usually, Sebastiano did not contribute to these sorts of inquiries. But I must say that his question held a veiled threat of menace that was infinitely more powerful than any I could have conveyed.

Mr. Smith trembled. "I am sorry, ma'am. I truly didn't." He blinked. "Frankly, I've been looking for those two I don't know. I don't want them telling the grand jury about me. But I haven't seen them again. Honest, I haven't."

Sebastiano, Angelina, and I looked at each other. We all seemed to have come to the conclusion that there was nothing more to be learned from Mr. Smith. We bade him farewell and walked back to the buggy.

Out of the corner of my eye, I saw Mrs. Costa watching us. As I looked again, I saw that she had a grim smile on her face.

After Sebastiano helped us into the buggy, I nodded slightly toward Mrs. Costa.

"She seems... Not happy, but as if something has pleased her," I said, glancing again at Mrs. Costa while Sebastiano got Daisy going.

"She was wearing a man's boots," Angelina said. "But where would she have gotten the ornament? Besides, I do not think she participated in the riot."

"I don't either," I said. "Although, she is definitely hiding something from us."

"If I had to make a guess," said Angelina. "She's afraid because she's been left alone so much. She seemed most angry when she was talking about that part."

"She doesn't have light hair or a beard," Sebastiano said from the seat.

"Could it be that we are looking for two different malefactors?" I asked.

"I suppose we could be," Angelina said. "It would account for the different attacks. However, it does not account for the fact that we've seen the same boot print at the scene of every attack."

"Even then it doesn't make sense," I sighed. "It is a pity we couldn't get a glimpse of either Mrs. Costa's or Mr. Smith's boots, though."

"It is," agreed Angelina. She frowned. "That ornament we found. It seems fine enough that someone would be looking for it, nor does it seem like the sort of thing that Mr. Smith or Mr. Sanford would have."

"I agree about the latter," I said. "But if the villain knows where he lost the bijou, he would hardly want to let anyone know lest he expose himself as the killer."

Angelina's face wrinkled as if she smelled something nasty.

"Perhaps we could place an advertisement in the newspaper," she suggested.

"Do we want the killer to know that we have something that could identify him?" I asked.

"No," Angelina sighed. "He would want to kill us, and if we asked him about it, all he would have to do is lie."

"On the other hand, it could eliminate some fellows simply because they are less likely to have the wherewithal to have such an item."

"But wouldn't the fellow who has that kind of wherewithal also have the wherewithal to get his boot fixed before he got such a huge hole in it?"

Sebastiano laughed. "Is it not possible that our villain had money once, but does not now? Or perhaps the ornament was a gift."

I pressed my lips closed, fervently longing for the release of strong language.

"In other words, we cannot overlook somebody simply because he is a common laborer," I complained. "Perhaps we should speak with Mr. Fletcher again. Except that it probably will not do any good. He refuses to admit that he was present, and Mrs. Fletcher told me that it's entirely possible that he simply does not remember. He has been giving in to the temptation of strong drink since last summer, and that can cause one's memory to falter."

"That it can," said Sebastiano.

We rode toward the center of the pueblo in frustrated silence. Angelina pulled her lists from her dress pocket and shook her head as she re-read them.

"Wait," I said, putting my hand on hers. "I have just now realized that we have a piece of information we did not have before."

"What?" asked Angelina.

"We have some idea of what the villain looks like. He is tall with light hair and a neat beard. There are several in the pueblo who could be described that way. Mr. Gluck, for example."

"It's true," said Sebastiano. "Mr. Gluck's hair is very light in color."

"I cut half of his beard away when I stitched his cheek closed." I frowned. "Even if that were what Mr. Pugh would consider a neat beard, Mr. Gluck was still in the hospital when Wei Chin was killed. Nor could I imagine he felt well enough to attack Wang Fu or me, for that matter."

"Mr. Handley has light hair and his beard is not quite so wild," Angelina said. "I suppose it is possible that when we talked to him this morning, he was lying again."

"It most certainly does not seem likely," I said, looking over the list of laborers that Angelina held. "There. Mr. Dillman and Mr. Sanford. They are both fair-haired, although Mr. Sanford's hair is more red than blond. They have both been quite nasty about the Chinese, as well. And when I asked Mr. Dillman if he was near my rancho the Friday evening Wei Li was killed, he became quite angry and declared he didn't want any business from me."

Sebastiano snorted, then talked over his shoulder. "For all the complaints that the Chinamen are taking everyone's jobs, you would think that we would have had a line of men asking to come work for us. Are you sure you put that notice up at the mercantile, Maddie?"

"Yes, I did," I said. "And, as yet, we haven't had any responses?"

"Not one," said Sebastiano. "Where now?"

I looked at Angelina, but she was looking at the street and, following her gaze, I saw that Chin Tai was running toward us. He was a sturdy lad of about twelve. When he saw us, he waved and hurried over.

"Miss Medina, she sent note for you and Miss Wilcox," he told Angelina as he drew up to the buggy. "She say it very important."

"Thank you, Chin Tai," Angelina said.

She took the paper from the lad and sent him on his way.

"Well?" I asked.

"Sebastiano, we need to pay a call on Mrs. Medina,"

Angelina said. "She has discovered something."

Sebastiano chucked the reins and pushed Daisy to a trot.

CHAPTER FIFTEEN

Sebastiano pulled Daisy up about a block before Regina's house. It may have been a house of ill-repute, but it was also a beautiful dwelling, with white clapboard, built against a hill. Tall bushes grew around it, so that it was difficult to tell who was coming in or out of the place.

I led Sebastiano and Angelina through the private back entrance that I always used that led to the kitchen. A young Irish lass led us to Regina's study.

It was a surprisingly cramped room, with a desk pushed up against one wall, a small chair and little else, except the shelves, which were filled with ledgers bound in gray-blue cloth. I deeply feared what would happen if the so-called honorable gentlemen of Los Angeles ever found out about those ledgers. But it was how Regina chose to run her business, and she certainly knew more about it than I did. And while I could not approve of what she did, I had no right to complain or worry about how she did it.

Regina, herself, was firmly ensconced in the one small chair. Upon seeing Angelina, Sebastiano, and myself, she signaled something to the Irish lass, then shooed myself and my companions to another, somewhat larger sitting room off the kitchen.

This was quite obviously not a place where Regina normally did business, as it was quite Spartan in its furnishings. There were only three wood chairs, bereft of cushions, no art on the walls and one blacked out window.

"It's where I put the drunks," Regina explained as

we waited for the Irish lass to return. "I don't normally have the chairs in here but thought that we might make use of them."

I shuddered to think of how we might do such a thing, but then the door opened and one of Regina's girls was pushed inside.

She was a lithe young woman, with a full figure, easily visible through the silk dressing gown she wore over her unmentionables. Her rich, golden tresses fell over her shoulders and down her back. Her face was round, her eyes a peculiar mix of brown and green.

"This," Regina said sternly. "Is Annie LeGuine. I seriously doubt that is the name she was born with, but I normally have little to no reason to discern the validity of those particular facts. However, I have reason to believe that Annie has not been telling us the truth about a great many things even beyond the name she was given."

Miss LeGuine shivered, looked around the room, then scurried to one of the chairs and sat in it almost defiantly.

I sighed. "As you have suggested, Mrs. Medina, people lie for all manner of reasons. Just because Miss LeGuine has not been honest about her true name does not mean that she is engaged in some nefarious activity."

Regina snorted. "Not usually. However, I do believe the silly thing has fallen in love, and as a result, has been withholding valuable information regarding one of the individuals who may have been responsible for the murders of your field hands."

"I don't know what you're talking about," Miss LeGuine said with a snort.

Regina's eyes rolled Heaven-ward. "They never do."

"Miss LeGuine," I said, fighting to keep my voice even and calm. "We are seeking the villain who killed two of my field hands, attempted a similar killing on a third, then accosted me in a most unseemly manner.

The man in question has left behind a very distinctive boot print in the dirt around where his heinous crimes were committed. This is why Mrs. Medina has asked you and your sisters about the bottoms of boots of late. Consider well, Miss LeGuine. Even if you find the object of your affections a companionable sort at this time, such a brute could turn on you and hurt you as easily as he tried to hurt me and my field hands."

"I do not have any object of my affections," Miss LeGuine said. "Nor have I seen anyone with holes in his boots."

"Miss LeGuine," said Regina, her voice utterly bored in tone. "I have owned this enterprise for almost twelve years. I have seen any number of young women come and go. I know what it means when a young woman's eyes light up, as yours have, at the mention of a certain man. I know that when a young woman who is otherwise honest starts lying about a certain man that she does so for many reasons, not the least of which includes protecting him. And, yes, Miss LeGuine, you have been lying about Mr. Dillman and your interest in him. I could go on, but the signs are rather obvious that you have fallen in love, and given your insistence that such has not happened, I strongly suspect that your feelings for him have been reciprocated."

Miss LeGuine regarded Regina with a stony stare. I, however, tried to calm the fervent beating of my heart, which had started with the mention of Mr. Dillman's name.

I sighed. "Miss LeGuine, have you considered the possibility that we are trying to protect you? If you tell us what you know about Mr. Dillman, we can keep you safe from his predations."

"He is not a predator!" Miss LeGuine exclaimed, then flushed. "He is not. He is a kind and gentle man. A sweet man. He is even willing to overlook my many sins to marry me. Why would anyone call him a predator?"

"There, there, Miss LeGuine," Regina said. "I am sure he has been most tender in his regard for you.

Why don't you prove it by telling us the truth about his boots and anything else you know about him?"

"But he is innocent," she groaned.

"We know he participated in the riot," I said. "We had confirmation of that from several people."

"That was one night," Miss LeGuine said. "And he was terribly shaken by the event. He has done no one any harm since. I am certain of it."

"And how do you know that?" I demanded.

"I... I... I don't know how I know. I just do." Miss LeGuine blinked back tears. "Mr. Dillman is a gentleman, even more gentle and kind than many of the supposedly finer sort of man in this town. You must believe me!"

"What is it you fear, Miss LeGuine?" Angelina asked softly.

"What?" the girl asked.

"What is it you fear by telling us what you know about Mr. Dillman?" Angelina said. "If he is truly as kind and gentle as you say, and if you are so certain that he is innocent, then why do you hesitate to tell us the truth of it?"

Miss LeGuine looked away and the tears slowly dribbled down her cheek.

"He can't be the villain who killed your field hands," she whispered. "Please don't let him be. He's my last hope."

"You mean you hope to escape from your life here, with him," Regina said softly.

Miss LeGuine nodded.

I sighed. "Miss LeGuine, there is always hope. And if you wish to leave Mrs. Medina's employ..." I paused. "I can house you and find you more suitable employment. It won't be easy, but marriage is not your only choice."

Miss LeGuine looked at me, her face clouded with both disbelief and hope at the same time.

"Why?" she asked softly.

"If I am to claim the title of Christian, then I must

follow the example of our Dear Lord. And if he forgave and cared for the prostitutes and sinners, then I must, as well."

I do believe I saw Regina roll her eyes at that point. Miss LeGuine did not seem entirely convinced of my reasoning, but she nodded and sniffed.

"I do love him," she said. "I really do. And I truly do not think he killed your field hands. But the day that first field hand was killed, he suddenly stopped work around two o'clock that afternoon and left without saying why."

"What about that Saturday night when Wei Chin was killed?" I asked.

"I do not know where he was." Miss LeGuine shrugged. "I was working."

"And he had already finished his job here," Regina interjected. "I think it was that Monday after the second killing, so neither of us would have cause to know his whereabouts in the pueblo in the days following."

"And what of his boots?" Angelina asked.

Miss LeGuine began sobbing. "They... They had holes in the bottoms. And he had them repaired almost a week ago."

I pressed my lips together. I glanced over at Regina, Angelina, and Sebastiano.

"You may go back to your room, Miss LeGuine," Regina said. "If you wish to leave, speak to Sybil, collect your wages, and wait for Mrs. Wilcox to finish here. If not, then be ready to receive by five o'clock, as usual."

Miss LeGuine hurried from the room.

I swallowed. "It would appear that we have our villain."

Angelina had been counting days. "Mr. Dillman finished his work here on Monday, the thirteenth, which was the day after Wei Chin was killed and we found the boot print with the hole on Wei Chin's shirt. So, if Mr. Dillman had his boots repaired that Tuesday, they would have been whole again on Wednesday, when Wang Fu was attacked."

"And it would stand to reason that he would have the work done after he'd received his wages that I paid him," Regina said.

"I know," I said. I began pacing.

"It's not conclusive evidence, Maddie," Angelina said. "It will be hard enough to convince the jury that the boot print points to the killer."

Angelina was correct in that evidence of that sort was even less likely to be found then, let alone accepted, than it is now.

"Still, we need to get a good look at his boots," I said. "But how?"

"Maddie," Sebastiano said. "I think I know of a way. We have to bring him here."

"Of course, we'll bring him here," Regina said. "Hm. I know just how to do it. I'll return in a moment."

She left and returned, as she had stated, but a few minutes later.

"He'll be here soon," she said, with a rather frightening gleam in her eye. She then smirked at me. "Maddie, if you are going to undermine my business by rescuing my girls, then you are going to have to come up with a more believable excuse than your Christian duty."

I bristled. "And what if it is my Christian duty? Which it is."

Angelina giggled.

"That may be," Regina said with a chuckle. "However, I know full well that had you not married Albert Wilcox, you might have ended up offering the same services my girls do, and it was that fear that drove you to marry the unpleasant cur."

I looked away. "Even you, Regina, choose compassion. Why not remind ourselves that it is our calling as Christians?"

Regina snorted. Sebastiano and Angelina just looked at each other and shook their heads.

I do not know what specific means Regina used to compel Mr. Dillman to join us. In truth, I am not sure

I want to, especially in light of what happened when he did.

Now, as I am about to set down the actual events, do I realize the reason I have been so loath to recall them. It was not the horror of anything I witnessed, although that was bad enough. No, I remain deeply ashamed of the depths to which I sank.

Mr. Dillman was roughly shoved through the door. He was in his shirtsleeves and from the rumpled state of his shirt and his dazed eyes, I surmised that his jacket had been removed forcibly.

"What am I doing here?" he demanded.

"Sit down, Mr. Dillman," Regina ordered.

He puffed out his chest and stumbled toward her. Sebastiano reached out and grabbed Mr. Dillman from behind, Sebastiano's strong hands firmly gripping Mr. Dillman's upper arms.

"Mrs. Medina said to sit down," Sebastiano growled.

He turned and shoved Mr. Dillman toward a nearby chair. Mr. Dillman sat down but remained defiant.

"What in tarnation am I doing here?" he demanded again. "I didn't do anything."

"You are here to answer questions," I said, far more calmly than I felt.

"I don't have to say anything to you," Mr. Dillman said, adding quite a few vile epithets.

"You will answer the questions," Sebastiano said, his voice icy cold. "And you will tell us the truth."

"Dagnabbit, I got nothing to say to you!"

"Indeed," I said. "I can well imagine you do not want to tell me where you were two Fridays ago, on the third. In fact, when I asked you about it, you told me that you were nowhere near my place and that you didn't want any business out this way. And when I expressed surprise that you would not want business, you left immediately without answering my question. Now, why would you do something like that? Perhaps you had something to hide?"

"It's no business of yours," he snarled.

"Come now, Mr. Dillman," Angelina said. "Can you not see why we might find your behavior suspicious? All we are interested in is the truth of what you were doing. Perhaps you had some secret rendezvous that you wish to hide from Miss LeGuine."

"Do not mention her sweet name to me." Mr. Dillman started from the chair but Sebastiano, still behind him, grabbed the carpenter by the shoulders and shoved him down onto the seat. "That woman is a princess, a sweet, innocent girl taken in by evil influences." He glared at Regina specifically.

"Then where were you and why are you trying to hide it from us?" I asked. "Unless, of course, you were murdering my field hand."

"I did no such thing!" he exclaimed with much foul language. "I am an upright fellow. You cannot say otherwise about me."

"I most certainly can say otherwise," I said. "You have been named by several others as one of eight men who accosted Sebastiano and me the night of the riot. One of those men encouraged Mr. McKinley to shoot me, as I am a lady doctor and, thus, would get what was coming to me. Are you sure you don't remember that event?"

Mr. Dillman swallowed. "I don't care if you're a lady doctor or not. Why would I care?"

"Then you were part of that group?"

"I was not!" His bravado diminished somewhat. "You can't say that I was."

"And, yet, you have been less than kind regarding the Chinese in this pueblo," I said.

"Them little yellow—"

"Do not finish that sentence," I growled.

"They're taking our jobs! And they're heathens. They should all be packed up and shipped to their Chinee land."

I do not know how, but my hand had slipped into

my bag and had grasped one of my scalpels. I pulled it out and advanced on Mr. Dillman.

"They are just as human as we are," I growled and brandished the scalpel. "They are only trying to make a better life for their families back home. Is that not why you came to Los Angeles, Mr. Dillman, to build a better life for yourself? Why do the Chinese deserve to die and you do not? Answer me that!"

Mr. Dillman's eyes grew wide, as well they should have, given that I'd placed the point of the scalpel against his chest.

"Well?" I asked again. "Answer me! Why do the Chinese deserve to die and you do not?"

Mr. Dillman whimpered but could not form words.

"Mr. Dillman, I am a trained medical doctor. I know exactly how to cut you open without killing you and how to re-arrange your organs to guarantee a very slow and very painful death. I need you to be honest with me. Where were you on Friday, the third of November? Where were you Saturday night, on the twelfth, and three days later on the fifteenth? Where?"

"Maddie." Regina's arms were enfolded about me as she gently tugged me back.

"Mr. Dillman," Sebastiano said, his voice all the more menacing because it was quiet and low. "I can do only so much to keep Mrs. Wilcox from attacking you. As you can see, she is quite affected by this turmoil."

I pulled myself from Regina's embrace. "Mr. Dillman, I will accept nothing less than the truth. Where were you?"

"I can't say," he whined, his legs splaying outward and straight as he tried to back away from me.

"Where were you?" I pressed the scalpel against his chest again and applied just enough pressure to cut through his shirt.

"Maddie," Angelina cried. "Wait! His boots."

Regina again pulled me back and held me more firmly this time.

Angelina pulled up one of Mr. Dillman's legs,

almost toppling him over backward.

"He's not our villain," she said. "Look. The mend is straight, not on the diagonal and the heels are not worn in the same way. These are not the same boots."

I glared at Mr. Dillman. "Where were you?"

He blinked as his eyes filled. "I went to see a lawyer that Friday. I heard that the grand jury was being called. I needed to know if I was safe. He told me not to tell anyone that I had seen him. If I did, then the grand jury could get them to testify against me. That's why I ran. I don't want to be hung for killing no Chinaman. That's the God's honest truth. I swear it!"

"And what other boots do you have?" I demanded.

"None, ma'am. These are all I have. I had to wait for Mr. Johnson to fix them."

I turned away, shaking beyond all measure. Tears were forming in my eyes, as well, and I did not want Mr. Dillman to see, let alone anyone else in the room. I could feel Sebastiano's and Angelina's shocked stares.

"Get out," Regina said. "Go collect Miss LeGuine, if she'll still have you, then be on your way someplace else before the night is out. That's the least I can do for Miss LeGuine. But be assured, if you ever show your face in this pueblo again, I will know, and I will not scruple against letting people know what you did that terrible night."

I assume Mr. Dillman left quickly. I did hear the door open and slam shut in quick succession.

"Maddie," Regina said, sliding up to me and gently removing the scalpel, which I still held in my shaking hand. "It's all right."

"No, it's not," I said, crying. "It's not in the least bit all right. How could I have done that? How could I have threatened an innocent man with such meanness? Where were my womanly instincts? What kind of monster am I?"

Regina tut-tutted. "Monster? Maddie, my darling, would you call yourself a monster knowing what I am?"

"You didn't threaten that poor man with slow

painful death."

"I didn't get the chance," Regina said.

She gently helped me to a chair and had me sit down. Sebastiano and Angelina both seemed to be recovering from the shock of seeing me so out of control.

"I would say you were most justifiably angry with Mr. Dillman and his behavior," Regina said, her voice low with a very soothing purr.

"But what good did it do?" I asked. "If Angelina hadn't seen the bottom of his boots, I would have cut an innocent man."

"I would not call him innocent," Regina said. "He was part of that gang that accosted you. He helped to chase down and lynch otherwise innocent men. He was only innocent of killing the Wei brothers and the attack on Wang Fu and you."

I looked at Sebastiano and Angelina. "I apologize for exposing you to such an appalling display. I don't think I've ever been so angry or violent in my life!"

"We understand, Maddie," Angelina said, obviously still shaken.

Sebastiano laughed. "You were at least that angry at Schoolmaster Williams when he boxed Ramon's ears for no reason except that he didn't like the boy. Then there was the time that drunk chased Elena and Armando. It's a good thing that you did not have a weapon at hand."

I glared at Sebastiano.

"Hmm," said Angelina. "I have never seen you quite this angry before, but to hear that you have been so before does not surprise me."

"Oh, indeed, indeed," said Regina, with the hint of a smirk on her face. "Our dear little Maddie Wilcox is quite the formidable opponent when someone she cares about is threatened."

I sat up straight. "Who wouldn't be? That is a whole different subject than being in good control of one's passions, and I like to think that I am."

Regina snorted. "Madeline Franklin Wilcox, you

are the least in control of your passions of anyone I know, and I am profoundly grateful for it. If you were more in control, then there might not be room in your life for me, and that would be very dismal, indeed."

There was no good response to that.

CHAPTER SIXTEEN

Regina was forced to stay behind as Angelina and Sebastiano helped me outside to the buggy. My heart burned with the guilt of leaving her on the outside of our inquiries, especially after she had been so gracious in letting us use her home. But I could not change society, nor did I care to at that point.

I also faced a greater fury at that point in the day. We had missed our lunch, and Olivia took great pains to make sure we understood how greatly put out she was. I did insist on including Angelina in our meal. Logically, that should have incensed Olivia all the more. However, it did exactly the opposite in that Olivia's pride was assuaged. After all, it was not often that we had guests, and thus she seldom had the opportunity to show off her exceptional skills in the kitchen.

This does not mean that Olivia did not fuss at us for missing our lunch and complain that we had added a guest at the last moment. It merely meant that the scolding was not nearly as severe as it could have been.

The weather had warmed up to late spring-like temperatures. The sky was a brilliant blue expanse empty of all clouds. Olivia had set the table in the yard and served us chicken and mole with fresh flat corn breads, newly dug radishes and onions, and a cabbage salad dressed with tart vinegar and rich olive oil. There was plenty of claret, as well, and Angelina made sure I drank mine to soothe my shattered nerves.

We were lingering over the last bits of food and wine when the dogs began barking. The three of them ran to the gate in great excitement, and Hernan hurried from the winery to see who had incited such a ruckus.

It was Mr. Montero. Kind soul that he was, he stopped to pet all three of the dogs, bending over happily to pick up ChiChi. The ridiculous creature, who had bitten everyone on the rancho except Wang Fu multiple times, reveled in being held by Mr. Montero. Sebastiano immediately asked the tanner to join us at table, then called Olivia to bring more food and wine. Mr. Montero demurred.

"I cannot stay long," he explained, accepting a glass of claret, nonetheless. "I have news, though, and that is why I have come." He held up a ragged piece of leather. "I found this behind Mr. Johnson's shoe shop. It was one of many. So, if you have some picture of the boot you seek, perhaps we can find out if Mr. Johnson fixed that boot, and then you can ask Mr. Johnson whose boot it was."

Angelina looked at me and nodded. I pulled the journal in which she had drawn the mended boot print from my bag, as well as my original drawing of the boot with the hole. I presented these to Mr. Montero.

"Yes, there were not many discarded soles that had a hole this big," he said. "It should be easy to find, as Mr. Johnson is rather careless about the soles he discards. They make a huge pile in the alley behind his shop."

"Discarded soles," I muttered. "Holes."

It suddenly occurred to me that I had heard someone talking about holes in soles shortly after Wei Li's death. But I realized that I had actually heard something else. I looked at Sebastiano and Angelina.

"We have a visit to make," I said, then turned to Mr. Montero. "If you can find that bit of leather in Mr. Johnson's pile, it could help our case. And I thank you most heartily. You have reminded me of something that I should have understood early on."

Mr. Montero seemed pleased and went to do his search. Sebastiano directed Pascual to hitch Daisy to the buggy again and we were soon on our way into the pueblo. We stopped at the Gaines home. Fortunately, Miss Gaines was in. She seemed a little flummoxed by my urgency and by the presence of Angelina (we did ask Sebastiano to wait outside to make things somewhat easier for the young woman).

"Please, Mrs. Wilcox, Mrs. Sutton, be seated," Miss Gaines said, proving her mettle indeed. "Shall I ring for some tea?"

"It's not necessary, Miss Gaines," I said as Angelina and I settled ourselves on the couch of the parlor. "Pray forgive me for alluding in front of Mrs. Sutton here to something you told me in confidence, but I do believe it has great significance in regard to the recent murders of my field hands; and Mrs. Sutton, in addition to being exceedingly discreet, is very involved in finding the evil man who committed those murders."

Miss Gaines looked at me oddly. "I have full confidence in you, Mrs. Wilcox. You would not have brought Mrs. Sutton here unless you thought it was important."

"Thank you, Miss Gaines." I looked briefly at Angelina, then took a deep breath. "That fateful day when you told me about the various men plying their suits for you, you mentioned that one had a hole in his soul. I thought at the time that you were referring to his moral character."

"Oh," said Miss Gaines. "Not quite, although it would be an apt description of him. I have even heard that he was courting you, as well."

"Mr. Leighland," I said.

"Yes. Him. He was sitting quite casually by the fire sometime before I spoke with you, and I saw that there was a great hole in the sole of his boot."

"Yes," I said. "I have heard that his means are considerably straightened."

Angelina looked at me curiously, but I forbore to answer her and stood instead. Angelina and Miss Gaines also rose.

"Thank you, Miss Gaines," I said. "You have been very helpful."

I all but pulled Angelina out of the house and brought her over to where Sebastiano was waiting with the buggy. I told him about Mr. Leighland's boot.

"He is not only tall enough, but he has a very neat beard," I continued. "And silver might be considered light in color."

"I don't know if I've ever seen him before," Angelina said. "I probably have."

"But that was the other part of what Mr. Pugh complained about," I said. "A finer fellow who thought himself above everyone else, especially an older drunkard, such as Mr. Pugh. And Mr. Leighland does seem to put a great premium on appearing well-to-do."

Sebastiano snorted, which I well understood. Angelina shrugged.

"Never having met the man, I am forced to rely on your perception of him," Angelina said. "On the other hand, it would explain how he could have had that ornament we found on Wei Chin's body."

I looked at Sebastiano. "You wouldn't happen to know where he lives?"

Sebastiano shook his head. "We could try asking at the Uribe saloon. So many of the men from the riot were there."

We made our way to the back room, ringed by crates, with the sun filtering in through the one window. Mr. Sedonez looked up from the small writing desk and greeted us, Angelina in particular.

"Mrs. Sutton," he said. "This is a rare pleasure."

It came as no surprise to me that Mr. Sedonez was friendly toward Angelina, given how often his customers required her services.

"Thank you, Mr. Sedonez," she said, quietly.

"Mr. Sedonez," I said. "Are you familiar with a man by the name of Mr. Leighland?"

Mr. Sedonez snorted. "I should throw him out is what I should do. But he's mostly inoffensive, even if he can't pay his bill more often than not. I gave him lunch today and it's as likely as not that he has forgotten his coin purse and will have to pay me in the future."

"So, he is here now?" I asked, my heart beating.

"Yes. Would you like me to bring him in here?"

"Yes, please," I said.

I dug through my ever-present bag as Mr. Sedonez returned to the front.

"Oh, good, it's here," I said, pulling the ornament, wrapped in paper, from my bag.

"You were supposed to keep it safe," Angelina chided.

"It was safe in my bag," I retorted.

"Mrs. Wilcox, what a great pleasure it is to see you," Mr. Leighland said from the doorway. He advanced into the room, mostly ignoring both Sebastiano and Angelina.

"Mr. Leighland, I am glad to see you," I said. "I believe I may have something that belongs to you."

I unwrapped the bit of paper and held out the anchor ornament toward him. His face remained blank for several seconds, then he looked at me.

"I do believe I lost this the night of the party," he said, finally, with a big smile. "It must have caught on your dress somehow."

"It was lost the night of the party," I said. "But it was not found on my dress. It was found in the queue of my field hand Wei Chin, who was foully murdered that night."

Mr. Leighland's smile vanished, but then returned quickly.

"Good heavens, little lady, you can't possibly be accusing me?"

"Oh, but I can, Mr. Leighland. After all, you were in the neighborhood the night that Wei Chin died. You were also in the neighborhood the afternoon I was attacked and my other hand shot to death. You even volunteered to find the miscreant. You may have covered your face with a kerchief that day when you attacked me and the day you also attacked my friend Wang Fu—"

"You don't call them Chinamen friends," he snarled. "They are murderers and rogues."

"As are you," I said. "If not, why don't you show me the bottom of your boot?"

He smiled. "Of course, Mrs. Wilcox. I have no holes to hide."

He lifted his foot and I slid around behind him to look at it. It had been recently mended, but the heel remained worn down, with nails showing through. However, it did not match the print we'd drawn.

"Would you mind showing me your other boot, please?" I asked.

He sighed, putting that foot down and lifting the other. I waved Angelina over. The heel was a perfect match for the one we'd both drawn and the newly mended sole had a slight crack where the two bits of sole had been joined.

"Yes, that is quite a distinctive mend," I said.

"What?" Mr. Leighland whirled around.

"And you should have considered replacing your heel when you got the soles repaired," Angelina added.

"My only question is why did you kill my field hands?" I asked.

Mr. Leighland laughed. "I'm not saying I did, but why would I want Chinamen on land I hoped to acquire?"

"And what made you so certain that you would be able to acquire it, as well as my affections, before you had even met me?"

"Mrs. Wilcox, you have quite the imagination," Mr. Leighland said, chuckling in spite of the anxious light in his eyes. "I had nothing to do with your Chinamen. Why would I strangle a Chinaman with his own queue?"

"I have no idea, Mr. Leighland," I replied coldly. "However, that they were strangled, and how, is not common knowledge. So how did you know how they died?"

He gasped for a moment, then pushed toward me. "You are unnatural. McKinley should have shot you that night."

"Ah. You are admitting that you were part of that party."

"Nobody is going to take your word for what happened."

"They will take mine," said Sebastiano. "I was there too, and I am a citizen and I vote in this city.

Mr. Leighland shifted. "You are only a Mexican. Nobody will believe you."

"But there is also my testimony," Mr. Sedonez said.

He had been standing in the doorway, coming in behind Mr. Leighland, something I found out later.

Mr. Leighland tried to bolt, but Mr. Sedonez tripped him. Sebastiano started toward the fallen man, but Mr. Leighland rolled onto his back, his gun drawn.

Angelina screamed loudly as she ran for the back door. Mr. Leighland fired again and again, the report of the gun almost deafening me. I scrambled back and forth, trying to avoid being hit, only to trip on my skirt and land on my face. The gun fire stopped, and I could hear the men struggling behind me.

The back door slammed open.

"What's going on here?" I heard Mr. Lomax demand loudly. "Mrs. Wilcox! Mrs. Sutton!"

"I am unhurt," I said, slowly getting to my knees.

I turned. Mr. Leighland lay on his stomach and struggled as Sebastiano held his shoulders to the ground and Mr. Sedonez bound Mr. Leighland's hands. Behind me, I could hear the drip of liquor where a bullet had torn through a crate to one or more of the bottles within.

"Are you hurt?" I asked them. Without waiting for an answer, I turned and nearly collapsed. "Angelina!"

Angelina lay on her stomach, bright red blood seeping onto her blue cambric dress just above her waist and to the left of her spine. It took but a second for me to collect myself, although it felt as though it took considerably longer. I rushed to her side and grabbed her pulse. She moaned softly. I put my ear near her mouth and her breathing was labored, but not overly weak. Better yet, there was no blood in her mouth or nose.

"The table!" I cried, scrambling to my feet and pulling my bag from over my shoulder.

I grabbed the chair next to the small desk and rested my bag on it. I still thank our blessed and providential savior that Mr. Lomax had arrived when he did. We did not ever learn who had called the police, but it was no small grace that Mr. Lomax and one of the newly hired officers happened to be near the saloon at the time.

Leaving the young officer to help Mr. Sedonez deal with Mr. Leighland, Sebastiano and Mr. Lomax hurried to settle the back room's long table near the window. Sebastiano didn't wait to be asked and lit as many lamps as he could find and placed them on the nearest stack of crates. I pulled my surgical tools from my bag and dosed them with carbolic acid, then handed the flask to Mr. Lomax, who quickly wiped down the table, while I put on my work apron.

Only then, did he and Sebastiano gently lift Angelina and place her on the table. I gasped and tried not to cry as I prepared a cloth with ether and chloroform, then pressed it against her nose and mouth. Her face was ashen, but she still breathed.

I tore through her dress and had to struggle to get through her stays. They had been tied very tightly and I couldn't get my scissors underneath. I cut the laces first, which made it somewhat easier, but then there was a great deal of whalebone, which caught the scissors and hindered them. Once free of the stays, I was able to tear the unmentionables away, although I did keep as much of her decently covered as I could.

I reached for my flask of carbolic acid and went to pour it on the wound. The flask was empty. Nor was there another flask in my bag. I had made a note to purchase more the prior week, but events had conspired to put it from my mind.

"No," I whispered, then swallowed.

I did not have time for histrionics, not if I were to save Angelina, and there was, indeed, a passable substitute for the carbolic acid at hand.

"Whiskey!" I demanded, holding out my hand.

"What?" asked the young officer.

Sebastiano, however, knew immediately what I required and why I required it, as did Mr. Sedonez. The latter gentleman scrambled to his feet and swept a full bottle of whiskey off the top of the little desk. He tossed it to Sebastiano, who pulled the cork from the top, then handed the bottle to me.

I poured the liquor over the wound, dosed my scalpel again and began the incision.

With some difficulty, I was able to find the bullet and breathed a prayer of profound thanks when I found that it had landed next to one of the kidneys, but not in it. After removing the bullet, I went about stopping the bleeding as best I could, and all the other tasks one must complete when treating the victim of a gunshot. After closing the wound, I verified that there were no other wounds, then bent to the bandaging.

I do not know when Mr. Lomax and his officer left to take Mr. Leighland away, but they were long gone by the time I finished. Mr. Sutton and his men had come in, with poor Mr. Sutton's face almost as ashen as his wife's. He was a short, almost stout man, with graying brown hair and whiskers. The litter stood on end, ready to be unfurled as soon as it was needed. Sadly, the question remained: to which part of the house would Angelina be brought?

I checked her one more time. Her breathing was shallow but steady, and while her pulse was a little on the weak side, it was not so weak as to be worrisome.

"She's survived this far," I told Mr. Sutton. "Assuming she doesn't take sick, she should do well."

With Sebastiano's help, we got her onto the litter and home to her own bed. She began to come around shortly after we got her settled. She opened her eyes and looked at Mr. Sutton and smiled.

"Angelina," he whispered.

"Edgar," she whispered back.

"How are you feeling?" I asked.

"Maddie." She smiled at me. "Were you hurt?"

"I'm quite all right," I replied. "How are you?"

She swallowed. "Hurt. It hurts a lot."

"I don't doubt it," I said, and turned to my bag. "I'm going to give you a couple grains of morphine. That should help you feel better."

"Water?"

"Of course."

I gave her the injection, then helped her sip some water. She soon fell asleep, which was the best thing for her.

However morose Mr. Sutton was, he had the good grace not to carry on, and when I offered to stay and watch Angelina, he accepted with a great deal of relief. I began to wonder if I had misjudged the fellow.

Sebastiano arrived, as well, and with two fresh flasks of carbolic acid.

"I've ordered more," he told me. He nodded at Angelina. "How is she?"

"Good enough," I said, my stomach tightening. "But it's too soon to tell for sure."

It was a long night, indeed. Shortly after dusk, Angelina became feverish. I checked her wound, and it was red, but not oozing, so I dosed it with carbolic acid again. Fortunately, her fever did not climb, but it did not lessen, either. We gave her beef tea and water, which she took quite well. Still, her skin remained hot and her face flushed.

Mr. Sutton and I both sat with her all night, taking turns dozing. Angelina slept in fits, but still took water, which was a very good thing.

The next day, her fever continued. I checked the

wound, and it gave up a fair amount of pus, although I had seen much worse. However, there were no red streaks radiating from the wound, which would have been a bad sign indeed. I rinsed the wound again, this time with whiskey and boiled water and left my trocar in place so that the wound would continue to drain. Olivia came by with strong beef tea for Angelina and mole and chicken for Mr. Sutton and me.

I wrung out cloth after cloth to put on Angelina's forehead. The times she was awake, she seemed lucid enough, though in considerable pain. I dosed her with as much morphine as I dared. She was also able to take water and beef tea, which I took as a good sign. The contagion did not seem so bad that she faced certain death, but her failure to improve was quite worrisome.

As the day wore into the second night, Angelina's fever rose. It was not what I would have called dire, but I went ahead and bathed her in cool water and checked her wound again. It was still giving up pus, but that had, at least, lessened. I rinsed it again.

Mr. Sutton mostly watched. If he spoke, it was to Angelina, or to ask me if I needed or wanted anything. There was little more we could do but wait. I settled back into the chair by the bed, with Mr. Sutton sitting in a chair on Angelina's other side.

I was riding under the bright blue, cloudless sky, hurrying to talk to Dr. Skillen about germ theory. It was so fascinating. We could do surgery without people taking sick from it. We could find drugs that might actually heal people rather than risk killing them with our supposed cures. Then the sky grew darker and darker. I pushed Daisy onward. Instead, she slowed as row after row of tombstones grew out of the ground, all around us. Then Daisy was gone, and I was surrounded by shades that slowly formed into patients and friends. My mother, children with whooping cough and scarlet fever, women who had died trying to give birth, ranch hands and field hands who had come to grief. Will Rivers walked up, followed by William Warren and

Jeptha Bennett. Mrs. Gutierrez stood next to them, as did Leon Walters and Mr. Valdez. Then Angelina stood in the middle of them all. All together, they each raised a hand and pointed at me.

"I did my best!" I screamed. "I tried! Why isn't that good enough? I tried!"

"Mrs. Wilcox?" The soft male voice broke through the fog of my sleep.

"What?" I blinked as I came awake and realized where I was. "I must have dozed off."

"I know," said Mr. Sutton, from the chair on the other side of the bed.

"I'm so sorry," I gasped. My heart was still beating quite hard from the nightmare, and as I remembered it, I looked over at Angelina.

She seemed so still as she lay upon the bed. I swallowed, but then her chest rose ever so slightly, and I held my breath waiting to see if it would move again. A moment later, it rose again, and again. Softly, slowly, she continued breathing.

"Why are you sorry?" Mr. Sutton asked, a curious frown on his face.

"I fell asleep."

"Small wonder," he said. "You have not left her side since we arrived home. You must be worn out, and yet you stay."

"She is my friend."

"I know. And she loves you dearly for it." He looked down at her. "My poor Angelina. There are many that she is friendly with, but she has so few real friends, and all her family is in Santa Barbara. She never complains."

"Why don't you blame me for this?" I asked, although I was not at all sure that I wanted to hear the answer. "If she had not been helping me, this would not have happened to her."

"No. It might have happened to someone else, instead, perhaps even you. It still doesn't mean that the blame for what happened should fall on your shoulders. An evil man shot Angelina, one who did not scruple to try to harm you and killed two Chinamen and an Indian besides. I'm just grateful you were there when this happened, because if you hadn't been, she probably wouldn't be alive now."

"We may yet lose her." I looked at my dear, dear, friend, her face flushed and her forehead perspiring, and I let the tears trickle down my cheeks.

Mr. Sutton sighed as he gazed at his wife.

"Oh, you poor thing," I said, suddenly remembering that Mr. Sutton had even more to grieve over.

"Yes. First the children. Now this." He looked up at me. "You do know how we lost our little ones, don't you?"

"No. I'm afraid I don't," I said. "I did not know Angelina all that well until a year and a half ago, and you'd only been in the pueblo not many years before that."

"We came here in May of 1868."

"Angelina never speaks about the children."

Mr. Sutton shook his head. "No. She doesn't. She cries every night, though. It was a terrible time. We had our eldest, Betty, then James, then Bobby. Betty was four when James caught a croup and died suddenly. Bobby was just an infant, then. Then, after Betty turned five, she was playing with some other children and tripped and fell. It was the sort of accident any child might have, but that she struck her head on a rock and was killed."

"How terrible," I said, looking as Angelina stirred and muttered, then returned to sleep.

"It was," said Mr. Sutton. "We had thought Bobby was going to grow up, though. We never let him play near marshes or other fetid places. He'd had the croup, scarlet fever, measles, all manner of things and had survived them. Until he was six, when he caught typhoid and succumbed."

"I'm so terribly sorry," I said.

"We were living in Santa Barbara then. Angelina

was deeply grieved, and the doctors gave her laudanum for her melancholy, but it only got worse. My cousin, Jasper Morton, died and his widow, knowing of our plight, asked us to take his business."

"I remember Mr. Morton," I said, and suddenly bit my lip. That he had owned a funeral parlor seemed uncommonly apt, as he had looked rather cadaverous.

For the first time, I saw Mr. Sutton smile. "He did look like a vulture, didn't he?"

I couldn't help chuckling. "He did, I'm afraid. I always thought his appearance was singularly appropriate."

Mr. Sutton nodded. "His widow's offer was a profound grace, and so, we moved. Fortunately, once Angelina got here, she began to improve."

"Was she still taking the laudanum?"

"No."

"Then that's why." I shook my head. "It has many good uses, but it is prescribed far too often for complaints that it shouldn't be."

Mr. Sutton looked bemused. "I had always thought it was because she'd gotten away from all the reminders of our grief." He took a deep breath. "In any case, the reason I have told you all this is because you wonder that I do not blame you. But you didn't do anything wrong. I have lost three children, not one of them due to my or Angelina's fault. Blame does not ease the pain, nor does taking on guilt which does not belong to you. Angelina and I have learned that in the cruelest way possible."

"But she says you still grieve."

"I grieve because I cannot give her any more children." He looked at Angelina so tenderly. "I offered to give her a divorce after Bobby died so that she would have a chance to have another child or two. She took me to task quite thoroughly." He smiled softly at the memory.

Slowly, he bent over and pressed his lips to her forehead, and I blushed at witnessing such intimacy.

He pulled back with a puzzled look on his face.

"I think her fever has broken," he said.

"It has?" I got up and felt her forehead with my hand.

It was definitely cooler, but not that awful cold. Angelina stirred again, opened her eyes for a second, then sank into sleep again.

We waited a while longer, but the fever had, indeed, broken for good, and by the next morning, Angelina was awake, eating gruel, sitting up in bed, and chiding us for worrying about her.

Chapter Seventeen

Mr. Leighland was brought to trial some months later. He continued to insist that he was innocent. He convinced Mr. Fletcher to act as his attorney, however, it didn't matter. Between the evidence that Angelina and I provided, with the drawings of the boot prints, Mr. Lomax testifying about Angelina's discovery of the anchor ornament and Sebastiano testifying about the boot prints, and several other men who had heard Mr. Leighland complaining about the stain of the Asian devils, Mr. Leighland was convicted of murdering the Wei brothers and Mr. Valdez, and attacking me.

I did not go to the rest of the trial. Nor did Angelina, who had recovered quite nicely by that point. There seemed little point. Miss Gaines invited the two of us for tea the day Mr. Leighland was sentenced. She cleverly directed the conversation toward the unsuitable men her father had encouraged to court her. It was no accident that her father happened to be home at the time.

Mr. Leighland was sentenced to fifteen years in prison, which I thought was rather paltry. Then I learned that the heaviest sentence that had been imposed on the few rioters who had been found guilty was only five years. I was told that Mr. Leighland had gotten the extra ten years because he killed Mr. Valdez. He wasn't hung because Mr. Valdez had attacked him. If Mr. Leighland hadn't been attacking me, then Mr. Leighland might have escaped conviction for Mr. Valdez's death on the basis that he was defending himself.

I don't think we'll ever know what prompted Mr. Leighland to kill the Wei brothers. According to Mr. McKinley, Mr. Leighland wanted to clear "his" land of Chinese. At least, that's what Mr. Sedonez told me some days after the sentencing. I found it hard to believe anyone could be possessed of such hubris, but Regina said that she could well imagine it of Mr. Leighland. Mr. Wiley did tell me that Mr. Leighland had been prone to brooding over his losses and thought that was behind the killings.

Mr. Leighland didn't serve his full fifteen years. Instead, three years into his sentence, he died of the flux, so perhaps there was some justice after all.

As for the riot, Mr. Johnson, the shoemaker and the presumed ringleader, was among those indicted. His trial was held, and he served some jail time, but it seemed sorely lacking as a punishment. As I noted above, the sternest penalty was only five years. The men who had accosted me and the others with me that terrible night somehow managed to avoid being indicted, let alone tried for their part in that awful night. The lynchings remained a black mark on the reputation of the pueblo for many years. Sadly, this did not mean the deplorable prejudices against the Chinese improved any. Indeed, some years later, the federal government would ban the immigration of all Chinese people.

Wang Fu prospered, however. He gave up working for me, setting up his herbal shop at the end of the Calle de los Negros closest to the Plaza. That way, he could treat both the Chinese that remained in the pueblo and the several Americans and Mexicans that sought his cures. Wang Fu assured me later that spring that one of the companies had seen to sending the money the Wei brothers had collected to their family. Wang Fu and I continued to challenge each other regarding our preferred cures and remained fast friends.

We did eventually find new field hands in three

young cousins of Sebastiano and Enrique. I was perfectly happy to extend employment to some of the Chinese laborers, but those that remained in the pueblo had found employment elsewhere.

The nightmare that haunted me so fiendishly finally ebbed, although it has been known to revisit me every so often. Perhaps it is just as well. I do like to think that I am in good control of my passions, however unlikely that is to be true. As Regina reminded me, there may be some benefit in that.

As for life lessons, my sweet grandniece notwithstanding, I do not think I have gained anything beyond remembering that my temper is not nearly as sweet and even as I would like to think. As for justice to the memories of those we lost, I gravely fear there is none to be had.

COMING SOON

The next book in the Old Los Angeles series is **Death of an Heiress**. Miserly land agent Mr. Robert Gaines has finally gone on to his reward, alas before he can marry off his daughter, Lavina. However, he has made provision for her by leaving her half his fortune in his will. Lavina's brother, Timothy, manages to take over her portion, leaving her with nothing. Then Lavina is brutally murdered and Timothy asks Maddie to help find the killer. After all, Timothy had nothing to gain by her death. Maddie isn't quite so sure but agrees to see what she can find.

And don't forget the previous two Old Los Angeles books:

Death of the Zanjero – In Old Los Angeles life was cheap and water could cost you everything. When the body of the water overseer, Bert Rivers, floats up out of her irrigation ditch, winemaker and healing woman Maddie Wilcox finds herself defending the town's most notorious madam. To save the one person she knows is innocent (at least, of the murder), she must find out who killed Mr. Rivers, a chase that will uncover the terrible truth about the people she thought were her friends.

Death of the City Marshal – When the city marshal gets into a gunfight with his deputy, winemaker and physician Maddie Wilcox is on hand to care for the marshal's wounds. Then the marshal is smothered in his bed the next morning, sending Maddie on the hunt for a killer prepared to do the worst to keep that most basic of human desires: a home.

Other books by Anne Louise Bannon

Please check out my other novels, available in print or ebook at your favorite retailer:

Freddie and Kathy Series:
Fascinating Rhythm
Bring Into Bondage
The Last Witnesses
Blood Red

Operation Quickline Series:
That Old Cloak and Dagger Routine
Stopleak
Deceptive Appearances
Fugue in a Minor Key
Sad Lisa

Mrs. Sperling
A Nose for a Niedeman

Brenda Finnegan
Tyger, Tyger

Fantasy and Science Fiction
A Ring for a Second Chance
But World Enough and Time

I would be honored if you left a review for this and any of my books on GoodReads or any other retail site. It really helps.

Connect with Anne Louise Bannon

Thank you for sticking it out this long! Please join my newsletter. It's the best way to stay up-to-date on my upcoming projects, blog posts and even games and giveaways.

Sign up here: http://eepurl.com/zH0Ab

Or connect with me on your favorite social media platforms:

Visit my website: http://annelouisebannon.com
Friend me on Facebook: http://facebook.com/RobinGoodfellowEnt
Follow me on Twitter: http://twitter.com/ALBannon
Favorite my Smashwords author page: https://www.smashwords.com/profile/view/MsBriscow
Connect on LinkedIn: http://www.linkedin.com/in/annelouisebannon
Follow me on Pinterest: http://pinterest.com/msbriscow

About Anne Louise Bannon

Anne Louise Bannon is an author and journalist who wrote her first novel at age 15. Her journalistic work has appeared in Ladies' Home Journal, the Los Angeles Times, Wines and Vines, and in newspapers across the country. She was a TV critic for over 10 years, founded the YourFamilyViewer blog, and created the OddBallGrape.com wine education blog with her husband, Michael Holland. She is the co-author of Howdunit: Book of Poisons, with Serita Stevens, as well as author of the Freddie and Kathy mystery series, set in the 1920s, the Old Los Angeles series, set in 1870, and the Operation Quickline series and Tyger, Tyger. She and her husband live in Southern California with an assortment of critters.

www.ingramcontent.com/pod-product-compliance
Lightning Source LLC
Chambersburg PA
CBHW070921190726

48292CB00004B/1057